Two forces in a race agai

After a whirlwind roma

woman, Lara Petrova,

businessman—Derek Harrison. Unbeknown to

Derek, a seemingly successful business owner under immense pressure to keep his business in the black, has agreed to collaborate with the Russian secret services against Lara's son Alex.

Alex, is studying nuclear energy science for his doctorate at Stockholm University, and has invented an important new source of energy, which could remove the need for fossil fuels for any country which becomes the owner of this ground-breaking technology. The Russians want the invention at any cost, Japan would be more than interested, but the British want it, too.

Alex just wants to stay alive...

Acknowledgments

My greatest "Thank you" is to my beloved husband John and my dearest children Maxim and Olesya for their moral support and encouragement during the writing of this book.

Assisting in development of the good ideas in this book, editing my writing, giving me creative suggestions and spending his valuable time, I always will be in debt to an intelligent wonderful man, director of an IT department, Robert OConnor. And I would like to express my major "thank you" to him, without whom this book would not reach the readers (his photo is on the back cover).

Also I would like express my huge thank you to my friend Elena Smith in supporting me, give me generous aid to start writing and editing in the beginning. I wish also to thank Vanda Gregg and her husband Ian, whose interest in my book, reading chapter by chapter with comments, stimulated me to continue writing.

And last but not least, a huge thank you to Susan Humphreys and her excellent team at Black Opal Books for their effort and creative support in publishing this book and bring it to the attention of readers.

appear! And I still have no idea why. What do you think, Alina?"

"You do realize that some foreign men just like to play games, Lara. We don't really know anything about your Derek, although, I must say that when I was helping you to translate his emails, he did seem very genuine and I was inclined to trust him more than not. It really is odd that you have heard nothing. Maybe you should try and call him—something might have happened to him?"

Lara was torn by the idea of chasing after Derek and decided to call her son in Stockholm, first.

"Hi, darling, it's Mama—how are you? I could really do with a little advice from a man of the world."

She explained about her missing guest and asked if Alex would call him on her behalf. He would do this better as his English was much better than hers. She gave him the number, and hung up, still not sure if she was sad or angry.

A few minutes later the phone rang. "There was no reply, Mum. I think it might be best if you just try to forget him. He doesn't seem very reliable to me."

She was hoping for a charming, decent man who would be faithful and devoted to her. She wanted someone who would share her life and whose values were the same as her own. She needed something more than just a good secure job. She wanted to be with someone—her own man! After her first marriage ended in divorce, she had not met anyone with whom she could even consider a lasting relationship—all the decent men were married.

Her circle of friends mainly comprised of powerful business people with good social positions and although they were very understanding and always willing to help her, she wanted love, affection and intimacy—she was aching to give her heart to someone.

Lara breathed deeply, taking the small pile of his letters from her bureau. As she read, she thought he sounded sincere enough…two grown up daughters, neither married yet, but both living with partners—one had a small son.

Derek had been married twice, which did not sound too good, but his last wife had died suddenly, so it was not his fault that he was single again. He certainly came across as an honest, caring man without the usual emotional baggage. And he had a lovely telephone voice—he had even called her princess. Hardly how she saw herself, but flattery is very pleasant for any woman. He seemed to be sincere and wrote beautifully, with a strong, masculine hand. He'd had a business for 26 years, which suggested both ability and stability. Lara didn't really understand exactly what he did yet, but his company seemed to be doing well, which was the main thing. Everything had looked so promising—except, where in God's name was he?

She snapped out of her reverie.

What am I thinking about? I really am losing my head! This man failed to show up, without a word, and here I am still thinking about living with him. Am I insane?

It was getting late and she was feeling hungry so went to her comfortable kitchen to rustle up something quick for supper. She was admiring her stylish granite worktops, and thinking about a glass of wine when the phone rang! A call at this time of night was unusual—she ran to the phone, her heart beating wildly.

"Oh, Thank God. It's you! What on earth happened? Where are you, Derek? Yes, yes…All right—I'm writing the number down now. Don't worry, everything will be all right. You found me—I won't let you go now. I'll call you straight back at your hotel."

Her face was getting hot and red with excitement, her

heartbeat quickened with pleasure, and her hands were trembling a little from the shock of such an unexpected surprise. At last he was here! It was magical. She hurried to the kitchen for a glass of water then grabbed the phone.

"Hello, Derek. I was so worried about you. Where were you? Tell me what happened."

She was so thrilled to hear his voice that she only partly listened to what he said, and certainly didn't understand every word. However, despite her excitement, she had a very acute woman's intuition, and had a worrying feeling that he was not telling her the whole truth, that he was holding something back.

"Derek, it's very late now and I cannot come to your hotel tonight. If you can wait there alone for a few more hours, I will come in the morning. It is about a two-hour drive from Balakovo to you in Saratov, so I should be there by ten. Is that good?"

"I'll be fine here till the morning, Lara, but I cannot wait to see you! I am looking forward to it so much. Till tomorrow—sleep well."

Despite the late hour, she picked up the phone again and called her secretary

"Olga? I am so sorry to disturb you at home so late. Look, I need to take some holiday. I am going to the Saratov tomorrow, but would prefer to keep it quiet. Please, will you find the letter, at my desk, that needs to go to the Regional Office and make sure it is sent tomorrow? Thanks. I'll keep in touch while I am away to check on things."

Lara began to pack quickly, her mood buoyant. She tried various clothes in front of the mirror, smiling to herself, and imagining their first meeting.

ꟸꟸ

The day dawned clear and sunny, birds were singing gaily in the trees. The building where Lara lived was on an avenue in the greenest part of town, close to the banks of the river. Normally she did not notice the birds, but this morning her own heart was singing in unison—maybe even more loudly than the birds.

As expected, it took a little over two hours to reach the city of Saratov. The driver, Peter, was quiet during the journey thinking about his own domestic problems. His wife had no job, and he had two little girls to bring up, his salary was barely sufficient to feed everyone. Despite his troubles he could not help but notice that his boss was in an unusually happy mood, singing to herself most of the way. Obviously, something pretty dramatic had happened since last night. Once in the suburbs, she asked that he drop her at the Metropole Hotel and return to the office. She mentioned that she would be taking a short holiday and that her secretary Olga would let him know when to come back. He was very pleased when she also said that she was looking into the possibility of giving him a raise, despite the normal rates being fixed by the government.

As she got out of the car, Lara's heart was jumping almost out of her chest. This man, whom she had liked instantly from his letters and photos was waiting for her in this very hotel! She had decided that nobody should know about the new man in case she did not get on with him as well as hoped. This was why she had sent her driver back instead of having him drive them both to the airport. She asked the receptionist for Mr. Harrison's room number and followed her directions to the lift. She checked her hair and make-up in the mirror and trying desperately to remain calm, she went along the corridor to his room.

She knocked in the door and in the next moment the

door opened, revealing a good looking, man in his early sixties. He had a short grey hair and was casually dressed in a fawn, V-necked cashmere sweater and matching slacks. He had a charming smile, and opened his arms to embrace her.

"At last! I am so glad to see you!"

He held her back at arm's length admiringly.

"God, you are really beautiful—so much more so than your photograph. It's truly wonderful to finally meet you, Lara."

"Welcome to Russia, Derek—welcome to my country."

Smiling happily, she put both her hands in his hand and could already feel the passion rising within her from his touch.

Chapter 2

A day earlier, shortly after dawn, Derek stepped out of his front door into a light drizzle. The morning was chilly and he wore a fawn windcheater over his slightly old-fashioned business suit. He had on a fresh white shirt and carefully polished black brogues, but was not really at ease in any sort of formal clothing. *However* he thought, *needs must. I have to make a good impression.*

He threw his bag into the green Jaguar XJ and backed slowly down the sloping drive onto the road. At that time of day the roads were almost empty, which would cut almost an hour off his journey time to Heathrow. Once he reached the M6 and could cruise at a reasonable speed, he began to relax.

His thoughts were with his new lady friend, whom he was going to see that day. In her photographs she looked sophisticated, elegant, and intelligent. From her letters she gave an impression of warm-heartedness and sincerity. Since his wife had died just over a year ago, he had dated a few women, and even slept with one of them, but none had touched him like this beautiful Russian lady. He desperately hoped that she would be the woman with whom he could rebuild his life. During the past year, he had learned how terrible it was to be lonely. His life felt empty when he came home from work to a cold house, he missed the companionship of a partner, someone with whom he could walk his dogs and go on holidays. He really felt the need of a woman's touch for himself and his home. Derek was also aware that it was, perhaps, a bit soon to be involving himself in a serious relationship. Maybe he was not entirely ready for another person in his life just yet. May be he was trying to replace one woman with another, and this might be difficult, and even hurtful, for a new person to deal with. Still, he was sure that he had to share his life with someone, if he wanted to feel fulfilled.

Despite the difficulties and dangers, he was already smitten, and embarked on his adventure happy and excited, determined to give it his best shot. He just needed to stop daydreaming, put his foot down, and get to the airport in plenty of time.

As usual the airport was busy. He parked in the long-stay car park and took the bus to the terminal. A few minutes later he was in a short check-in queue and the formalities were quickly dealt with. With some relief he went to the bar and, hot and thirsty, ordered a pint of lager.

"Jesus, if the weather is this hot here, what will it be like in Russia?"

He remember that Lara said that August is normally very warm there. They better have plenty of beer.

His flight was called and he squeezed into the small seat and looked around. There was no one he was inclined to chat with, so he closed his eyes.

ᘓᘐᘓᘐ

He was awakened by a stewardess, asking if he would like some lunch. He hadn't eaten for nearly six hours, so he dropped his tray-table and soon finished a rather bland, fiddly meal. In truth he could easily have eaten two had he been offered more, but this was economy class with a very small "e."

After coffee, listening to the engines low rumble, his thoughts returned again to Lara.

Where is she now? I hope she is as nervous and excited as I am. God, I feel like a drippy teenager again. He was returned to earth with a bump, when he remembered all the obstacles and difficulties he had had to sort out in his factory, before he was able get away. One of the moulding machines was on the blink and a spare part had had to be couriered down from Scotland. Fortunately, it had arrived in ten hours and the problem had been solved. He was lucky to have a reliable workforce and a couple of brilliant workers, so there was no cause for concern. He would call in regularly to make sure that everything was working normally.

There was, however, a much bigger fly in the ointment, which would not be so easy to deal with. He had two grown up daughters from his first marriage. He had divorced their mother many years ago and they both liked to have their say where his activities were concerned. He had always been generous towards them both, probably too generous! The outcome of this was that they now relied on him to supplement their incomes and certainly had their eyes firmly on the main chance should anything happen to him. They had made him feel guilty for destroying their family life, and he had tried to make amends by paying out for every little thing they asked. As a result, he had no savings to speak of and for some years had spent very little on improvements to his own home or even fulfilled any of his own wishes and ambitions. It had even put a strain on his relationship with his second wife who was childless.

Their marriage was not long lasting—and now she was dead.

He was fully aware that a third, new wife would want to make changes to his household and that he would need most of his income to give her the sort of life he would wish for her. He was almost at retirement age now and too old to start saving for the future. He felt a twinge of resentment that his children, who were now adults with life partners, still depended on him for handouts. By now, they should be standing on their own two feet. He had done everything a good father could reasonably be expected to do, but enough was enough, he now wanted nothing more than to enjoy his life with a new lady. Hardly surprisingly, his girls felt threatened by the whole thing, seeing their promised inheritance going down the drain. Derek had explained to them that if he remarried and anything happened to him, only fifty percent of his estate would pass to his new wife, the remainder to be split between them. This did not go down at all well—they were spoiled and greedy, and tried to insist on having all of it.

At this, he had put his foot down and said that his decision would stand, take it or leave it. He knew that this would make future relationships with his children difficult, both for himself and Lara, but thought it would be a price worth paying if he found the happiness he longed for.

He was snapped out of his daydream by an announcement.

"We are about to land at Moscow Sheremetyevo, the air temperature is…"

He left the aircraft, collected his baggage and went through immigration surprisingly quickly considering the horror stories he had heard from others, who had visited Moscow. But he was in Moscow for a second time and did not believe those stories.

He filed out with the other passengers into the huge arrivals hall, where there were people standing on both sides waiting for visitors. Many were holding up signs bearing the names of the guests or clients that they were waiting for. He was somewhat taken aback to see a sign with his name on it, as he was not expecting to be met. He thought it odd, but he walked towards the sign anyway.

"Excuse me, my name is Derek Harrison. Are you meeting someone else of that name or?"

The good-looking middle-aged man wearing a smart grey suit smiled at him "Ah, Mr. Harrison! Yes. I am waiting for you. You're the guest of Lara Petrova? Good. My name is Nicolai and Lara asked me to meet you and take you to the domestic airport—my car is just outside."

Derek was slightly confused, but Nicolai's English was good and he seemed genuine enough. He had also mentioned Lara by name so he must be OK.

Once outside, Nicolai explained that he was an old business friend of Lara's, now living in the capital. Yesterday she had phoned him and asked if he would kindly give a lift to her friend, who was arriving from England. "She said that her friend, meaning you, spoke no Russian and would need to get to the domestic airport. She thought he might have problems organising a transfer."

"You do know that your plane to Saratov is from another airport?" he said.

"Yes, I know. It's very kind of you to help me like this. I'm really grateful, I wouldn't have had the foggiest idea where that domestic airport is located."

When they arrived at the car, Derek was slightly apprehensive to find another man sitting in the back.

Nikolai quickly reassured him,

"No problem. This is my friend Vladimir. After I drop you, I have to attend to some business with him. Let me put your luggage in the boot and you can sit in the front and see the sights as we go."

Derek felt himself relax—his trip was going very smoothly. In an hour he would be on his next plane and two hours after that would meet his new lady friend.

He nodded at Vladimir as he took his seat, but only received a grunt in return. He assumed that his other companion did not speak any English, and settled back to watch the scenery.

For many years, Russia had been on his "to do" list. He had longed to visit the country, especially its great capital. On this, his second visit, he was going to make the most of it.

Nicolai drove carefully as the traffic was very heavy, but from time to time he asked Derek about life in England—prices, politics, the weather—he was a likeable companion and they immediately hit it off. Derek had imagined that the capital would be a huge metropolis but was still surprised as they sped through street after street. Finally, they left the city center and were soon heading through the suburbs on a motorway. He asked how far they were from the airport.

"Quite close, won't be long." he said.

The car took the next exit from the motorway onto a secondary road and Derek was suddenly alert.

"Is this the quickest way to the airport?"

He asked, unable to keep a hint of panic out of his voice.

"Don't worry, Mr. Harrison. Another five minutes and all will be revealed."

At this, Derek began to really worry. Who were these people? Where were they taking him? He started to sweat—something was definitely not as it should be.

"Nicolai, would you please go straight to the airport? I have a plane to catch."

Nikolai ignored him and drove on in silence. Derek quickly understood that he was completely helpless. A sixty-two year old with two quite strong looking men—he was now very frightened and just wanted it all to stop. He had no idea who these two really were or what they wanted. But he could do nothing but wait anxiously for their next move. After a few more miles, the car turned between two heavy stone pillars. Immediately beyond was a security barrier, which automatically rose to allow them access. They drove up to the front of a large brown stone house that looked as if it had been built in the last century. Derek hardy noticed—by now he was scared for his life.

Nicolai turned to him.

"Mr. Harrison, we want to assure you that you are quite safe. If we wanted to do you any harm, it would have happened already.

"You have been invited here by a very special Russian organisation—they wish to talk to you about some very important business. I'm sorry, we were obliged to use subterfuge, but we could not afford a scene at the airport. All will be revealed in due course, meanwhile just relax, keep calm, and do as we tell you, and there will be no problems."

The imposing front door was opened by a muscular looking young man, dressed entirely in black. Once inside, even in his petrified state, Derek was impressed by the sumptuous furniture and decoration. Faux Louis XV chairs and commodes, crystal chandeliers and heavy embroidered curtains. It was more like a small palace than a private house. A young man in a business suit approached them and spoke to Derek in immaculate English.

"Good day, Mr. Harrison. My name is Oleg. I'm sorry that it has been necessary to bring you here in this manner, but, please, understand that you are in absolutely no danger. We would be obliged for your understanding and cooperation. But please don't do anything stupid," he added darkly.

"We shall take you to a room, where you can drop your luggage, and then you will have some lunch with Nicolai. After that, my bosses would like to have a chat with you. Don't worry about the flight to meet your lady that will be sorted out for you tomorrow."

He was pleasant, but serious and official, without any hint of a smile, he was also obviously used to being obeyed without question.

Despite his conciliatory tone, Derek was still shaking with fear and sweat was running down his back. He had been kidnapped, but why? What had he done wrong in this country? What could they want from him? And what would Lara think when he wasn't at the airport? He felt totally helpless.

Moments later he was escorted to the first floor and into a spacious room as luxurious as any 5 star hotel he had ever been in. It was beautifully furnished in the same opulent fashion as the downstairs, thick plush carpets and gilt framed paintings on the walls. Derek dropped his bags and took a seat in silence. Nicolai did the same.

"If you need a toilet, it's through there."

Derek went to the bathroom, which was as impressive as the other rooms he had seen. He closed the door, not surprised to find there was no bolt, and threw open the window. It was barred on the outside! All he could see was forest. He had heard that there was a massive circle of woodland around Moscow. So—no way to escape, even if he could get out of the house. Despondently he washed his hands and returned to the bedroom.

He was taken down to the ground floor again and then into a large dining room. A waiter approached, invited them to sit down and handed each of them a menu—Derek's was in English.

Nicolai insisted that Derek choose something to eat although he felt so nervous he wasn't at all hungry. They finally ordered some soup which, when it arrived, smelled and tasted delicious. They ate in silence. Derek was still very apprehensive, and Nicolai was wondering what orders he might be given concerning his captive.

After lunch they returned to the hall and Nicolai knocked on one of the doors.

"Come in!"

Derek's heart was thudding his chest, but he stepped forward into the big room, staring around with wild eyes.

"Welcome to our company, Mr. Harrison."

Chapter 3

Professor Yakomoto was an elderly Japanese man, with short, greying hair and a wispy moustache. He was the head of the nuclear science department at the Royal University in Stockholm. Although slightly stooped, his dark, intelligent eyes were still bright and commanded immediate respect from all who met him.

He was finishing his report for a conference, which would take place in the USA. Some colleagues from the university in Boston had invited him to give a speech about global fuel problems. He had a free week coming up and was really looking forward to his trip. His wife called, as usual, to remind him what time dinner would be—in that way he was a fairly typical professor. He was not the only one working late that evening.

Two friends, Alex, from Russia and Swedish Michael, two talented researchers, were also in the building. The professor locked his room and looked in on the laboratory where Alex was hard at work.

"Bye for now, Alex. Remember, tomorrow will be a long and important day, so perhaps you should finish here now and go home for dinner. Take care."

The car park was almost empty at that time of night and the professor was able to locate his Volvo without his usual problem of trying to remember where he'd left it! It normally took around forty minutes for him to drive home and he was in the habit of using the time to think about his students—especially the gifted young Russian. He remembered when Alex had first enrolled as a student at his facility. There were many bright young people competing every year for an opportunity to continue their education at this university. Its reputation in the field of nuclear physics was among the best in the world. Alex had sent in a very competitive application for a visionary method of conserving and processing nuclear waste and was unanimously awarded the scholarship that year. The professor had liked Alex on sight. The young man was a complex mixture of modesty, kindness, strength and tenacity, and had an astonishing capacity for logical thought. The professor would have been a happy man if all his students were as talented and diligent.

Professor Yakamoto had noticed, however, that during the last couple of weeks Alex had changed. He was not as open and light-hearted as usual, the laughter and jokes had disappeared. The professor made a decision that when he got back from his conference, he'd take Alex for a drink and see if he could get to the bottom of what was worrying him, the boy had even appeared a bit secretive when he'd looked in on the laboratory that evening. Something was definitely troubling him.

Alex had, in fact, been in the middle of checking an important part of his research when the professor had interrupted him. He didn't want his boss asking him any awkward questions because he was not yet ready to answer them. He was very excited—his brain had been racing non-stop for days. He knew he was on the verge of a potentially world shattering discovery. It had come to him with seismic clarity during his ordinary research work and he had spent the last month checking and rechecking his data. Alex's experiments held the promise of an epoch making discovery in the domain of energy production. He found this difficult to believe himself, and could think of nothing else. Absolute certainty was the next objective and this was presently being pursued relentlessly.

If he was right, the discovery would be a means of bringing about major changes to industry and even the climate of the planet. The potential was so momentous that he was afraid to tell anybody about it. He kept all his calculations in his head and backup on a single memory stick, which he kept hidden in his rented room. Nobody knew about it so nobody would be looking for it. He would keep the news to himself until he was sure.

Alex decided that his professor was right and that he had done enough for tonight. He went next door to find his friend, Michael. These two had become very close in recent months, they were both very keen on karate and practised regularly in the university gym. Alex was far more experienced than his friend, having achieved his 1st Dan black belt when at university in Saratov, but they were still able to have a good workout on the mat, and Michael had improved by leaps and bounds with Alex's help and instruction. No gym tonight though, they were both too tired.

"Michael, you look wiped out too. How about a couple of beers and some supper in that café around the corner? I could eat a horse and a half!"

"Brilliant, give me a sec to tidy up and I'll be with you."

Michael quickly cleared his desk, picked up his jacket and they left the building. Normally, at this time, there were not many people near the university, just an occasional dog walker or solitary jogger. Alex and Michael turned towards the café which was famous among students for its cheap beer and good cooking. On the way they chatted about various aspects of their work and university life. Alex noticed a man who had stopped by a window, apparently greatly interested in an advertisement. He had a fleeting thought that the chap was behaving rather oddly.

Ten minutes later the two friends were sitting in the café behind a couple of large beers, waiting for their orders. It was a busy place, patronised mostly by young people, who came in for a quick bite or a drink with friends. When the waitress brought their meals, they both fell on the food like gannets. Alex was enjoying his soup and Michael was fully occupied with his favourite fish when he suddenly said quietly, “Alex, who is that bloke on your right? Don’t look now, wait a bit. He seems interested in us—looks like he’s watching us. Do you know him?”

Alex deliberately dropped his napkin to the floor and, as he bent to retrieve it, took a quick look as he sat up again.

“It’s the same guy I noticed earlier when we were walking here. Don’t worry, mate. I think you are studying too hard. Take it easy! I’m sure it’s nothing. He’s just bored and looking around.”

Although he reassured his friend, Alex had himself become a bit uneasy and couldn’t help but make a connection between this stranger’s interest and his research. He began worrying about the safety of his memory stick and was suddenly anxious to be home.

“Hey, hey. Alex! Are you still with us? You’re looking pretty stressed. Is something wrong?” Michael smiled at him, waiting for an answer.

“No, no. Just tired. Overworked really and anxious about my dissertation. Let’s get back, I’m ready for bed.”

They left the café, said their good nights and separated.

was clearly in the air.

After lunch they went together to book the sleeper train back to Moscow, where they wanted to have time together. Derek insisted that they travel 1st class, and paid for one compartment for the journey. Now, standing in the corridor staring through the train window he was suddenly consumed with happiness. He just couldn't believe his luck. *She is so lovely, lovely. Warm, always smiling and very bright. I definitely want to know her better—I want her to be my friend and lover. Maybe even more than that.* He had already decided that, at the end of his visit, he would invite her to his home in England. He desperately wanted Lara to accept his home, his two dogs and his children. He was also thinking of how she might be an asset to his business, she was certainly very savvy. If he had any reservations or worries deep down, he did not allow them to come to the surface—he wanted nothing to spoil this magic moment. Any problems could be sorted out later.

She called him from the compartment—"Are you coming back to me? I am very lonely in here." She had wrapped herself in a blanket and tucked her legs up onto the narrow bunk. She appeared to be looking forward to another long chat with him. Her eyes were sparkling and she was in a very happy mood. She didn't want him to see how tired she was, and how much the emotions of the day had affected her. This was a very special time—their first day together. So full of possibilities, first impressions, and new beginnings. "So, Derek—are you good now? You look tired."

"Yes, sweetheart, I am, a little. But I'm just so happy to be here with you. I was really taken with you from our Skyping, and now it does seem as if there is a real chemistry between us—I only hope you feel it as well. Don't say anything for now, but I so want you to like me.

Let's spend a little quiet time together so that we can really get to know one another?"

"Of course, my dear. Don't worry. Perhaps I should not admit it so soon, but I already feel a strong connection between us."

Suddenly her face clouded slightly as she remembered. "You were going to tell me why you missed your plane."

"Oh, yes," he said, somewhat reluctantly. He shifted to a more comfortable position and began the story.

"Well, you already know that my flight was through Switzerland and there was a four hour gap between flights, so I bought something to eat and drink and wandered around the airport. I was so happy to be meeting you I didn't mind the wait. When I finally went to board my flight, you wouldn't believe it. I was stopped at the gate and told I would not be allowed to continue my journey to Moscow. I got quite angry, but was quickly informed that it was because my visa was single and invalid for this trip! I'd applied months ago for a multiple visa but the one in my passport was a single. Some idiot in the Russian embassy had got it wrong, and I hadn't noticed. You remember I told you that I'd visited Moscow on business some time ago, before I met you. I assumed the visa was still Ok, did not checked properly, and no one at Heathrow had noticed that it was already invalid. Unfortunately, the Swiss did, and stopped me. I was so frustrated and disappointed and I couldn't think what to do. I found a hotel for the night and went to the Russian Embassy the next morning, paid for an emergency visa, and got the next flight that evening."

"My God! What an adventure! You must have felt so helpless. You cannot imagine the horrible thoughts that were going through my mind when you didn't turn up. Car crashes, heart attacks—it was awful. But why didn't you phone me?"

"Unbelievably stupid! In the rush to the airport, I left my address book and phone in the car, so I had no idea where you were. Just imagine! I really felt like a fool! Arriving in a strange place with no note of the address I was to visit and no contact numbers—that takes a special skill!" Derek said with excitement.

"Yesterday, I suddenly remembered that I'd made a note of your number on an old business card—that's how I managed to call you eventually. Otherwise, I'd still be running round the city searching for you."

They laughed together until Derek said, "Ok, Lara, we should try to rest now. It has been a long day for us both—pleasant and happy, but very long." He was feeling really wiped out and ready to sleep. He gave her a chaste peck on the cheek, stretched out on the narrow bed shelf and flexed his tired feet, hoping that sleep would come quickly.

However, no such luck, despite his tiredness. The train rattled and bounced around. The whistle sounded every now and then, and there was the whining sound of the wind whistling past the train like a mini tornado. He just couldn't drop off. The movement of the train made him feel insecure on his bunk, and he found himself hanging on to the edge to stop himself from falling out. He also had a lot to think about, conflicting thoughts were whizzing in circles around his brain and not all of them pleasant.

I am really very fortunate. She's charming, intelligent, and very pretty. Gorgeous green eyes. And she does seem to like me too. That's all very well but what am I going to do about this bloody FSB business? I'm sure that's who they were although they didn't actually admit it. Their English was good, but I'm sure I could hear an accent. What in Hell's name can I do about it? They're sure to be keeping an eye on me. And what is wrong now, is that I will be building a relationship with this lovely lady on a base of deceit and lies. Watched by God knows who all the time. What bloody choice do I have? Do I do what they want or let my business fall apart? I've already lied to her. My Switzerland delay "tale" I told her so that she would believe my reason for being delayed. At least, Lara knows that I have been to Russia before on business, so it won't be too suspicious if I suddenly go off to somewhere on my own. Christ, I'm so tired. I need sleep.

The night train brought them eventually to Moscow, where they had a leisurely breakfast at one of the station cafés. Lara made calls to friends trying to arrange somewhere for them to stay for the next ten days, until Derek had to fly home. She quickly managed to rent a flat at a price that made Derek smile when he thought of UK prices. An hour later they were exploring an old fashioned Moscow flat with two rooms, high ceilings and decent decoration. They both liked it. It was close to Red Square so Lara suggested that after lunch they do some sightseeing. Derek was very happy to be lead around, and they spent a delightful afternoon wandering the streets. He was generous and kind and Lara soon found that she was not allowed to pay for anything.

Later, at "Praga," a famous Moscow restaurant, they had dinner to the accompaniment of romantic gypsy music, played by two black clad violinists with a pianist in the background. The restaurant had a romantic atmosphere and Derek was glad he had dressed up for the occasion. He simply loved it here—everything about it. Lara insisted he try the famous Siberian red caviar, which is made from salmon roe. Derek was astonished by the unique taste, especially when washed down with a glass of Champagne. Lara teased him.

"You do not know how it is made, do you? I will tell

you later, it will be quite interesting to you because I had a lot of experience with making caviar like we are eating now." She smiled confidently at him.

Derek became totally fascinated—he was becoming increasingly smitten by this amazing Russian lady, and could feel himself falling in love.

The rest of their dinner was excellent and all the waiters were helpful, but unobtrusive. He allowed his thoughts to wander. *This is a fantastic place. Everything is just right here. This is the life I am meant to lead! My beautiful Lara looks gorgeous in her black dress with my pearls shining around her neck. God, she looks so sexy.* It seemed so long since he had been intimate with a woman that he found himself trembling with excitement for what might be.

After dinner they returned to the flat by taxi, joking and laughing together and holding each other close.

Lara finished her bath and, wearing just her bathrobe, was heading for the bedroom she had chosen for herself, when his voice from the other room stopped her.

"Lara, my dear, could you come in here for a moment? I get a bit scared sleeping on my own in your country. Would you come and hold my hand for a bit?"

For a split second she thought he might be serious, but quickly realized what was happening, and said with a smile, "Just give me a moment."

With her heart beating rapidly she went to her own room, took off her bathrobe and, with trembling hands reached for her silky, almost transparent nightdress.

ꕥ

The next morning, they had a cosy breakfast together. Derek couldn't believe how delicious even the simplest food was. Wonderful dark bread, fresh unsalted butter, jams and honey bursting with natural flavours, cheese better than any he had ever tasted—this country was exceeding his wildest dreams. After they cleared up, Lara suggested they visit some of the famous monasteries tombs, warrens, and caves on the outskirts of the city. It was a famous tourist attraction and people came from all over the world to see the fabulous churches and ancient icons and tombs. There was also an immense underground warren of passageways, where the nuns used to perform their devotions and hide in times of danger. Derek thought that it was fascinating.

A taxi was quickly ordered and they were on their way. It was huge—gleaming belfries, cloisters, and churches with bells ringing non-stop. Derek was fascinated by its beauty and complexity, but found it difficult to concentrate, knowing that they were probably being watched. He couldn't stop himself from continually looking round for anyone or anything, which looked remotely suspicious.

They took in all there was to see above ground and then joined a queue of tourists, each holding a candle, for a visit to the caves. Underground it was very dark and distinctly chilly. The caves were labyrinthine, with tunnels and branches running off in all directions. There were ancient icons on the walls and notices in various languages describing the various points of interest. Derek had moved on slightly ahead of Lara—a painting had caught her attention and she stopped for a few moments to look at it. Derek strolled on ahead and came to a fork where he turned right and after a few metres followed another right fork. He suddenly realized it was very quiet and turned to look behind him. There was no one there, and no one in front. He was quite alone in the silent darkness. He began to feel panicky and slightly silly—far too embarrassed to call for help. He decided to retrace his steps. He turned round and bumped straight into another man, who had silently materialized behind him. "I do apologise, I thought I was lost for a moment."

"Yes, I thought so, too, Mr. Harrison." Derek felt his heart sink. There was now no question that the blighters were watching him. He tried to feign indifference.

"Do we know one another?"

"I hope you remember us Mr. Harrison. We have been keeping an eye on you—just to ensure your safety, while you are in our country." He turned away and walked back as silently as he had come. Derek hurried back along the tunnel looking for Lara.

"Derek, darling, where have you been? You just disappeared! I have been calling but there was no sign of you. Please don't wander off again, I was really worried. Here, give me your hand, let me go in front. I don't want you to get lost again." She was paniced.

By the time they had seen everything it was late afternoon and they were tired and hungry. Derek was also very edgy. Despite the encounter in the cave having unnerved him, he still couldn't bring himself to tell Lara the truth. Instead he changed the subject, "Lara, you did talk about getting tickets for the ballet at the Bolshoi. Did you have any luck?"

"Yes. For the day after tomorrow. We will have to dress up, I think, in my country a visit to the theatre is always considered a great occasion—especially the Bolshoi Theatre." She smiled at him and kissed his cheek. "If you hang up your suit for a couple of days, the creases will fall out." Derek supressed a sigh of relief that he'd even brought a suit with him!

The Bolshoi Theatre is an extravagantly beautiful white stone building, important both historically and architecturally, and Derek caught his breath as they entered. The huge mirrors were reflecting light from the enormous crystal chandeliers, and everywhere were gilded furnishings and rich carpets. Before the performance they had time to wander around, looking at the pictures of the famous dancers, actors, and singers who had played there. From their seats in the balcony they had an amazing view of the beautiful neoclassical interior. Throughout the performance Derek held Lara's hand tenderly. Sometime during the second act, Lara whispered to him.

"Darling, are you enjoying it?"

""Yes, I am," he said. "And I feel as if I'm falling in love."

ઌઌ

On their last night in Moscow they talked late into the evening about their lives and hopes for the future. He asked a great number of questions about her son and daughter and she was happy to talk about her children, who were so close to her heart. She told him about Alex, studying hard in Stockholm, and her daughter Oleva, who was also studying at the university there and married to a charming Swedish man, Michael. He could hear the pride in her voice as she spoke about them, and was happy to agree with her suggestion that perhaps they could go there together soon. She so much wanted them all to meet and get to know one another. Derek said honestly, "I'm so full of admiration for anyone who has managed to raise two children almost alone and, from what you've told me, made them understand the importance of education and hard work. I only wish I could have had the same success with my two. I'd love to meet them, sometime. Where does Alex plan to work after university?"

"I don't know, but he is talking about a research post at a top university in Japan. They have a big interest in nuclear sciences, and many of the best professors in that field work there. He has already been invited to continue his research in Tokyo and become a professor there, if he wants. One more year in Sweden and then he will make up his mind. But, he is a very clever boy and I think he will choose the right thing."

Derek was suddenly serious. "Lara, I think we've really hit it off and I'd dearly love you to come and visit me in the UK. My house is a bit of a mess, living on my own, but I'm sure a woman's touch would soon sort that out. Please say yes—it would be so much easier for me to go back now if I knew that I'd see you again soon."

"It's all been very quick for me too. I'm not sure what I'm doing any more. Can I answer you tomorrow?"

ꕥ

The airport was huge and very modern. It was cool and calm, despite the large number of passengers milling around. Derek thought how much cleaner and sharper it was than the scruffy mess that Heathrow had become of late. As they stood in the line for checkin he held Lara close, thinking sadly that he would soon have to leave this lovely woman.

Sensing his mood, Lara turned to him and said suddenly, "Derek, my dear, I have to thank you for your kind invitation to England." She looked suddenly very serious and he feared the worst. "I would love to come and visit you. I very much want to see you again." She smiled at him knowingly, "As soon as I can get a visa and some holidays, I'll get on the next plane." She threw her arms around his neck and kissed him passionately. "Will you wait for me? I promise I will be on the plane." She said with a cheeky grin.

"Oh! Sweetheart, you make me so happy! Of course, I

will wait for you! And when I get home I'll send the money for your ticket. No arguments please, I'd love to help."

"Thank you very much—you are so generous, darling, you know that international flying is expensive." She admitted.

All too soon, he had to leave her and go through security, turning and blowing kisses as he went.

Formalities over, he headed straight for the bar feeling relieved that he had gotten this far without any disasters. He still had a niggling worry about his departure. He only knew about the old KGB from novels and films, but he was fairly sure that this was close to the true picture. He felt himself sinking out of his depth and would remain uneasy until he was safely on the British Airways plane. The information about his visit must have come from somewhere, and he was sure that even in modern, so called democratic Russia, the FSB could still do more or less as they pleased with anyone they were interested in. Who was to know? They might have already changed their plans and decided that he would just disappear.

For God's sake, Harrison, stop being so bloody paranoid. Everything is fine—I'll be on the aircraft in an hour. I just need a drink. He sat on a stool at the bar and ordered a beer.

"Can I get that for you?"

The slightly accented voice came from an enormous man with a bull neck and close-cropped hair, who had sat on the next stool. Derek turned in surprise. "I'm sorry? Are you offering to buy my beer?"

"Yes." The stranger was smiling grimly at him, now.

Derek thought angrily, *Jesus Christ almighty, won't these buggers leave me alone even for a minute. Here we go again.*

"Mr. Harrison, I hope you remember that you have

very powerful friends here. We thought that we should accompany you to the aircraft steps to ensure security for us all. I do hope you understand. Remember, we need you to help us. You do remember that we met when you arrived here?"

"I'm hardly likely to bloody forget, am I?" He said with unconcealed irritation in his voice.

The stranger smiled again "Just call me Misha, please. I rather like my name. In Russia, it's usually associated with a bear. Rather suitable, don't you think?"

Bear, or the "Incredible Hulk," he thought, not without some apprehension. "Ok, Misha," he said with unconcealed sarcasm. "So what you want me to do now?"

"Mr. Harrison, you know very well. We want you to find the quickest way to get to Lara's son. As soon as possible, Mr. Harrison."

"Ok ok. Your boss told me all that before. Things have to be taken slowly. I like Lara very much and have invited her to visit me in England, where I fully intend to propose to her. I certainly can't do anything until after that."

"That will be all right, Mr. Harrison. In fact, just what we wanted to hear. Well, have a good flight and a safe landing, but before you go, would you like me to introduce you to the best beer in Moscow?"

Derek glanced across nervously and forced himself to smile, "Ok, my friend—Oh, I do apologise, Misha, let's have that drink."

Chapter 5

Around the corner from the Lubyanka—the old KGB building, which still struck fear into those old enough to remember its sinister past, is an anonymous looking, thirty story red brick building. That evening, behind a heavily curtained window on the eleventh floor, five men in military uniform, were sitting at an oval wooden table. They all looked very serious and there was an electric tension in the air. An older man, who was obviously in charge, demanded, "Captain Ivanov, bring us up to date with the situation regarding Alex Petrov in Sweden."

"Yes, Comrade General. I'm afraid I have not a lot to add at this stage. We continue to watch him carefully, but he appears to lead an uneventful life outside his studies. A thorough search was made of his flat, but nothing of interest was found. We are sure he has a disk or memory stick, with details of his research, but so far, have been unable to locate it. He may even be carrying it on his person. But, do not worry Comrade General, we shall find it soon."

"Are two agents enough for this case?"

"Yes, General. Two officers should easily complete the job."

"Good—I hope so! Now, some information for all of

you. One of our agents in London, with responsibility for Swedish affairs, has reported no increase in traffic from Sweden to London and no activity to suggest that the Swedes have any idea about this student's discovery. Therefore, for now, we can confidently assume that British Intelligence is in the same position, they do not know about this. This gives us a singular advantage, which we must make all efforts to retain.

"We have to find Alex's file. At whatever cost." He added ominously.

"We must also make sure that no harm befalls him, as he will be required to oversee the production of our first production plant. Once we fully understand everything, he can be dispensed with."

There were knowing nods around the table.

"In a further development, we have acquired a new 'recruit' to our operation. He is an Englishman called Derek Harrison. He has already been approached, and has agreed to cooperate. We have high hopes of him. He is a weak willed character, and easy to manipulate. He plans to marry Alex's mother, if she will agree, as soon as possible and take her to live in England. He will then have close contact with Alex, which we shall obviously use to our advantage. He is presently in Moscow with Alex's mother, but returns to England next week.

"Major Kosinskiy. It will be your mission to shadow Harrison in England, reporting back and activating our plan for him as soon as it is practical. We'll have a private discussion after this meeting and you will be given any necessary details. You should be ready to go to Britain in two days. If the operation lasts longer than six months another officer will replace you. The rest of you are dismissed. Go!"

The officers stood up promptly, saluted and left. Major Ivan Kosinskiy remained at attention, anxious to learn the

details of his mission. It would undoubtedly be good for his career, but he knew it would be a risky assignment.
"At ease, Major. Wait here a moment, please."

The General left the office and returned a few minutes later with a Lieutenant-Colonel from the foreign reconnaissance department.

After brief introductions, the General said. "Operation Fulmination starts officially today. We are confident that this Englishman will do everything we need to achieve our goals. You will have two operatives on the ground and will report back at a fixed time each week. For now, I'll leave you two to discuss the finer details, while I check that your travel arrangements are in order. Are there any questions?"

"No, comrade General."

The General, Vasily Litinov, was an attractive and powerful man in his late fifties. He was tall, had a full head of silver hair, and retained his military bearing, despite being a little overweight. He had been working hard today, and was looking forward to going home.

A lift whisked him down to the ground floor, where he wished the duty officer a soft "Good night." The officer jumped to his feet and stood to attention as the General left the building.

His driver was waiting and saluted smartly as General Litinov climbed into his official car. With a squeal of tires and a throaty roar from the engine, they shot off into the streets of Moscow. It was late evening and traffic was light, there was no need for the driver to use the siren. The General spent his journey home thinking about his lovely wife, who would already have gone to bed. Maybe she was still awake, reading a book, waiting for him. He smiled softly. He always thought tenderly of his wife, whose life with him had been far from simple. It was not easy to be the wife of a career officer. He spent most of his time travelling around the world on duty, and had rarely been there to help her at home even when their children were young. He appreciated her tolerance and patience and truly loved her. Perhaps surprisingly, for a man with his charisma, he had never been interested in any other woman in his life. And now he was beginning this very important operation, which would probably be his last before he took retirement. He could have taken his pension much earlier, but had not wanted to. He enjoyed the responsibilities and challenges, and also the status and privileges that his position brought. But now, he felt he had had enough—this would be his swan song.

ꕥ

After an hour's discussion with the Lt-Colonel, Ivan Ivanovich stood up and declared "The task is fully understood, comrade Commander?"

The older officer saluted in reply and the two left the office. Ivan was in a buoyant mood and felt very confident. He was in his early forties and still viewed the future with optimism. He enjoyed his job very much. It had been a childhood dream to become some sort of spy, and he had finally made it. When he finished university, he became an electronics engineer, but always hankered after a more clandestine life. After three months, his disaffection was brought to the attention of the then KGB, and he was offered a provisional place at a training center. He already had quite good English, having been to a specialist school, and he was soon recognised as a promising potential agent. He worked hard, with great enthusiasm, and was soon rewarded with a position in Europe. It was hard and interesting work to which he applied himself diligently. He always had glowing progress reports form his superiors. Now he was going again, and to Britain this time. Foggy Albion—misty landscapes, sheep and cows, a country of many animals and birds, as the Russian encyclopaedias described it. He would soon find out.

He put on his coat, locked his private cabinet and went out into the long corridor, where the offices of different highly secret departments were located. His steps echoed along the empty, wooden floored passage. He took the right turn leading to the special lift. He remembered that lift from his very first visit and the wonder and pride he had felt then. A very limited number of personnel had the right to use that lift because it descended to a highly secret place—an underground passage almost thirty miles long, leading to an underground bunker located north of Moscow. It was the Reserve Headquarters, maintained by his organisation, from which the government could function in the event of a world conflict. Ivan, of course, dare not ask any direct questions about anything there, but felt privileged to even know of its existence.

Three years ago, he had been moved from the far east of Russia to a bachelor flat in Moscow on the order of his superiors. He had no family life—even the pretty girl he had been dating since his student days in Irkutsk, had been forced to stay behind. She had waited for him for a couple of years, but his life had turned in a different direction and eventually she wrote that she had met another man. He still missed her in quiet moments, but was sanguine about it and applied himself to his job with renewed vigour. Since then, he had been almost continuously away on various assignments and any romance had had to take a back seat. Ivan now knew that his life would be solitary and he could not involve any woman in it permanently. He rarely dated, but occasionally an attractive girl would serve to remind him that he was still young and virile, and he would amuse himself temporarily, making use of those who offered themselves.

Ivan's two bedroomed flat, on the twelfth floor of a contemporary block, was comfortable and relaxing and, when he was in Moscow, he took pleasure in its anonymity. Once a week a woman came in to clean and deal with the laundry. She was a pleasant, middle-aged woman named Polina and, like all such domestics, had a high security clearance. He liked her—she was discreet, quiet and unobtrusive. Sometimes he invited colleagues back for a drink and a bite in the evening. They often talked long into the night, arguing gently on many subjects. In fact, about anything at all except work—that topic was strictly off limits, and walls had ears, especially in Moscow!

Later that evening, after the meeting with the General, he returned to his flat. He opened the curtains onto the great cityscape, gazing in wonder at the panorama below him. He thought again how much he loved this city, which was now a twinkling vista of light outside his home. He switched on the TV news and went to make a cup of tea. Suddenly he became aware of a news item, which caught his attention. The newscaster was telling of a new diplomatic row with the country of his next assignment—Great Britain. It seemed that a British spy had been caught operating in Russia and had had some sort of "accident." There was now the usual posturing between the two governments and the likelihood of "tit-for-tat" expulsions. *This may be trouble,* he thought tetchily. *All my careful planning may be out of the window.* The telephone interrupted his thoughts.

"Major Kosinskiy? You are to work two hours earlier than usual tomorrow"

"Understood," he answered, and rang off abruptly.

I wonder what that's all about, he thought. *Bet, it's something to do with the British agent on the news.* There had been no further details about him, or his "accident." It must have been severely botched to have even made it onto the television. Normally, this sort of thing was totally unreported. *These bloody amateurs did not have my efficient approach to work,* he thought. *But something closer to home must have happened for him to be summoned to work early. This was becoming serious.*

Chapter 6

Derek turned back, halfway up the aircraft steps, to take a last look at Moscow. His visit was over, and not without considerable relief in a certain quarter. He moved along the aisle looking for his seat. There were few passengers on the flight, so he was able to find a seat on his own, where he could stretch out and sleep without being disturbed. He closed his eyes and let his thoughts return to Lara.

She is such a lovely lady and I'm so lucky to have met her. She has a beautiful smile and genuine affectionate ways. Everything about her feels so right—I really couldn't bear to lose her. But what the blazes am I going to do about this other business? Of course you read all this KGB stuff and see it in films, but it doesn't happen to real people. Never, in my worst nightmare, would I have gotten myself involved in this sort of caper. And what on earth do they want with Lara's son? He's only a poor research student—what can the mighty FSB want that badly that they would use my romance to get to him? It sounds like a fantasy—none of this can be real! he thought. *Then why the hell did those guys go to all that trouble to kidnap me? And all that bloody pretence.* "You are in no danger, Mr. Harrison." *Maybe not, as long as I do what they say. I'm not sure I can cope with all this crap.*

His brain was now working overtime. *I was scared to death at that first meeting. I'm sure I'd have signed my own death warrant if I hadn't agreed to work with them! Please, God, they'll soon realise that I can't do anything for them and they'll get off my back. For Christ's sake, stop worrying Harrison, and pull yourself together! But maybe it's not so simple. Suppose they do not leave me alone? What can I do? Do I have any choices? I am afraid I may not. There's no way I'd do anything against the interests of my own country. You'd be hard pressed to find anyone who loved England more than me—the very word "traitor" gives me the creeps. Why, for God's sake me? What have I done to deserve this? Although, maybe I wouldn't have to do anything that would harm Britain—their offer to help me expand my business into Russia is certainly very tempting. It would get me out of a hole, and would be beneficial to both countries. Any extra exports have to be good for all of us.* He tried, in vain, to justify his position. Suddenly overcome with tiredness he lay back, trying to relax.

First, I need to find out what is going on at home, he thought. *Last time I called the factory I got the feeling there was a problem there that they were not telling me about. And what is Lara going to say when she finds out that I've been lying through my teeth? She'll probably finish with me. God, that would be just terrible. What a bloody mess. Fat chance of me getting any sleep on this flight.*

ଓଓ

The following morning, after a restless night at home, he hurried off to the factory much earlier than was usual for him. The place was already unlocked and Jim, who normally arrived first, was already there, pushing buttons on the biggest moulding machine. He was concentrating hard on trying to start the program. Suddenly the huge machine began to throb and throw out moulds. He turned away and saw Derek, who was standing, watching him with a very worried look etched on his normally pleasant features.

"Oh! Morning, boss. Pleased to see you alive and well!"

"Hello, Jim. Glad to see you too. We need a pow-wow as soon as possible. Can you do it now or a little later? Is Gina in yet?"

"Yeah, she's making a cup of tea."

"Well, stick one on for me too, please, and ask her if she's OK for a quick meeting in ten."

Jim shot off and Derek walked into his office. Everything looked just as it should—filing done, post sorted, all pretty shipshape, he was relieved to see. Thank heaven for Gina—she was a real godsend. As well as keeping the production line functioning, she found time to make sure that the office jobs were kept up to date and she made the tea! He made a mental note to thank her. He would also give her a little bonus for keeping everything under control, while he was away. And he had a little gift from Russia for her. Lara had helped him pick out a silver pendant of the St Basil's Monastery in Red Square as a souvenir.

"Oh! Hi, Gina! Unusual for me to be away so long—I hope you haven't forgotten who I am?"

"Hi, Boss—of course I haven't forgotten you—my salary was paid on time, wasn't it?" she laughed. "Still, pleased to see you back, there's a few things need sorting... Here's your tea."

"Great. Look, we need to get together with Jim, for a catch up. Shouldn't take more than half an hour to bring me up to speed." Jim scurried into the office. "Right on the nail, as usual," said Derek. "OK—you first, Jumbo."

Derek listened carefully. He had good reason to be grateful that he had such a good worker to leave in charge of the business. Jim, like Gina, was absolutely invaluable to him. He seemed to be able to resolve any problem thrown at him. During the time Derek had been in Russia, one of the machines had suffered a broken condenser, which slowed production temporarily, and resulted in threats from two important clients to take their business elsewhere. Jim had poured oil on the water and then, with his little team, had worked a couple of twenty-hour days to get production back on track.

"Brilliant—I really owe both you guys—many thanks. There will be a little bonus for each of you this month, but keep it quiet or everybody will want one. My trip to Russia was really wonderful—I've fallen in love with the place and can't wait to go back again. Look, here's a little gift for you both."

They left and Derek turned his attention to work for a while, but soon became bored with reading reports. He desperately wanted to find someone he could talk to about Lara. He picked up the telephone and called his youngest brother.

"Hello, Tom! Yes—got back last night. Yeah-h, it was wonderful. And my Russian Princess was amazing. She's a real doll, a lovely person, I can't wait to see her again. Oh, yes, I'm definitely going back there. First, I need to make sure that everything is chugging along smoothly here, and I have a couple of things at home to sort out. Then I plan to arrange for her visit over here, in fact I already invited her.

"God, I feel like a bloody fifteen-year old, brother! No, you just wait till you meet her. She really is a stunner, and very nice with it. I'm sure you'll be as smitten as I am. We'll set up a family meal at that restaurant in the village—what'd you think? Such a pity Dad's not around to join us, but with you and Peter and the girls. It'll still be great. I'm a bit pushed at the moment, do you think you'll be able to set it up for me? I'll give you some dates, nearer the time."

"No problems, mate, I hope you're serious about this one—we don't plan a family meal for every floosy you take up with. Ok, sorry, bad choice of word. No, no, of course I don't mean anything, you dope, but I just want you to be sure that you know what you are doing. There's no fool like an old fool, and you certainly wouldn't be the first near geriatric to get his knickers in a twist over a nice pair of boobs. Seriously though, if you are thinking of talking on a foreign wife, you should realise that it isn't going to be all roses. Apart from the language problems, there'll be all sorts of cultural difficulties. I hope you understand what a responsibility it will be. Uprooting a woman from her friends and family and dumping her in a strange country, where she can barely make herself understood. Big learning curve, mate—not to be undertaken lightly. I don't know her, but I know you, and if you are just playing games with her you could find yourself up to your ears in the brown, smelly stuff. No, no. I'm sure you've thought it all through. If this is the real thing, then we will all be delighted to meet her. Sure, sure. Bye for now. Catch you later."

H-mm. Derek put down the telephone and thought hard for a few moments. *Well, it would be better call daughter Jane and get it over with.*

"Hi, Sweetie! Everything OK? Have you got a minute?" He told her briefly about his visit with Lara. His tone was excited and bright and he really wanted to share all his experiences with his beloved daughter. He hoped, without much expectation that she would be excited for him. No such luck, of course. She interrupted him in full flow.

"Listen, Dad, I'm glad you're back, but I can't be as excited as you about it all. Why did you have to go to Russia for a bride, anyway? There are plenty of single women here, just look around! You only have to whistle and they will come running. And do you really need to marry again anyway at your age? Why not just live together if you fancy her that much? Sorry, Dad. Ok ok. I don't want to upset you but you did promise to help me with your grandson's school fees and maybe, with a new wife to support, you won't be able to?—Your priorities will be different.

"Look, Dad, it's not too late to step back from this. The private schooling was your idea. Look if its help at home you need, I don't mind coming over occasionally, to give the house a bit of a clean. I will even cook a few meals for the freezer if you like. Dad, please—Are you listening to me?"

"Yes, I am listening, Jane, and I have to say that it makes me very sad to hear that you can be so selfish. I have already given you and your family so much! Do you really want me to remain single for the rest of my life, simply to support you? I'm disappointed in you, Jane! Why shouldn't I have someone to hug and kiss? To give me a good morning smile? I'm only sixty-two, for Christ's sake. Who? You? No, absolutely not. I'm afraid you just make me feel like an extra source of income, rather than a father!"

Derek was thundering with anger and disappointment. His daughter had slammed the phone down on him not waiting to hear his last words.

What a bloody ungrateful little bitch! Although he hated thinking of his daughter like that, it was what she had become. *Well—we will see! She can pay her own bloody bills for a change and see how she likes that! If she can't afford the private fees, she'll have to use the state school! In any case, things are different now. Even if I were not thinking of marrying Lara, money would be tight. When said I might take on these wretched fees, business was good, and they would have been a drop in the ocean. Unfortunately, times have changed. God, after all I've done for her, I cannot believe what an unpleasant, selfish little cow she has become!*

He was absolutely sure that he wanted to marry Lara, but he was equally sure that things would have to be done to his home before he could ask her to live there with him. He would need quite a bit of cash to sort it out. He tried to visualise the house through her eyes—the whole place needed decorating, the fence around the garden was falling over, the garage roof was leaking quite badly. She'd undoubtedly be very disappointed. *Ok Harrison. Stop feeling so damned sorry for yourself and get back to work. You need to earn some money and pretty bloody quickly!* He left the office and wandered around his factory for a while, watching the automatic machines and checking the production line. It was noisy and smelly from burning raw materials, but he always got a feeling of satisfaction from his creation. He was so proud of it! And to think he had started it thirty years ago with just a hundred pounds in his pocket. He went off to have a word with Gina and then returned to his office to really begin work.

ꕥ

Some days later, Derek returned home from work in a very depressed state. He had had a meeting with his accountant, who had warned him that the financial position of the factory was pretty precarious. He had fretted about this all day, and spent much of his time trying to think of a way out. Derek decided on his way home that there was only one possible course. Against his better judgement, he would make a call to that agent from the Russian security service, who was supposed to be his "contact" in England. He didn't like it for a moment, but feared it was that or going under. He took out the small notebook, which was tucked away in his briefcase and, with a shaking hand, dialled the number. A pleasant, mellow voice answered immediately in unaccented English.

"Hello, can I help you?"

"Hello. My name is Derek Harrison. Is this the right number?"

"Oh yes, Mr. Harrison. I was waiting for your call. I need to talk to you urgently, but not on the telephone. Where can we meet? I'm not far away from your place."

"Oh—OK. Err…Somewhere in Birmingham, say? Do you know the Shish Kebab Balti House in New Street?"

"Don't worry, I'll find it. Can you manage this Thursday at six in the evening? Good, I will be waiting for you. Don't worry, I'll recognise you. I know what you look like."

"How?"

"Please don't ask unnecessary questions, just be there."

Derek was still shaking as he put the phone down. But soon, having made both the decision, and the phone call, his mood changed and he began to feel a little better. *This deal with the Russians was quite straight forward,* he thought, *and would certainly change his business fortunes, maybe even get him out of the hole into which he seemed to be sinking. Anyway, he wasn't doing anything illegal—how can it harm anyone.* Feeling better than he had done all day, he picked up the telephone again.

"Hello, Sis! I hope you are all well. I have so much to tell you." His sister, Anne, listened patiently while he told her about his recent trip and his plans for the future.

"Derek, I don't know what to say, but it's lovely to hear you so happy. If you are sure that she is the right girl for you then go ahead and marry her. At your age, you don't have a lot of time to waste! I am really looking forward to meeting her when she comes over. If you'd like to have a chat about her beforehand, why don't I call Lisa, and we can all have a drink this weekend? It will have to be Friday, we are going to a wedding on Saturday."

"Yes, OK. Look, I was going to call Lisa next, but I will wait 'till I see you both. Bye—love to everyone."

ꕥꕥ

Thursday. Derek found a parking space close to the Shish Kebab House and hurried to his meeting. Suddenly he got very uneasy feelings about everything. At this time of the evening the place was almost empty so he had no problem picking out his man, who was sitting in the window alone, reading a newspaper.

"Hello. I'm Derek Harrison."

The man who stood to greet him was tall and powerfully built—as all the Ruskies Derek had met seemed to be. He wore a dark suit with a black polo neck shirt and had crew-cut blonde hair. With a charming and friendly smile he said, "Good evening, Mr. Harrison. My name is Ivan. I am happy to meet you at last. Come and sit down. We have much to discuss and I trust you will speak freely to me. Especially about your problems at work."

Derek was impressed by Ivan, his appearance, his urbanity, and his manners. He was easy to talk to and had very good English. He had barely a trace of an accent and it would have been difficult to place him if you didn't know he was Russian. He listened intently while Derek went on and on about his business troubles. Finally his question was—were they still prepared to help him to expand his business into Russia, as they had discussed in Moscow?

"Right," he said. "I understand everything you have told me and now you must listen carefully to me. We have already put things in motion to help you. You need to be back in Russia as soon as you can make it, and you must do exactly as I say without any questions. Please make some notes so that you have everything clear. But first, let's eat something? The food looks pretty good here."

When they had finished their meal, Ivan moved the empty plates aside and began to talk. It hardly qualified as a conversation, more a list of instructions. When Derek next goes to Russia, he should immediately buy tickets to Komsomolsk in the Far East region of Russia, where he would be met by an agent, who would introduce him to the biggest car component makers in the country. He would meet the managing director and thereafter would remain in direct contact with that man. All his business difficulties would be resolved there. The deal was already in place for him. A portfolio of orders was already fixed up.

"Is everything clear?"

"Yes. Wonderful. It sounds almost too good to be true, but I'm afraid I shall not be able to go for a while. I have already arranged for Lara to come to visit me first, before I return to Russia, and I need to get my house sorted out.

I'll let you know when I'm ready to go again."

"OK. And is there any chance of you meeting her son?"

"I think during his mother's visit, I may be able to invite him over from Sweden to join us for a couple of days. I'm sure I'll be able to find a good reason."

"Right—that will be all for now. I will contact you if necessary."

Derek felt really invigorated during his drive home—he was excited by the prospect of a lucrative business deal with a top Russian company. He would take samples of his production with him to Russia and his certificate of quality.

With any luck, he'd have enough money both to support his new wife and keep his daughter happy by paying her son's school fees. It all boded well for a bright future with Lara.

ଓଓ

Since his return from Russia, Derek had spent every evening on Skype, talking to Lara. They laughed and cooed like a pair of old turtledoves, over their web cams.

"What did you do this evening, my sweet?"

"Nothing really special, darling. I just came back from a party. There was a lot of wine and dancing—you know we always dance at parties? There always seems to be something to celebrate here. Many invitations—sometimes it is difficult to refuse. But I was tired tonight and anyway, I couldn't concentrate, my thoughts kept coming back to you and my visit to England. When I come over, I hope we will to go to a typical English party. You can show me what parties are like in your country, yes? It will be very fascinating for me."

Derek was feeling slightly jealous at the thought of her

dancing with other men. "You really are looking forward to visiting me?" He asked.

"Yes,—of course, yes, my love—I can't wait to see you again. We both want to see each other so much, don't we? I want to see how you live and what is life is like for you. And your children—I'd love to meet them both. By the way, you have told your children about us, haven't you? What do they think about me, about us, about future? Are they happy for you if you get married again? No objections, I hope!" She laughed briefly.

"Oh Lara, I'm afraid that might be a bit sticky, and I'd rather wait 'til you're here before we go into it. Don't worry, there's nothing that can't be sorted. Before you come though, I will have to do some stuff in the house. Even to an old bachelor like me it looks a bit of a dump. But don't worry—I'm going to change a lot of things before you come. It will take about a month to smarten things up so that the place is fit for a 'Princess' to stay. I will book your flights for the beginning of September—can you manage that?"

"Oh, Derek. Please do not worry about the house. I will be coming to see you, my darling, not painted walls. I can help you with whatever you doing. My dear, I do love you and miss you so much."

"I do love you too."

ɞɞ

Over the next few days Derek was extremely busy. Some his more troublesome customers were demanding meetings, where he would have to supply quotes for new orders—these were jobs he could not delegate to Jim or Gina. He also wanted to organise work on his house. He was very pleased to find two decorators who could start immediately, but he still needed to choose paper and paint—not something he was ever very good at. He did think of asking Gina if she would come round and help, but she was so busy at work, he didn't think that was fair. Later that day he was speaking to one of his workers in the garden. "How quickly can you finish this job? We need a new fence and gate. Don't worry about the shed—we can deal with that later. Keep the gates the same black, but I would like them electric, if possible. The guys working on the house reckon three weeks, can you do the same?"

"No problem, Mr. Harrison, but I must have your agreement to my quote in writing. I have to buy some pretty expensive stuff for this job."

"You will have it in writing today, but can you just get on with it?"

Derek turned away and went out into the street at the front. He stood for a few minutes looking at the house and garden, trying to picture how it would look when everything was done. Of course, he should have done it years ago, but at least he had a real reason now—a cosy nest for his beloved Lara—for ever, with any luck. Enough day dreaming! Get back to work you silly old bugger or you won't be able to afford any of it! There's the meeting to prepare for tomorrow—Acheson's give me a quarter of my business, so I have to keep them sweet!

The electronics firm, Acheson & Co, had already had a bad batch of work from Derek and had tried to buy in mouldings from another source. Those had proved to be even worse, and they were ready to be persuaded back. With any luck, they were going to be a bit "cap in hand" tomorrow, he thought, but still had to be convinced of Derek's quality control. Another mistake and they would be history. Thank heavens Jim had been there to work on the immediate replacements. But the relationship still needed to be carefully handled. At least there had been no orders lost that time. No matter! He would be happy to listen to what they had to say, but it was always better to have an argument prepared!

ଓଓ

Derek's sisters, Anne and Lisa, were sitting in a cosy bar in a small town, waiting for their brother to arrive. Although they were both in their fifties, and casually well dressed, they would never have been taken for members of the same family, let alone sisters. Anne, the younger of the two, was slightly plump and a jolly, merry woman, always ready with a quip or a helping hand if required. Lisa was tall and thin with a pinched face, which usually looked as if she had recently smelt something unpleasant. She was much more serious and reserved than her sister.

They were exchanging family news and gossiping a little about people they both knew.

Anne said, "Listen, love, I'm a bit worried about Derek's business. How do you think it's going? He's been a bit quiet about it lately."

Lisa replied haughtily, "I think he's still ambitious, but not as successful as he ought to be. He's been getting a bit slapdash lately, especially since this Russian woman came on the scene—more or less letting Jim and Gina run things. He has to get a grip or he will be in trouble—the world is much more competitive now than when he started. Look how he is done nothing to that ugly old house of his—he doesn't seem to care anymore. I always think a nice house is one of the first things you should have when you have made a bit of money. He's really been letting things go since Margaret died. Of course, he hands out too much to those dreadful girls of his. He's is not getting any younger and I don't think he has a lot to fall back on. Mind you, he was always good at squandering money."

"M-m. That is certainly true—but I do think he is quite keen on this Russian lady! Ah! Here he is, the old reprobate."

Derek was threading his way through the tables smiling at them.

"Hi, my babes!" He gave each a peck on the cheek and sat in the chair opposite. "So, what would you like to drink, girls?"

He brought a gin and tonic and a mango juice back to the table, along with a pint for himself, and the three spent an hour or so chatting together about everything and nothing. Anne was her normal bubbly self, but Lisa tended to be a bit aloof and remote most of the time. The sisters were anxious to hear all about his new love, but contained their curiosity, waiting impatiently until Derek himself mentioned the subject. Out of the blue he suddenly said. "So, will either of you be coming to Russia with me for my wedding? Anne? Lisa? I do hope that at least one of you can be there."

"I am afraid it won't be me," said Anne. "I have just too much to do at home. But I will help with the arrangements here so that we can all celebrate together when you bring your new bride home. Derek, sweetie, are you really sure this is the right thing to do? You know I'll support you, whatever you do, but a lady with foreign ideas and little English? It could easily be a disaster. Wouldn't you rather find an English girl instead? Maybe it's worth trying a matachmaking agency?"

Lisa was even more forthright, "Well, I really don't agree with any of it—I think, it is madness and quite wrong of you. If you are still determined, I will be polite and treat your chosen wife as a sister-in-law, but I cannot pretend to be happy about it! I've always thought your behaviour with women was flippant, and this affair has done nothing to change my mind."

Derek felt his temper rising, "Well, Lisa, you are entitled to your opinion, but whatever you think, I shall propose to her when she visits me and if you don't like it, I'm afraid you'll have to jolly well lump it! It really has nothing to do with you, anyway. I'm amazed and very hurt that my own sister is not prepared to allow me a little happiness." This outburst had made his face really red and he stomped off to the bar to order another pint, willing himself to calm down. He didn't want to have a heart attack, and neither did he want any bad feeling with his sisters. He went back to the table, calming down a bit and apologised for his outburst. He added, "I'm sorry, Lisa if you don't like it, but I'm going to marry Lara if she'll have me, come what may. Even if you won't come to Russia, I hope we shall be able to have a civilised family meeting together, when she comes to England next month." With this agreed, they parted reasonably amicably, and Derek went on his way, still unhappy with Lisa's attitude.

So much for family support! he thought. *I shall just have to rely on myself in future. If their hopes come to nothing and their peace is disturbed, so be it! Let them all go hang, is what I think! I only want one thing now, and that is to know that my darling Lara will be there to wave me off when I go out in the morning and welcome me home in the evening. I want to travel with her, stay in good hotels, do things together like every other couple and that is exactly what I'm bloody well going to do.*

The following morning he was still feeling grumpy and gave his decorators a bit of an earful. The three weeks were almost up and they only appeared to be about half way through. They assured him that it would all come together soon and they would be finished on time. He drove into the town center and went to the Western

Union Office.

“I’d like to send some money to Russia, please.”

Chapter 7

"May we come in?" Alex and Michael were peeping round the door of the professor's office. It was lunchtime and he was alone with his usual cup of coffee and a sandwich. He never went out at lunchtime, preferring to stay at his desk and work through.

"Hello, professor Yakomoto. Sorry to disturb you, do you have a moment?"

"It's OK. I've finished lunch and I'm really pleased to see you both—let me ask you a question first. I am reporting to the faculty tomorrow about my visit to the Boston conference. It was very interesting and some of our American colleagues made some extraordinary claims about nuclear research. I have an intriguing statement to pass on from a big international player in the business and I think you boys will be very interested to hear it." He smiled as he spoke to them, obviously pleased with himself. "I wanted to ask you if you would be prepared to assist me with my report. The whole thing will only take about three hours, and I think you might find it illuminating—how about it?"

"Sure. We'd be glad to help. When would you like us to start? Will we need a briefing first?"

"I would like you in quite early tomorrow—can you

manage eight o'clock?" They nodded their agreement. "I will fill you in on everything tomorrow. Now, gentlemen, what can I do for you?"

The boys glanced at each other and Alex said.

"We'd like to ask if you would be prepared to give a short talk at a student's discussion evening. We know you're really busy just now, but it would be great to hear about the Boston conference first hand, and ask questions less formally. It'd only have to be about twenty or thirty minutes and could be any evening that you can manage. All the guys are really hoping you will do it, I'm sure you'd have a full plate. Is there any chance?"

"Mm-m. I'm sure I can manage it—I feel honoured to be asked—I'll let you know when I am free"

ೞೞ

The next morning after having spent an hour with Alex and Michael going over certain points, the Professor stood on the rostrum in the spacious conference hall to deliver his report to the entire faculty. His voice vibrated with excitement and passion for his subject. When he finally stopped speaking he looked intently at his silent audience. Before they could break into the usual polite applause, he began to speak again.

"The Americans have announced that they want to open a world-wide competition, which anyone can enter, on ideas for how best to produce safe energy in the future with minimum influence on climate change. If all the countries pool their resources, perhaps something can be found that will be less destructive to the planet than the present systems. The rewards are high—they have set aside five hundred million dollars in prize money."

He waited a moment for the buzz to die down and then continued. "They have a committee of world famous scientists, economists, and financiers. The competition has already been open for a week, details were published in most of the scientific magazines with terms and conditions, etc. So, all you young people have a great opportunity to showcase your talents, and, who knows, one of you may become very rich indeed!"

With this he finished his presentation, and there was now some applause and a few cheers from the students. For most, this competition would just be a pipe dream, but one student, at least, took the announcement very seriously indeed.

Late that evening, Alex sat at the back of the almost empty bus with his eyes closed. He liked the night bus because it was quiet and he could look out at the streetlights and think about his day, good or bad. Today had been very good indeed. It had been long, it was true, but it had been very satisfying. He was now coming home from a students' party, which had been good fun. Lots of beer, good humour, and dancing. He was a bit of a show off and liked dancing. He knew he was good at it and he often noticed girls watching him. He was a tall boy with a strong athletic figure. He was well aware that women found him attractive and he was not averse to playing on the fact. It gave him a kick and pandered to his male ego. He thought of the beautiful blonde with enormous trusting eyes whom he had spent most of the evening with. She was very sexy and he had found her irresistible. Alex had been tempted to take her back with him to his flat, but had not suggested it as he still hadn't finally finished with Natalie. Their relationship was definitely no longer working, especially since he still thought she had probably blabbed to her father about his research. She had phoned him a couple of days ago and asked if he would meet her the next evening at a nightclub they both liked—he guessed that she was hoping to save their relationship. He had agreed to go, although he didn't really fancy her any more. Alex was a decent enough guy to come clean before he took up with someone else and he was also fairly confident that the blonde would keep for a day or two!

The following evening found him at the nightclub, Natalie had chosen. As he stepped through the door, he saw that it was already quite full, with a number of young people dancing on the glass floor. Alex quite liked this place with its cosy soft lighting and up to the minute dance music. It was not too dark for him to quickly locate Natalie. She was sitting at a table near the dance floor. He waved to her and walked over.

"Hi! How are you? Sorry I am late."

"Don't worry. Would you like a drink?"

She looked elegant and sophisticated. She had beautiful grey eyes, long black hair and an expensive looking black dress, which didn't leave much to the imagination. Alex had been really smitten with her once, but she had got a little drunk one night and slept with another guy when he'd been away. Although she had tearfully confessed the next day, his ego had been dented and he'd angrily told her to get lost. He was still hurting from the break up and, when Natalie had asked for this meeting, he thought it would be a perfect opportunity to finish with her.

Natalie started straight in, "Alex, darling. I'm really so sorry for making such a stupid mistake. You know that Claus didn't mean anything to me, I was just a little drunk and you weren't there. I feel such an idiot. Oh, baby, you mean so much to me and it's really breaking me up not seeing you." She had tears in her eyes as all this spilled out. "Alex, we were so good together, please give me another chance. I promise I'll make it up to you."

Alex felt his resolve weakening. She was a stunningly

beautiful girl, and they had had some wild times together. "You've got me really confused now," he said. "I came here determined to finally break it off. Look, leave it for a bit. Let's try to enjoy ourselves for a couple of hours. Come on, let's have a bop. I can't stay late—I have to be at the University early tomorrow."

They joined in the fun on the dance floor, quickly letting their hair down. When a slow tune, was played, Natalie was happy and even a bit hopeful, when he held her close. Before long the mood overtook them, and Alex felt his desire rising, it was so relaxing to speak in Russian again.

Natalie suddenly said. "By the way, Alex, I was in Russia last month visiting my parents and I told them all about you."

"Really, what did you tell them?" he said, suddenly interested.

Natalie blushed and smiled "I told them how clever you are, and how proud I am to have you as my boyfriend. I told them about your little secret and they were amazed that I could know anyone so clever. My father was especially intrigued. They said I should bring you with me next time I go home. I know a fantastic place we could go—it's just forest—trees, birds, and peace. My parents own a little dacha on the edge of a lake. Alex, please come there with me. We could spend the whole-time swimming, sunbathing, and making love. It would be perfect."

Alex pulled himself up. "Look, Nat, I know you're trying to butter me up and you know how I hate that. It's a very kind invitation, and the dacha sounds great, but we are not really still together. I just don't know if I want to go through all that again. It got pretty grisly last time, if you remember. As for all that boasting about inventions, well, it was nothing, just a bit of nonsense brought on by too much beer and wanting to show off. Please, just forget all about it."

Her face darkened. "All right, Alex—have it your own way, I'm not going to beg. I hope you live to regret passing me up," she said spitefully. "It was you I liked anyway, not your bloody job. Just leave me alone!"

He made to leave, but being polite, asked if he should see her home.

"No thanks," she said. "Some of my real friends are over there so I'll go and enjoy the rest of the evening."

She walked away, without looking back.

The next morning, Alex was up very early. He was going on a field trip of energy faculties located in the far north of Sweden with a group of students. Once on the university minibus, he relaxed and stretched his legs. He'd had a disturbed night with all his problems with research and women flying around in his head and was soon nodding off. The bus was very comfortable and travelling slowly north. They had left the good roads over an hour ago when they passed Torne Trask and, according to the driver's announcement, it would be another hour before they arrived at the remote cottage hotel on the extreme northern tip of Sweden, where they would be staying.

A week ago, the university had convened students who were interested in a field trip to look at a major wind farm and a hydroelectric station in the far north. With any luck, they should see the Northern Lights as well. Most of the students were from the energy faculty, as they had been given priority, and the group of twenty or so young people were now relaxing on the long journey north.

After a comfortable night in the cosy hotel, they had decided to trek to the power station they had come to see, rather than go in the bus. They set off in high spirits, with the usual joshing and teasing among the group. The nights were frosty at this time of year, but the days were usually crisp and sunny. Today, there was brilliant sunshine with just a light northerly breeze in their faces. Alex had thought yesterday how lovely the country was up there and even in summer the panoramic view of the mountains, already white with snow, was quite stunning. The mountains here were not especially high, but seemed to invite climbers onto their gentle, forested slopes. It was all just fantastic and everyone was jumping with excitement.

After a while they could see a number of wind turbines on the horizon, and before long they began to hear their low droning noise. Alex found this noise increasingly disturbing and wished he had brought some earplugs. He found himself wondering how the workers here coped with it, and he felt a little spurt of satisfaction that maybe, in the future, it would all be different. No more noisy windfarms, or scary nuclear power stations, and no more dirty thermal ones. His dream was of a new energy source that would be different from anything we have now—it would be a great innovation and join all nations together in a wonderful technological and economic revolution—economies would be stable, people would thrive. While he was revelling in his fantasy, he strode on purposefully, happily inspired by his great dream.

ᘛᘚ

Most of the students were sitting near the big open fireplace trying to catch a little of the warmth, some were on a bench and others on the armchairs around it. Alex was talking with a girl he had gotten to know on this trip. To anyone watching it was clear that they were getting along very well together, they laughed as they chatted and looked into one another's eyes rather more than was entirely necessary. As they continued their banter, Alex was asking himself how he had not noticed her before, she might make the trip north very interesting indeed! And who knows? He was a free spirit now—there was a vacancy that she might be prepared to fill. Blonde? What Blonde?

"Quickly, hurry up everyone! All of you—outside!"

A member of the party had been on watch outside and now he alerted the rest of the party to the Northern Lights, which were just appearing in the sky.

"Look, look!"

"God!—fantastic."

"That is just so beautiful!" They were all outside, staring at the sky where vivid colourful waves rolled over and over. It was a symphony of quite stunning beauty, which they found impossible to describe in words. Although many of them had seen the phenomenon before, no one had seen such a spectacular occurrence, they were all blown away by the breath-taking vision. It continued for half an hour or so and it was a smiling, happy bunch of young people who eventually made their way back into the lounge to continue their evening.

Next morning the coach was ready for the excursion to the hydroelectric power station. A guide was available to tell them about everything they would see over the next two days and Alex was especially interested in this part of the trip. His mind was already full of the changes he hoped it would be possible to make to energy production in the future.

Their trip to the north proved to be a remarkable success—everyone enjoyed themselves hugely. On the way home, the bus rang with the sounds of laughter, singing, and even some serious discussion on all that they had seen.

When Alex returned to the university, there was some good news waiting for him. He received a letter from the Central Office informing him that he had been chosen to attend an international forum of young professionals from the field of energy production, which was to be held in Croatia early in the New Year. It was a considerable feather in his cap, especially when he discovered that the university would pay for the whole trip. He was anxious to call his mother and share his good news. He really missed her and knew he should call her more often, but he had been so busy that they had fallen out of the habit of daily conversation. Even so, he tried to speak with her at least once a week. He picked up the phone.

"Hello, Mum, oh, yes, yes I am." He told her about his trip north and the conference in Croatia. As usual, she was pleased and very proud of her clever son. He then asked, "How about you? What about your romance with the Englishman? Oh, really? Brilliant! Of course I'll be home for English Christmas and New Year to meet him, did I get that right, Mum? I think we are all coming over together, Oleva and Michael and me it will be brilliant—we can sort out the arrangements next week?"

He rang off and thought about his mother. It was great that she was so active and positive. He had always thought he had the best mum in the world. The mother/son bond was very strong between them, and he loved her dearly. She had an easy-going nature and, although she never interfered, she was always ready with clearly thought out advice, whenever she was asked. She never nagged, and was always quick to help, whether with words or deeds. He felt truly pleased for her trying to rebuild her life and was looking forward hugely to going home. He then called his sister to make sure it was OK to visit them next week.

After lectures Alex and the other students went to their

laboratories to continue their research. Alex had brought his secret memory stick with him and sat at his computer to continue his calculations. He returned again and again to the same point.

However he checked the figures, the result was always the same—there could now be no doubt about it. The process would work! The world would be free of its dependence on fossil fuels, and even possibly nuclear energy. It was such a fantastic prospect that he still could hardly believe it himself most of the time. Whichever way he looked at it, facts were facts, and he was sure he'd made no mistakes. Any government that adopted this system would instantly become a world power—the financial implications were almost beyond comprehension. His process would become an enormous economic weapon, and he would have to take great care how, and to whom it was made available. The ecological benefits alone would change the planet. A clean world and a reversal of climate change—it was almost too big to think about—his head was spinning with the enormity of it all. However, that was in the future. For now, he had to finalise his research and refine his thesis. Then his formula would have to be tested under the most stringent of laboratory conditions. He went back to work.

It was dark when he heard the sounds of students leaving the building and he realised how tired he had become—it was time to go. He usually did all his work in the lab, but he needed a shower and something to eat. He decided that he would not take important papers and the memory stick to carry home, it was very late. He headed to the bus stop.

After getting off the bus he had a short walk, which took him for about a hundred yards or so past a small park. As he drew level with the gate two workmen suddenly confronted him. Without warning, they jumped at him. He saw a sudden flash behind his eyes and everything went black.

ꕥ

He could hear voices a long way off. They came nearer and he opened his eyes to see a pale green room. He knew at once it was a hospital as his brain rapidly kicked into action. He remembered being attacked by two men, but the rest was a blank.

"Hi, there. Wakey-wakey!" A young nurse was smiling at him. "Do you feel better now? You were picked up by a passer-by who called an ambulance. You had passed out and we thought you were just one of the usual drunks, but the doctor who examined you thinks you have had an electric shock. You will be fine, so don't worry, but the doctor would like a word with you before we let you go. There's also the usual paperwork, of course."

"Thank you for everything, but I need to get home as soon as possible. I had a briefcase with me, do you know where it is?"

"No. The chap who brought you in said you had nothing with you."

Alex immediately became anxious. He was fearing the worst. "Can I go? I have things I must do."

"Yes, as soon as the doctor has seen you, we'll provide some transportation for you."

In the ambulance, on the way back to his flat, he checked his pockets for his wallet and other possessions. Nothing was missing! What he had feared all along, became a certainty. This had been no ordinary robbery. Whoever it was had wanted only his briefcase. But he had nothing important there! That robbery could only mean one thing—

Chapter 8

The band was playing gentle music on the little stage at one end of the tastefully decorated hall. Coloured fairy lights twinkled over the dancing couples and the night air was full of the scent of the flowers, which were dotted about the place on the tables around the dance floor.

"Lara! At last! Will you dance with me?" He smiled at her. "I have been watching you dance and waiting my turn patiently. You are looking quite radiant—has something happened? A new man, maybe?"

"Now wouldn't you just like to know." she smiled. "But, I have to admit it, Sasha. You are very perceptive, as always. I never thought it would happen but I've met someone really special."

"Lara, my dear, that's truly wonderful! Do I know this lucky man?"

"Not yet," she said with a smile. Lara could open her heart to this man. She had known him for many years and, unusually for someone so handsome, he had never once tried anything with her. She truly valued his friendship and excitedly told him all about her romance with Derek and how the Englishman had visited her and swept her off her feet.

"I hope I'll have the opportunity of meeting him

before too long." He danced a little closer so that he could whisper in her ear. "I must warn you before you go back to your table. I think you should know that the chap sitting opposite you is one of the big chiefs at the station, and he is well known for having a bit of an eye for pretty women. He has already asked about you. The frosty looking lady next to him is his wife, and she's a bit of a harridan I'm afraid. So, if he starts flirting or askingyou're your phone numbers you would be well advised to ignore him. We can do better without a scene here tonight."

"Thanks for the warning, Sasha, I already caught him leering at me. At the moment, I'm only interested in one man. Anyway, your big cheese is fat, bald, and rather sweaty—not exactly my type,"she laughed. "Let's go back to my table."

She was smiling and gay as he accompanied her back across the floor. He bowed and said gallantly, "Thank you for the dance, Lara, you are a wonderful dancer."

Sasha was the deputy director of a huge nuclear power station close by. His was in a prominent position in the neighbourhood, which enabled him to have his fingers in a number of lucrative pies—shops, restaurants, building projects and the like. He was extremely wealthy, but did not let this go to his head. He was a true gentleman—quiet, friendly and always helpful to those less fortunate than himself. Lara had known and liked him for many years. They had collaborated successfully on many community projects and always got on well together. He ensured that she was on the guest list for the official parties that were a necessary part of the business life of any Russian town. After her messy divorce, he had helped, both in business affairs and as a shoulder to cry on, but had never attempted to be anything more than a very good friend. This suited Lara perfectly, and she felt very fortunate to be part of his circle of acquaintances.

When she finally got home, she filled the bath with cool water and, with a sigh of relief, soaked her aching feet. *Too much dancing in stupid shoes,* she thought. *I think my toes are warming the water up, not the water cooling them.* She was sitting on the edge of the bath feeling tired, but in a good mood after a fun evening. She would prepare for bed now, and then have some special time talking to Derek on her computer. She always thought of this time as her little reward and as compensation for any problems she had had to deal with during the day. So, sitting in her pyjamas she called him up. When he answered she began laughing and teasing him and pointing the web cam around her room.

"Really? Have you redecorated your house just for me? I am so proud of you! That's wonderful! I hope you planning to change cars for me, too? I think a Maserati would be very nice. OK! OK! You should know by now when I am only joking—the house will be good. Thank you very much, sweetheart. I will—I will like it. I go to bank tomorrow and deal with the transfer. Then I can buy my ticket. I am looking forward so much to seeing you again. It's OK. Yes, of course I love you and can't wait to see you, and England and everything." She squealed with excitement, "Don't worry about my visa, darling, I have friends here who can fix anything. I am so happy—look at me? I'm grinning like a 'Cheshire cat.' Isn't that what you call it in England?"

A few days later, as she left her office, she called to her secretary.

"Olga, I shall be off on Monday, so if anyone calls from Headquarters can you tell them I'm unwell and at home. I'm actually going to Moscow on some private business, but I want no one to know about it. I'm sure I can rely on your discretion?"

"Of course, Miss Petrova. I will look after everything here, and go to your deputy if I really must. Good luck with your business, and have a good weekend."

So, that was that. She'd send her driver to pick up plane tickets and then went home to sort out the arrangements she needed to make. Tomorrow, an old girlfriend was coming from the next town to visit her for the weekend. Lara always looked forward to her visits, she hadn't seen her for about four months. Lara had told her about Derek over the phone, and her friend had immediately asked if she might come and stay for a night to hear all the news. Lara was delighted to think that one of her oldest friends was so happy for her, and had bought a nice bottle of wine. She planned to cook something special for their supper.

That evening, however, she was going out to dinner with another man friend. She thought with amusement, that she did seem to collect odd men. Lara was sure that most of their wives were not too pleased about it at all! Still, she never led any of them on, and it was very good for her morale that they all seemed to delight in her company. Lara had known this particular man, Vasyli Ivanovitch, for a number of years and had been rather surprised when he had phoned, out of the blue, insisting that they meet.

Her driver Peter arrived at her door with the tickets. She put them quickly in her bureau and went out to the car. "I'd like you to drop me at Momo, the restaurant on the corner of Gorky Street, please."

It was a dark, drizzly evening and anyone sensible would have stayed at home in a cosy bed with a good book, but she was hungry and had promised to go. Lara jumped quickly from the car and hurried into the restaurant. It was warm and very luxurious. Momo had a reputation for excellent food, discretion, and expense!

Fortunately, her friend was very wealthy, so she didn't have to worry. Vasyli was the director and owner of a big transport organisation in her town, he was influential and rich. He had a reputation for honesty and decency, and was well liked by everyone who knew him. He had the added advantage of good looks and charm, and, although Lara was a couple of years older than him, she had always felt that he rather fancied her. The big drawback was that he was married but unhappy. It was well known in their social circle that he and his wife had not got on for years, but were sticking things out for the sake of their children. Lara felt quite sorry for him, but had never entertained any thoughts of stealing him, however willing he might have been to be stolen. She simply never dated married men—it was totally against all her beliefs. So, today, whatever he had to say, she would tell him about Derek.

"Hi, Vasily. Have you been waiting long?"

"Hello, Lara." He rose and looked into her eyes as he kissed her hand. "Thank you for coming. I hope you are hungry. Will you let me order for you?"

"Yes, but, Vasily."

"No buts, Lara, I understand why you are nervous, but no one knows you are here. My secretary arranged this evening for us supposedly to talk about the unemployment situation in our town, so no one will think anything untoward. We can talk all evening about anything and you need not feel uncomfortable about spending time with a married man. Did I guess right?" He smiled at her.

"Ok, ok, Vasily. Let's not worry about that, I'm here now. Shall we order something to eat?"

During their meal, they chatted about the local gossip and the different people they both knew. There was a small band, a girl singer and two musicians, which provided gentle background music and, together with a glass of champagne, helped Lara relax a little.

She could tell what was coming from the soft expression in Vasily's eyes. This, for him at least, was far removed from a business meeting. Suddenly, he reached for her hand and said. "Lara, I have to speak to you seriously. You have been in my thoughts and my heart for many years. Whenever you visit my office, I find myself agreeing to do anything you ask. So often I have wanted to hold you close to me. My darling, I would like you to come away with me. A holiday somewhere in Europe. Please, please don't refuse me. I'm sure you must be lonely, living as you do, although I do realise that you have plenty of other opportunities. Please give me a chance, you won't regret it. I have a very good position and money enough to support my wife and children, with plenty left over for you and me to have a full and happy life. I would buy another house for us and I swear I'll protect you forever. You know I have a wife in name only—we've had separate rooms for the last five years and agreed long ago that we would divorce when the children completed their university courses. Our youngest does his finals this year, so I feel that I have at least a moral right to discuss this with you. Lara, I'm not asking for an affair, I want to build a life with you."

She looked at him, her eyes wide with surprise and sadness. *He's too late.* she thought. She had already fallen for another man, who now filled all her thoughts and dreams. But what was she to say now to this sad, gentle man, whom she counted as a friend?

She tried to soften the inevitable blow. "Vasyli, I am so confused right now. I had no idea that you felt like this. Can I have some time to think about what you have said? Meantime, let's not waste this lovely music. Dance with me?"

While they danced she managed to avoid looking directly at him. She decided not to make him unhappy this evening, but to telephone him the next morning, so that she would not have to face his disappointment. Although Lara was tough and efficient in business, she was a real softie when it came to personal relationships. She hated to see anyone hurt. Of course, this was pathetic and cowardly, but he had been her friend for a long time and she couldn't face turning him down tonight, especially as she was bursting with love for Derek. She still hoped to find a way to avoid losing him as a valued friend. If she had learnt anything in life, it was that true friendship is precious, especially for the unattached. Although, at this moment, she was so besotted that she hardly considered herself single.

At the end of their evening he drove her home and, outside her apartment asked if she would ask him in for coffee.

"No. Not tonight, Vasyli. I am waiting for my friend to arrive for the weekend." She smiled at him as the white lie made her refusal more comfortable for them both. "Thank you for a lovely dinner," she said, and added with a mischievous grin, "and especially all your wonderful ideas to ease unemployment. They will be very useful." He gave her a slow smile and drove off into the night.

ꕥ

"Hi sweetie! I should be with you in half an hour."

Lara had nearly finished cooking the pilaf, a Georgian dish of slow cooked rice and vegetables with lamb. She tasted it—mmm—pretty darn good. It was one of her favorites. She had a good bottle of red Georgian wine, which had been given to her by a grateful client, and tonight would be a perfect opportunity to drink it. She was sure that Zhannet would be impressed.

"Hi Lara! It's been ages!" They hugged one another on the doorstep. Lara's guest was the same age, with blond hair and the low husky voice of a heavy smoker. They had different personalities but were both strong, independent women. They respected each other and always got on well together.

After supper they lingered at the kitchen table to talk and Zhannet picked up her cigarettes. As usual she sought her friend's permission before she lit up, "may I smoke here Lara?"

"Of course you can, but just open the window behind you a little first? How about some coffee? I'll put the kettle on."

"Lara, I've listened to your big news, and now must tell you what I really think. To be honest, I'm shocked."

"Zhannet!! Why ever?"

"Why, Lara? Just think about it. Do you really want to abandon your country to be with this so-called beloved one? Let me tell you something. I hope I can be honest with you." Lara nodded, dumbly. "I know how romantic and soft hearted you can be—even naive sometimes and, because you have had an easier life than most…no, no, let me finish. Just listen and let me say my piece! I have a lot of friends who are far worldlier than you. Older women like us, but who have been around a bit. And they have some real horror stories to tell! I have heard quite a lot about international marriages, and all I can say is 'look before you leap.' If you think I'm exaggerating just go on the Internet and read what some of these 'brides' have to say. Please, my dear friend, I beg you, slow down a bit and really think before you marry this man."

Lara sat quietly, stunned by her friend's words. She knew Zhannet to be passionate in her views, but she had not been prepared for this onslaught, and was truly shocked by it.

Her friend ploughed on. "Do you know what kind of men come to Russia to look for wives? They are usually men who have violent tempers, or filthy habits and think that Russian brides will consider them worth the hassle just for the sake of a western passport. Not just Russians, of course, girls from other places are just as stupid. Look, these men start by being kind and charming and generous and then, after they have got you safely married and moved to their home, they turn into monsters. They lose interest and force their new wives to be little more than housekeepers. Insults, abuse and worse! They cheat and lie and just go on leading the lifestyle they want. You'll be treated like a second-class citizen until the inevitable happens—the marriage will fail. And then where will you be? In a foreign county with no friends and no support!"

"I'm sorry Lara," she continued. "I'm not trying to frighten you, I just don't want you to end up being humiliated and used as a domestic servant. You are worth so much more than that. I have known you for such a long time and I'm really frightened about what might happen to you. Of course, any relationship can fall apart and some of these marriages do work out, I admit, there are some real love matches out there, but it doesn't seem to me to be very many."

By this time, Lara was barely holding back her tears.

Zhannet softened slightly. "You've told me all about him and I'd love to believe that he is a decent, honest man, who will love you for ever. You know that if you stay here, in your current position, you will have no financial worries at all, and a good pension to look forward to when you retire. But what will happen to you over there? You have no idea. Do you think that 'love' will provide for your old age? You must sort out everything before you get married.

"Ok I'm sorry, I know I'm looking on the blackest side, but Lara you just can't be sure. Maybe he only wants you to look after him—what if there are problems with his daughters. Do, please think carefully about this before you jump in. I would want a legal financial settlement, before I'd do anything so drastic. If he won't agree to that first, don't marry him. You have too much to lose!"

By now, Lara was sobbing uncontrollably. She just couldn't believe that her dear friend would attack her like this in her own home, and she took a few deep breaths, trying to regain some composure.

"Well, Zhannet. I hope you've finished.

"I must say I'm very hurt that you can't just be happy for me. I have a new love and possibly even a new life and you seem to think I am so stupid that I have not considered all this. I know that behind it all you just want the best for me, but please grant me some intelligence. Next month I am going to visit him in England. Believe me, if I'm not absolutely certain, there is no way I'll stay with him. I'm 100% sure he really loves me, but I will remember your warnings."

"Lara, promise me that you will come straight back if he turns out not to be the man of your dreams. Remember that you will always be my friend. If you have to come back here I can help you. If needs be you can come to work for me. Please believe me, I am not saying all this because I am jealous of your new love. You know I'm no longer interested in men and have no wish to marry again. I just worry about you and your safety."

Next day, when Zhannet left for home, they parted as friends, but Lara was still a bit resentful after her friend's tirade. She went about her usual weekend tasks in a sombre mood, counting the hours until she could settle down to talk to Derek.

When the time to call finally arrived, her computer did not want to boot up. Very odd! She'd never had any problems before. One of her neighbours was an electronics engineer and she picked up the phone to speak to him. And the phone didn't work. Lara now became seriously concerned when that was dead too.

She was beginning to panic a bit, but then remembered that the tele-communications system in Russia was not the most reliable at the best of times—it was probably simply an unfortunate coincidence that both phone and internet had gone down together.

She could do nothing until the next morning, so went to bed, hoping that Derek wasn't too unhappy not having heard from her as usual. The next day, she arranged for a visit from a telecom engineer to check out the equipment. The pleasant young man checked all the external wiring and, finding no problems, began to look inside. Lara waited impatiently. She had work to do and was worried that she had been unable to let them know at her office that she would be late. Finally the engineer called her.

"Please come and look at this. There, behind this wardrobe. Can you see those two wires? They have been deliberately cut!"

"What? Cut? Are you sure? Could it not have been accidental?"

"No, I don't think so. They have been cut deliberately and quite recently. Has anyone else been in the flat?"

Lara's head whirled. surely Zhennet wouldn't have done such a thing—

"I can't believe it! Just to stop me speaking to Derek?" Lara was shocked and angry.

The engineer reconnected the wires and checked that everything was working normally.

As soon as he had gone, Lara phoned Zhennet.

"Did you interfere with the phone wires in my flat?"

There was a pause.

"Did I what? No, no, of course not—how could you think such a thing. Lara, what has happened?"

"Somebody deliberately cut the phone and internet wires. Are you sure you weren't trying to stop me talking to Derek?"

"Lara! I did no such thing—that is an outrageous thing to think I would do to a friend! I'm really very upset that you could even think such a dreadful thing." With that, she slammed the receiver down.

Lara did not know what to think after this conversation but deep down she knew that even if Zhennet had not been responsible for the damage, she was still very bitter about Lara's romance, and was not the true friend she pretended to be. Lara decided then and there, that Zhennet would not be a guest at her wedding, if it ever happened!

Her driver was knocking at her door. "Miss Petrova! I am ready to take you to Saratov, to the railway station now. Where are your bags?"

Lara had spent the last month making arrangements for her trip to England. She had sorted out her visa, booked tickets, and arranged holiday time off. She had been shopping for gifts—not just for Derek, but for his family too. She wanted to start off on the right foot with them, especially his daughters. Only one of her suitcases contained clothes for her visit, the other was full of presents. Derek had called her last night, full of excitement and anticipation. He told her that he had set up a dinner party at a local restaurant for her to meet his brothers and sisters.

"Sweetheart, I want so much for you to like England

and my home."

He had sounded so sweet and loving and she couldn't wait to see him again. If she had had wings she wouldn't have waited for an aircraft, she would have simply flown straight to him. *Soon, soon I shall be there!* Her heart was full to bursting.

Her driver had decided to take a short cut to the railway station which was in the regional city and he suggested that they take a scenic route along some country lanes.

"That would be lovely." she said. "We have plenty of time—take me along that road where the sunflower fields are. It's beautiful there at this time of year and I don't think they will have been harvested yet."

An hour later the car left the motorway and turned onto a concrete secondary road. The sun was low in the sky and on each side of the long straight road were fields full of bright yellow sunflowers. It was a truly magnificent sight and Lara was overwhelmed by the natural beauty round her. She definitely spent too much time in the city!

The driver suddenly said, Boss, would you mind if I stop for a moment? I need to...mmm…go into the field." He sounded very embarrassed. But he was obviously in some discomfort.

"Of course not—we still have loads of time."

They pulled over and Lara also got out of the car to stretch her legs. Peter was gone for several minutes, entirely hidden from view by the dense wall of flowers. The air was still and there was nobody else around. Lara felt relaxed and at peace.

The sound of an oncoming car suddenly interrupted her thoughts. A black Pickup roared down the track and screeched to a stop by Lara's Zil. The doors flew open and four tough, athletic looking young men jumped out.

They ignored Lara and they lined up at the edge of the field where her driver had disappeared into the flowers.

Lara became very frightened, what on earth did these thugs want? She had no idea who they were, but she could see from the expressions on their faces that they were very unhappy about something—they had not stopped here to pass the time of day. At that moment her driver reappeared, carrying a bunch of sunflowers. When he saw the men, his smile rapidly disappeared, and he froze with fright. The guy who seemed to be in charge approached Peter threateningly.

"Did you plant these sunflowers? Do you spend your time looking after them? Who gave you permission to take those heads?"

"I'm sorry," he said. "I just wanted a few for my wife. She is pregnant, you see, and I…" his voice trailed off as he looked at the ground—probably hoping it would open up and swallow him.

"Well, we have ways of dealing with thieves. We'll teach you to steal…"

They turned towards Lara's car and deliberately let all the air out of the tires. They then removed the valves and pocketed them. Lara screamed.

"Please, stop. I have to get to the railway station which is a ways away. I'll pay for the flowers. My driver realises what he did was wrong. He's truly sorry and will never do it again! Please, gentlemen! It will be dark soon and we have no spares. We are really sorry!! Please, I beg you!"

They took absolutely no notice of her pleas, and got back to their own vehicle. With a sardonic smile and a wave, they sped off in a cloud of dust.

"Miss Petrova! I am so sorry! What can I say to you? I only wanted a few flowers for my wife. God, what an idiot I am. They must have been watching and guarding the crop!"

"Peter! Stop wailing and think what we can do to get out of this. We have to get to the station very soon. In another hour I will miss the night train to Moscow. And possibly even the flight to England. Just think of something."

Peter went to the boot to see if by any remote chance he had any spare valves. All Russian cars are obliged by law to carry a foot pump, but that is no use if the tire valves are missing. Lara suddenly called to him.

"Look, Peter, there on the horizon. There's a car coming. We must stop it quick, wave it down."

As the car drew nearer they saw with horror that it was the same black Pickup, still full of thugs. It ground to a halt and both Peter and Lara were paralysed with fear. A window opened and the valves were thrown onto the ground in front of Peter. Without a word, they screamed off again, leaving the driver scrambling in the dust for the precious valves. Lara and her driver were alone again.

"Good grief, Peter! What a start to my holiday! For heaven's sake get the tires pumped up quickly and get me to the airport."

Chapter 9

Moscow! Her favourite city, without a doubt. She had been here so many times, both on business and to take in its unique culture—the Bolshoi, the Tretyakov Gallery, the Vorobyov Hills. It was a wonderful place especially with time to soak it all up. But not today!

Today she was in a hurry to leave, to get to Sheremetyevo Airport and to England—to her beloved Derek! Lara left the train and joined the crowd of passengers moving from the platforms to the upper level of the huge Moscow Railway Station. Although she was a little travel weary from the twelve hour journey, and was wheeling two pieces of quite heavy baggage, she still looked very elegant amidst the throngs of travellers. Lara's good mood made her face radiate warmth and happiness. She crossed the concourse towards the stairs to the street level and the taxi rank.

"Hey, lady! Just a moment!" A young girl, who looked like a student, was approaching Lara.

"Did you drop this? It looks like money in here!"

The girl was holding a white envelope that certainly looked similar to the one Lara had been given by the bank with her dollars for the journey. She was sure hers was still tucked safely away, but opened her handbag to look just to make sure. In an instant, a young lad, ran up to them. He had a worried look on his face and began to speak very quickly,

"Oh! Ladies! Thank goodness—you've found my money. It must have fallen out of my pocket when I was searching for my passport."

As the boy approached them, Lara was astonished to see the girl quickly slip the envelope into her pocket and look away. Lara was momentarily confused and didn't know what to say or do. The young man suddenly became very angry. "What have you done with my envelope," he shouted. "Open your bag! I think you might have hidden my money in it?"

Lara suddenly found her voice, "Young man, I know nothing about your money, I think you should ask this young lady." She pointed to the girl, who feigned innocence and flatly denied all knowledge of any envelope. Lara couldn't believe what was happening.

The young man repeated his demands and threatened to call the police. Lara was already quite short of time and had no wish to spend the next few hours discussing the incident with policemen. Very reluctantly, she opened her bag. The girl suddenly began shouting at Lara, distracting her, as the young man poked his fingers into her envelope to check its contents. The boy's attitude immediately changed and he respectfully apologised for doubting her and walked away. The girl had somehow melted into the crowds of commuters too. What a peculiar thing to happen! Then it hit her! Lara opened her bag and checked the envelope—of course, she had been robbed, most of the money was gone. How I could have been so stupid, she thought. Her mind had been too much on England and seeing Derek again. There was a police post nearby so she went in and told her sorry tale to the officer on duty, embarrassed by being taken in so easily.

"You are not the first, love, and you won't be the last, I'm afraid. There are several groups of street robbers working the stations, but they're very sharp and we haven't been able to catch any of them yet. They move from station to station—not just here, but all across Europe, unfortunately. Leave your details, but don't hold out any hopes. You're very unlikely to see your cash again. Put it down to experience and be more careful next time."

Lara swallowed her pride and headed for the taxi rank feeling very angry and annoyed with herself.

ᏣᏣ

The flight to London was uneventful and the food was the usual plasticised, airline rubbish. Was it really beyond the wit of man to serve passengers something simple, fresh, and appetising?

Some years ago, when Lara lived in Far East of Russia, she frequently had to fly on business, so being airborne held no terrors for her, she hardly noticed when they encountered some slight turbulence. The journey was spent gazing out of the window and going over in her mind what happiness—or sadness, might be awaiting her. Crossing the Channel her excitement grew as she watched the coastline of England emerge through the mist.

Lara came out of the customs hall at Heathrow to find Derek frantically waving his arms to attract her attention.

They embraced and Lara said, "At last, my love! I am so pleased to see you again. I am now standing on the soil of your motherland and I am very much happy to be here with you, my Derek."

They left the brightly lit airport buildings and walked to Derek's Jaguar, which was parked in the multi-storey parking structure nearby. Once cocooned in the warm leather interior, Lara tried desperately to stay awake—she wanted to talk, but her eyes would not stay open and she dropped off almost as soon as the engine started.

Derek turned the music down and drove carefully into the night almost unable to believe that she was here with him at last. Tomorrow, she would see some of his world, and hear about all the plans he had made for them. Once on the motorway he put his foot down and 3.5 litres of supercharged engine rocketed them smoothly into the starlit night.

ɞɞ

Bright sunlight was streaming through the windows when Lara woke the next morning. She could smell coffee and hear a dog barking. Derek came into the bedroom carrying a tray of coffee and toast.

"Here you are, my darling. Good Morning!" He kissed her cheek,

"I don't think you remember much about going to bed last night, you were pretty well out of it. You certainly seemed to sleep well, I don't think you moved all night. I was afraid I would wake you when I got up to take the dogs out, but you were out like a light."

"I slept like a baby. I was very tired and, sorry, I did not talk with you."

"Don't worry, sweetheart—relax and make yourself at home. I'm really sorry, but I have to call at the office for a couple of hours—I should be back by about eleven-thirty. We can have some lunch out if you like, and plan the rest of the day. Please, feel free to look around the house and the garden. Don't worry about the dogs, they're big softies and quite harmless. The shower and bath are through there and there's loads of food in the fridge. Have anything you want for breakfast—I will be back as soon as I can."

Lara showered and went downstairs to find two beautiful little dogs sitting on the sofa, watching her intently. She smiled and approached them, holding out her hand cautiously to stroke them. "Hello little dogs, let us be friends. You are very beautiful, but it is not good manners to sit on the sofa. Come on, I will give you both a treat. I hope there is something tasty for you in the fridge."

Through the windows of a spacious conservatory, she could see a pretty garden and a riot of autumn colour beyond the fence, where the property gave onto ancient woodland. She stood transfixed for several minutes enjoying the view. It was really an amazing setting, almost like living in the forest. It was a beautiful blue and gold end to a September morning, with barely a breath of wind. As she watched, two grey squirrels were chasing each other around the shrubs. They ran across the lawn and over the wooden fence that formed the boundary. She smiled contentedly at their antics, happy to be in such a lovely place—so much more beautiful that she had imagined.

Her thoughts returned to Derek. He must have worked so hard to get everything ready for her visit. The house was tidy and spotlessly clean everywhere, she felt a sudden rush of affection for him. If he took so much trouble over his home, he would surely care even more for the person sharing it with him. A wife, maybe? Who knew? She would find out eventually. Maybe this visit would come to nothing, but so far everything had been more perfect than she had thought possible—even in her wildest flights of fancy. Derek really seemed to be very much in love with her—she was sure he couldn't just be playing games. Lost in these thoughts, she was suddenly aware of the doorbell ringing.

ᔓᔕᔓᔕ

At Derek's factory, everyone could feel that the boss was in a very good mood. He laughed a lot and told them all about his new lady friend, who was visiting from Russia. He even promised them an early Christmas party in a swanky local restaurant. The staff were buzzing with his news and wondering if they were going to hear wedding bells soon. Derek quickly cleared up the bit of work he had to do, and shot back home as fast as he could.

He ran into the house and grabbed Lara, kissing her gently on the mouth.

"My sweetheart, I'm still having trouble believing that you are actually here—I rushed home to make sure I wasn't dreaming," he laughed.

"Let's go and have a drive round and I'll show you the area. There are some really pretty villages in this part of Midlands, and then later we can go and eat at a restaurant, which I'm sure you will like—what do you think?"

"Of course, we will go anyplace what you want. Everything is new and interesting for me and I believe in your taste, Derek. I'm already acquainted with the house and with your lovely dogs, I like everything so far to be honest with you, my dear. So, what should I do now? Preparing to go out? OK. Give me one hour please. Oh, I forgot to tell you, a lady rang the bell and something told me, which I did not understood in detail, sorry. She wanted to talk with you, she is a neighbour, I think.'

"Ok I know who it was and what it was about. It's not important, darling, go and put your glad rags on.'

A few days later Derek's brother Tom arranged a party for the whole family at a famous hotel nearby. It was originally built in the early 1900s, for a wealthy landowner, in the style of a French chateau. About ten years ago, the house had been sold to a local millionaire and opened as a luxury hotel, specialising in weddings and other celebrations. The restaurant had a Michelin star and was the place to go in the locality for an elegant night out. There were several acres of wonderful grounds with streams, a waterfall, and beautiful formal gardens spreading down to a small lake, complete with swans and ducks.

Derek had thought long and hard about including his daughter in the party. Most of the family lived fairly close by, but for Jane it would mean a three-hour drive just for dinner. The most practical solution would have been for Jane and her family to stay overnight with him.

"Lara, would you mind if Jane and her tribe came to the dinner party at The Chateau, and then stayed the night with us?"

"Of course not, darling! What a question. I will be absolutely glad to see them in your house. The next day I could to cook a nice meal for them. They will not confuse me. Don't worry."

But, in the end, Derek decided that he didn't really want daughter there, putting a damper on everyone's mood. Lara was pleasantly surprised by Derek's thoughtfulness in asking her first. It all just added to how she felt about him and how genuine he seemed. Lara was seriously falling in love and hoped desperately that it would not all fizzle out to nothing.

At first sight The Chateau looked like something out of a Walt Disney fairy tale. Turrets and towers brightly lit against the night sky, and all nestling comfortably into the forest background. The enormous, arched entrance was also a blaze of welcoming light, Lara was spellbound by its beauty. However, there was little time to stare, as they were greeted as soon as they walked in by a smiling group of people, who were waiting for them—Derek's family.

Lara was introduced to everyone, and made a big effort to remember all the names. Soon she was trying to speak to them all, using her limited English as well as she could. They all seemed very friendly, but she couldn't avoid the feeling of being under the microscope, with everyone reserving judgement for the time being. She guessed that she was the latest in the line of Derek's girlfriends, who had been through this vetting process.

That's fine, she thought. *I don't suppose many of them have met a real live Russian before. I'm a rare thing—a bit like a monkey in a zoo, I suppose. Just keep smiling, Lara.*

They stood in the bar, drinking and chatting until called to their table. The dining room was beautifully decorated and there was a jazz piano playing softly in the background. Lara was hungry and really looking forward to her dinner. Derek's sister, Anna, quizzed her throughout the meal. She wanted to know all about Lara's family, her children and her job. Lara had to work hard, searching continually for the right English words to get her answers across without making a total fool of herself. She knew it was important, for Derek's sake, as well as her own, to make a good impression on them all. It felt a bit like an examination, but she also had the feeling that both Anna, and Derek's brother Peter, were trying to help her to join in, and to feel comfortable with them all. Derek's younger sister, Lisa, was a rather different matter. She seemed to be watchful and reserved and Lara could read the distrust and resentment in her eyes, which she made no attempt to disguise. *Ok lady.* Lara thought silently. *You're first in line for the Lara Petrova charm offensive—just watch out!*

Out of the whole group Lara particularly liked Tom's wife. She was very elegant with a sweet smile and friendly eyes and seemed genuinely warm.

Derek whispered, "Lara, don't eat all that if you don't want it—it's only a starter. There is a main course to come."

Lara was really surprised by this as she had assumed that such a plateful must be her dinner. Ah, well—another English lesson—they eat very large portions over here!

When the main course was served Lara couldn't believe the size of her plate. It looked like enough for everyone, and was far too much for her—there was also the pudding trolley to come.

She whispered to Derek, "I am sorry but I cannot to eat all this. It is very wonderful taste, but too big for me."

"Don't worry, sweetheart—just eat what you want."

The rest of the family continued to chomp down their food as if they had no idea where their next meal was coming from. Lara just put it down in her mental notebook and decided that next time she would make sure that less was ordered.

Elder brother Peter tapped at his glass to get their attention.

"Right, Guys! You know it is my birthday next month so we're taking this opportunity to invite you all to ours for a party. Anyone who can't come?" There was instantly chatter and discussion around the table. Lara thought sadly that she wouldn't be able to come as she would already be back in Russia. Pity, it would have been fun, and another chance to meet everyone!

At the end of the evening, after all the goodbyes had been said, Lara was totally drained, both physically and emotionally. Trying to follow the various conversations, whilst appearing pleasant and interested in everything, had been difficult. However, it had still been a wonderful evening and they were both happy and laughing when they returned to Derek's house.

"So, what did you really think of them all? You certainly seemed to charm everyone, especially my brothers." He said, with a slight hint of jealousy.

"Yes. I very liked all of them. Tom's wife is nice lady, but your sis Lisa was a bit cold to me at the beginning. I hope I can make her to like me before very long."

"Great, I'm sure it will all be fine. I'm very proud of you. It can't have been easy with everyone gabbling away at the same time. I think you were just brilliant. And thank you, darling, for making such an effort.

"I don't know what you think, but maybe we could go up to the Lake District tomorrow? It's a really stunning part of the country—mountains, lakes, forests, and it's only a couple of hours north. There's a lovely little hotel that I've stayed in a few times. Wonderful location, on the shores of Lake Windermere. Very cosy—delicious food and very good local beer—not that that will interest you too much," he laughed—"it's not as wild or remote as Russia, of course, but still pretty special. Actually, I want you to see all of Britain—Wales, Scotland, everywhere. We could even drive up to Holyhead some time and take a ferry over to Ireland. It's very lovely there. Miles and miles of wild natural countryside—and it doesn't rain all the time.

"Thank you very much, with very pleasure, I look forward to tomorrow."

ꕥꕥ

The next morning was bright and sunny. Just as they

were about to leave the phone rang—it was his daughter Jane.

"Hi Dad! I'm just about to leave to visit you. Sorry for the short notice but I really want to talk to you—well, and see you, of course."

"Oh dear, Jane. I'm not sure, I don't know…just a sec. We were just on our way out to go to the Lakes for a couple of days. I need to talk to Lara." Derek covered the receiver and said, "Sweetheart, its Jane, my daughter. She says she wants to visit us today. What do you think? Will you be devastated if we put our trip off for a couple of days?"

Lara was sitting nearby, stroking the dogs. "No, no. Of course not, my dear. I want to meet her soon. We can go tomorrow or next day I think."

Derek was relieved, but also a bit miffed that Jane still obviously meant to come up, despite knowing that she had spoiled their plans. He said, "Jane? Yes, of course come now. We'd both like to see you—no problem, we can change our plans a little. See you in a couple of hours."

Jane rang off thoughtfully. *What was that all about? Her father had been a bit less welcoming than usual. Of course, this dratted Russian woman is running his life already. God, I bloody hate it. When he is on his own he is so sweet to us, so generous with his time and ready to drop everything for us. But whenever there is a woman in his life everything changes. Sister Carol is right. He is far too old to be having love affairs. And as for marriage! If he gets married, everything will go to his new wife. I want my dad around for a long time yet, but I don't want some foreign gold digger cashing in. What did he bring her to England for anyway? I'll have to talk some sense into him.*

If he's worried about being alone when he gets older,

he could get a housekeeper. If he gets ill we can find him a good nursing home. He's being a stubborn old fool—it's just not fair to Carol and me!'

ഗ്ദ

Lara suggested that she should begin to make some food for their guest. Derek was amazed and delighted at the way that Lara seemed to cope with everything that was thrown at her, and still come up smiling. He volunteered to help, but as some extra supplies were needed, left her happily clattering pans in the kitchen, while he went off to the supermarket. Lara, meanwhile, was thinking about her approaching meeting with Jane. She had no idea of the animosity that Derek's daughter felt towards her, and was truly looking forward to meeting one of his children finally. Lara, in her innocence, thought that Jane's absence from the family gathering last week had been due to her living so far away. Derek had neglected to mention that she hadn't been invited! As she prepared the meal, Lara mulled over how important it was for her to get on well with Derek's children. *I want to be friends with the whole family, but especially Jane and Carol. There does seem to be a slight coolness between Derek and his daughters—he never talks much about them. That is not good, but he's a strong man, and I'm sure it will all sort itself out. I will just do my best to be nice to them. It's odd, though, that one of the girls Carol has had nothing to do with him since their mother died. Such a pity she turned against him. Still, life goes on and maybe I can help to put things right.*

Lara set the table in the conservatory, not forgetting a pretty vase of flowers from the garden, and lunch was ready just in time for Jane's arrival.

"Hello, both of you." Jane kissed her father and turned

to Lara, “Pleased to meet you, Lara. I have heard a lot about you. My father says he is crazy about you—so take care! When Dad is mad about someone or something, he becomes dangerous!” Jane said this jokingly, but Lara could feel an undercurrent of antagonism and sarcasm beneath her words.

During lunch both Derek and his daughter complimented Lara on the food she had prepared and the meal progressed smoothly. Lara’s understanding of spoken English was improving day by day, and she felt much more confident joining in the conversation. However, there was still an unpleasant tension beneath all that Jane said to her, and Lara knew that however complimentary she was, it was not sincere, and the real reason for her sudden visit was to speak with her father.

After lunch Lara sent the pair of them off to talk, while she set about sorting out the kitchen.

Derek and his daughter stayed in the study for almost an hour, during which time Lara could not help but hear occasional raised voices. Suddenly Jane appeared from the room, red faced and angry, and stormed into the garden. Derek emerged a few moments afterwards, squeezing Lara’s shoulder as he crossed the kitchen. He said quietly, “Please don’t worry, darling, everything will be all right. I love you.” He then announced, “Jane isn’t going to stay, she wants to get back before it gets too dark. We’ll still be able to leave on our trip this afternoon, if you like.”

Jane came back in, having cooled down a bit, and said, “Dad, my Aunt Clare lives near Windermere and you know how well I get on with her. I’m sure if I asked, you could stay with her. It’s my fault that you cancelled your hotel booking—I’ll call if you like and set it up.'

“That’s kind, Jane. Lara, will that be all right with you?”

“It’s good. I do not mind where we to stay.”

With that Jane left, promising to call her aunt on the way home. Lara and Derek set off northwards.

ꕥꕥ

Once she was on her way, Jane called her aunt. Clare was Jane’s mother’s older sister and they had always been very close.

“Hi, Auntie, it’s me. Thank you. Yes, yes, I will. Listen, I’m on my way home from Dad’s. Yes it was awful. Auntie, he has brought an odd woman over from Russia and I think it is serious. He is besotted with her. No, I don’t like it either, or her, for that matter! Listen—They’re on their way up to the Lakes and I suggested that they might be able stay with you for a couple of nights. Oh-h, sorry, yes, I see. Well, it’s too late to change now—they’re already on their way. Really? Will you do that? Yes. No, I’m not bothered at all—serve them right! It’ll be a lesson for him and, with luck, might put her off. At least she will see that life will not always be a bed of roses for her. All right. Brilliant—Bye!”

ꕥꕥ

It was just getting dark when Derek and Lara arrived in Windermere. They had stopped several times so that Lara could admire the stunning views. She had been overwhelmed by the magnificent scenery and wanted to take more and more photographs. They had stood for a while on the shores of the lake with their arms around one another, both almost unable to believe how lucky they were to have found each other. When they finally pulled up outside his sister-in-law’s home, it was after seven. It was a traditional Cumbrian country house in a very rural location. The door was opened almost immediately by a thin faced, elderly lady.

"Oh hi, Clare. I hope Jane called you and that you are expecting us?"

"Yes, she phoned." Her tone was cold and very unfriendly.

"Derek, I'm sorry but you are no longer welcome here, whether you arrive alone or with some floozy in tow. No—I have no wish to discuss it. Please just leave!"

With that, she closed the door on them. Lara and Derek stared at each other in shock and amazement. What on earth had caused such an outburst? They had never been particularly close, but Derek had stayed there before on a number of occasions, without any problems. He was embarrassed and very angry.

"I'm so sorry, my dear! I'll get to the bottom this when we're back home, please try and ignore it. We need to find a B&B sharpish or we'll be sleeping in the car." They drove on to Caldbeck, and were relieved to find a farmhouse B&B, where they were shown into a delightful room looking out the hills. There was even a little brook gently murmuring outside the window—perfection.

They walked down to the village pub, where they had a delicious home cooked meal and then spent a happy hour talking to the locals. As usual, Lara caused quite a stir. When they found out where she was from, everyone was trying to buy her vodka!

In the morning Lara was enchanted to discover that the fields outside their window were full of fluffy white sheep, she had never seen them in such numbers before. She had another revelation in the cosy little dining room when she was faced with the 'Full English Breakfast!" *Only the English could eat a whole dinner at the start of the day!* she thought. The farmer and his wife suggested they visit Kirkby Stephen, where there were pretty shops for Lara to browse. She bought some mint cake and some woolly gloves to take back to Russia as souvenirs. The countryside was much softer that the great open wastes of Russia, but she loved the wild skies and gentle hills dotted with her 'little cotton-wool sheep.'

The rest of Lara's time in England passed in a blur. There was so much to see, and of course, her increasingly beloved Derek. They held hands and hugged non-stop, like a couple of starry-eyed youngsters. Four days before she was due to leave, Derek told her that they would be going out to a special restaurant that evening. All day he was especially sweet and attentive to her. She kept catching him smiling mysteriously at her, and he had insisted she wear her best dress that evening. What was he up to?

In the restaurant, Derek waited until they had been seated, and had a sip of the Champagne that was waiting for them. He took her hand, at once serious, and said, "My darling, I hope you will make today very special for both of us. Lara, I love you and want you to be my wife."

She stared back at him, a surge of joy bringing tears to her beautiful green eyes. "Oh yes, my wonderful Derek. I am very happy to marry you."

With a huge smile, he produced a tiny, gold-embossed leather box from his pocket and showed her a sparkling solitaire diamond ring. He slipped it onto her finger saying, "I am so happy, Lara. I cannot think of anything to say, except thank you so much, my love. I will do everything in my power to make you happy."

Derek asked Lara if she truly liked the ring that he had chosen. If not, he would be more than happy to take her to the very upmarket jeweller in Knutsford, where she could have any ring she wanted. She assured him that it was the best ring in the world, and she wouldn't dream of changing it.

The following evening, after a simple supper, they began to make wedding plans. Derek asked if she would prefer to be married in England or in Russia. "I think I feel a bit alone to be in England. It is better for me with all my friends in Russia if that is good for you.'

Derek just wanted to be able to call her his own and readily agreed.

"Perhaps we could fix it for Christmas?

"The factory closes for a week and I can come over to you. I hope your children will be there—I'm longing to meet them both. Then we will make application to register our marriage."

They spent the rest of the evening playing dominoes. Derek taught her "fives and threes," one of his favourite games. She had played in Russia as a child, but this was a little more complicated and there was a lot of laughter and joking.

The telephone rang, interrupting their game.

"Hello? What? I beg your pardon. Yes?" Derek covered the receiver. "Lara, it's someone from Russia for you. Sorry, I don't understand what they are saying, will you take it?"

Lara was immediately nervous as she was handed the phone.

"Allo? Who? What?" She let out a wail of anguish. "Oh, my God! Please no-o-o!! I cannot believe it. She did not wait for me to return from England! Thank you for calling me, I'll be back as soon as I can get a flight. Thank you for letting me know. Yes!"

She flung herself into Derek's arms, her face contorted with anguish, as tears flooded down her cheeks.

"Lara! Whatever has happened?"

"My mother died just one hour ago," she whimpered.

"Oh my dear!" Derek held her close, stroking her back softly.

"Can you change my ticket? I must go back for tomorrow."

Derek went straight to the computer and quickly organised a suitable ticket for the following afternoon.

When Lara checked in the next day, her eyes were still puffy and red from a sleepless night. "I'm so sorry, my Derek, but at the moment I just want to be in my motherland, Russia."

"Whatever you wish, my love. After the funeral, when you're feeling better, we can talk about our wedding. For the moment, take care on the journey, sweetheart. I am so sorry about your mother. Be strong, darling, and call me as soon as you land."

Chapter 10

Alex's sister, Oleva, was speaking to her brother on the telephone. "Hi, Alex. How're things? Sometimes I worry about you, buried in that laboratory—life isn't a rehearsal, you know. Look, what about Christmas? Are you going to be able to get home? It will be a chance to meet this Englishman of Mum's—what do you think?"

Alex said "I think it's brilliant—I'm really glad she's found a man who makes her happy at last—I don't give a monkey's where he's from. We should just be pleased for them both. I know Mom's still pretty dishy, but she's still lucky to find someone she really fancies at her age. Actually, if she does marry him it will add to the family's international flavour—Russian, Swedish, and now possibly English. I might even be on the lookout for a sexy African girl, you never know." He laughed and continued.

"Seriously, when we do get home we must visit Grandma's grave. I feel really sorry that we didn't go to her funeral. I know, I know, it was just impossible, but at least we can give her our last respects at the cemetery with some flowers."

"Yeah, you're quite right, Bro—let's do that. Do you want to book tickets for all of us at the same time? It would be neat if we could travel together. We could try and fix the Moscow bit the same day that Mum's Derek arrives and then we could meet him at the airport. I'll phone and ask her which flight he's coming in on. There can't be that many Englishmen flying to Russia for Christmas!"

Oleva was four years older than her brother and almost as tall. She had her mother's raven black hair, but now wore it in a smart bob as the respectable wife of a Swedish architect. She had always tended to treat her young brother as a child, but fortunately, he recognised that she was only trying to be helpful most of the time, so he usually bit his tongue and put up with it. Oleva lived in a small town about twenty kilometres outside Stockholm. Her husband, Michael was quiet, and perhaps even a little dull, in his taciturn, Swedish way, but they loved each other and most of the time enjoyed their pleasant, uneventful life together without any problems.

Oleva called her mother to finalise the details of their visit and to ask if she wanted anything from Sweden. Of course, Lara was buzzing with the news of her engagement, and that the wedding would be in Russia. Oleva was delighted, and mother and daughter spent the next hour chatting and laughing together, filling each other in on all the local gossip, both in Balashov and Sweden.

When Oleva finally hung up, she felt much better—confident that she need have no worries about her mother's choice of man, or her future happiness. She seemed to have had a great time with Derek and his family, who had welcomed her warmly. Oleva was delighted when her mother told her about the proposal and the decision to marry in Russia. And two Christmases—English and then Russian. *Party, party*

party! she thought.

Oleva and Alex both knew that their mother had been very lonely since her divorce. It looked now as if she had finally found a good man, and could begin to enjoy life again.

Oleva went to find her own husband. He was in his study, as usual, beavering away on his beloved computer.

"Michael, sweetie, brilliant news! Moms going to marry her Englishman—in Russia. We're all going to spend Christmas there to meet him. Alex is planning to join us—it'll be a real family celebration—I can't wait! He's going to sort out the tickets for all of us and, with any luck, the famous Derek should be already with Mom when we arrive. We need to talk about what clothes we'll need. It'll be far colder there—you've never experienced a Russian winter! It makes Sweden feel quite mild!! And we need to make a gift list for all of them." She put her arms around his shoulders and hugged him. "What do you think about Mom getting married again?"

"No problem! If two people love one another, why shouldn't they get married? You can make a mistake at twenty-five or fifty-five, it makes no odds. Most of it is luck anyway." And then he added with a smile, "Apart from us, of course, sweet light of my life. Actually, I can understand anyone fancying your Ma—she's still very attractive—and clever, and hardworking, and quite well off—Mr. Derek sounds like one lucky man to me. I may still have to give him a little advice though, about marrying Russian women. You know, how temperamental and strong-minded they are, how they're always right, and never at fault." He wriggled away as he felt Oleva grab his ear—preparing to give it a good twist for his cheek.

"Only joking Babe—you're all too wonderful for words. Isn't it about time for a little drinky-poo—what would you like?"

ઌઌ

Lara's return to Russia was, inevitably, very painful. It was true that her mother had been ill for some time, and had not been expected to live much longer, but it was still a shock, especially with her being so far from home. Lara's sister, Masha, who lived close to their mother's flat, had looked after her during her prolonged illness. She had been totally selfless, spending many hours comforting their old mother, and looking after her apartment. Lara had visited wherever she was free and had provided money to help pay for medicines and extra nursing care, when needed. She had phoned regularly before her trip to England, and her mother had been overjoyed to hear about Derek and Lara's hopes for a new life. It was just very sad that she had not lived long enough to hear about the engagement and to meet the handsome, charming Englishman, whom her daughter was going to marry. Instead of a wedding talk with mother, Lara had to help her sister to arrange a funeral.

She called her secretary from Sheremetyevo as soon as she landed. Olga was quickly briefed about all that had happened, and informed that Lara's return to work would be delayed for several days.

ઌઌ

The day after the funeral Lara went back to her office in Balakovo. She had a great deal of work awaiting her but she called through to her secretary first. "Olga, can you come in here please—I need to bring you up to date with all that's happened." Although Olga was only a secretary, they had worked together for a long time and had become quite close friends. Over the years, they had both had occasion to cry on one another's shoulders, but Olga was a true professional, and would never abuse Lara's familiarity.

"Oh Lara! I was so sorry to hear about your mother. If there is anything, absolutely anything I can do, don't hesitate to let me know. Please give my deepest sympathy to your children when you call them. You must have very mixed feelings—so difficult for you, to pick yourself up after your sad loss, and then have to think about wedding preparations.

"I don't know how you'll cope with it all. Everyone will be happy for you, but very sad as well."

"Sad? Why ever should they be sad?"

"Because it means you will leave your job and all of us forever. It will be really horrible for me—I will probably change my job. We have been together for so long that it will be impossible to work with a new director."

"Olga! Please don't say things like that! You'll break my heart! I sure that whoever replaces me will be decent and easy to work with, you will soon adapt. Please don't be sad, you'll make me cry too. It might be a bit tough at first, but I'm sure it will be fine once everything settles down. Now, listen. I have one more thing to tell you, but please, deadly secret until Derek arrives for our wedding."

ଓଓ

After some time, Derek fixed a date for him to come to Balakovo, where Lara and her driver would meet him—he promised faithfully to appear this time! It was a date closer to the English Christmas, closer to the big family, friends meeting. She was so happy making her preparations, a family, almost complete, sitting round a dinner table together—it would be a dream come true.

One more call, then, "Oh! Hi, Sasha—it's me. How are you? Good, good. Listen, would you believe? I'm going to get married again, and have a big favour to ask."

Apart from his position in the Nuclear Power Station, Sasha had several other lucrative strings to his bow. One of these was a large and very prestigious restaurant, universally acknowledged as the best for miles around. He immediately understood what Lara wanted, and agreed to take over the entire organisation of her family celebration in December.

He was genuinely delighted for her, and he was determined when the date of her wedding was known he would take care of her wedding party, this would be the wedding party to end all wedding parties, it was something he simply loved doing. Lots of people, all having a wonderful time, was his idea of heaven.

Christmas in Russia and England are celebrated at different times and in different ways. Lara wanted Derek to experience a real Russian celebration.

Her next call was to a friend. "Hi, Alina, yes, I am back. Mmm, really my trip was brilliant. Yes, he is a lovely man. In fact, I want you to come to dinner on the 25th to celebrate the English Christmas with us and the children. Yes, it'll be at that local restaurant, you know where we been with you before, and you liked very much.

"Oh, Ali, I have oodles to tell you—how about you come over to supper on this Friday? I am asking also a couple of the others, so we could have a girly evening. What do you think? Great!"

A few evenings later, anyone passing Lara's flat would have heard very loud music and lots of chatter and laughing.

"Lara, do tell us again what you did when his relative sent you both away from her house! God I hope all the English aren't like that. Where did you learn such a dreadful word? Surely not from Derek? Still, it sounds like the old dragon deserved it. What a miserable cow."

And Alina, as an English teacher, went on to suggest exactly what words she might have used, to an outburst of laughter and squealing.

"Lara, how would you describe an average Englishman? Do they dress well? Are they nice to women? Did you see any drunks?"

"Well, the ones I met were mostly rather quiet, a little reserved in company, but usually very polite. The majority of the men behaved as gentlemen. They all seem friendly enough, but I'm not sure it's entirely genuine. You feel that they are hiding behind a screen or something. It's difficult to judge if they mean what they say and they don't open themselves like Russian men. They are tied up with their families and respectful to their wives—in company, at least! You all know there is good and bad in every nation, but in general I rather like them. In some ways, they are quite like us—especially when they throw a party! Very loud music and enormous amounts of alcohol—maybe not such strong stuff as our men, but an awful lot of it. But they don't dance! They stand around, getting more and more emotional or telling very rude jokes between them, never in presence any woman.

"Well, Derek said they were pretty risqué. Maybe fortunately, I didn't understand most of them! But the young women! You wouldn't believe the way they go on—especially when they've had a few drinks. Whatever they think they are doing is beyond me! Many of them have no self-control. They'll snog anyone they fancy, without a care who's watching, and probably a lot more besides. And some of their clothes! They wouldn't be out of place in a Parisian brothel—not that I know too much about that." she laughed. "I guess they are heavily influenced by the TV over there. Amazing! Sex scenes in just about every film or play you see. I'm afraid it's going to be the same here before long, so maybe I should not be too hard on them."

Her friends were interested to hear everything about life in Britain. The most amazing thing to Lara was the seemingly hundreds of leisure activities that were available. Everyone was doing something in their spare time. Gardening, all sorts of dance classes—ballroom, disco, salsa, tango, there were amateur dramatic societies, choirs, painting classes, orchestras, gyms and swimming pools. Anything anyone wanted to do, there was a club somewhere. Lara felt that had she lived in England, she would never have time to be bored.

"And with all the family stuff to fit in as well, I don't know how they have time to do any work." she added. Eventually the evening drew to a happy, giggly conclusion, with Lara still telling her guests about England as they crowded into the lift to leave.

ઌઌ

Three young people left the Sheremetyevo arrivals hall and headed for the bar. One of them, Oleva, was looking very green. She suffered dreadfully from airsickness and needed a quiet sit to recover. Michael went to buy some drinks and Alex opened his newspaper. Oleva sat quietly, hoping she would feel better soon. At least the long flight was over. They had decided to go on down to Saratov by the overnight train to save Oleva from the agonies of another long flight. From Saratov, it was a very short local flight on to Balakovo but Lara wants to send her driver to pick them up from Saratov airport, which should not be such a problem. While she waited for her husband to return with her tea and lemon, she watched the passengers flooding out of arrivals. So many lives—where were they all from? Where were they going? This seemingly endless human convoy. She had not been in Moscow for a couple of years, so most things looked new and different. The airport was certainly much smarter now than she remembered it. There was plenty of time before their train, so she closed her eyes and tried to relax.

Derek felt a little more confident when he arrived in Russia this time. He knew that a "friend" would be meeting him, and he spotted him straight away. It was the same chap as before.

"Hello, Mr. Harrison. We meet again. My comrades are nearby and we won't keep you long this time. You will have plenty of time to catch your next flight."

There was a car right outside and Derek with Nicolai were whisked off to an apartment building about five minutes from the airport. They took the lift to the third floor and were let into a flat.

"Come in, come in, Mr. Harrison, we would like a little chat with you. Everything is going to plan so there's nothing to worry about. Would you like some tea? Or maybe one of our specialities—a little vodka with some caviar?"

They were smiling, but watching him closely.

"Tea will be fine, thank you." Despite their relaxed manner, Derek could not get rid of the feeling of tension which overtook him as soon as he was with these people. He was pretty sure that he was in no danger at the moment, but the men sitting opposite him were still FSB agents and probably with the power of life and death over him—hardly an encouraging situation.

The Russians got rapidly down to business. “So, Mr. Harrison, what progress have you made? Are you going to become Alex’s new best friend? Maybe you are already? Come, tell us all your news.”

However hard he tried to remain calm and business-like, Derek felt himself sweating and shaking. Speaking carefully, he told them about his intention to marry Lara and how that would naturally involve him with Alex. He mentioned the planned family party and how he would then meet both of Lara’s children.

“That sounds very satisfactory, don’t fail to keep us informed of any developments in that department. You may call at any time, day or night. Will you have time to visit the Far East whilst you are here? It would be very much to your advantage if you could. You will need five free days and we do all we can to facilitate your visit. You would be met at Komsomolsk airport and taken around the enterprise as promised. Please let us know the dates that you will be available, as soon as possible.”

“Nicolai will now take you to the domestic Airport. Please give our best wishes to your bride-to-be,” he added, with more than a hint of sarcasm. “But remember, Mr. Harrison, do not mention a word of this to a living soul, not even your beloved Lara. Nobody must know about our business dealings or it’s all off. And,” he added ominously, “Should you ignore our request, we shall no longer be able to afford you any protection during your time in Russia. Consider that very carefully, and don’t do anything stupid.”

ᏅᏅ

Derek was happy to finally arrive in Saratov and hugged Lara. He asked her about the her mother's funeral and if she still felt sad.

"Oh yes. Yes, of course I did. I still think about her all the time. But now you are here to look after me I'm sure it will get easier. Don't you?," Lara asked.

The crowd had thinned, Derek and Lara were almost alone, standing in the arrivals hall, kissing and hugging like teenagers.

"You know how sorry I was, darling. It was horrible seeing you so upset. But I'm here now, and soon we'll be married. We'll go to England and build a new life together." Lara had tears of joy in her eyes as he kissed her again. They walked slowly out to her car, where Peter was waiting patiently.

ꕤ

"Darling? Are you asleep?" she whispered to him.

"I completely forgot to ask about your children—do they agree you to come here and visit me?"

It was well after midnight and, although they had turned out the lights over an hour ago, Lara wanted to go on talking.

"Sweetheart, don't worry about it—it's my problem and I am doing what I need to do. Can we talk about them another time?—I'm really wiped out. Your children are coming tomorrow, so let us sleep so that I will be in a fit state to meet them."

He hugged her closer and they both drifted into sleep.

They next morning, they had to be up early as Lara's children were due to arrive shortly after midday. For very different reasons, both she and Derek were anxious to meet them.

The apartment, with its two bedrooms, was obviously

not big enough for everyone to stay.

After Lara had spurned Vasily's advances in the restaurant, she had had to use all her feminine wiles to keep cosy with him. His company owned a large, very smart apartment in the center of town, which was used to accommodate visiting dignitaries, important guests.

Over the Christmas holiday it would be empty, and Lara had managed to persuade Vasily to let her use it for her guests also a minibus with driver in case she needed. Beautiful women do seem able to get their own way in this life, most of the time, at least!

The eventual reunion at the airport was a typically Russian affair. Flowers, hugs, kisses, laughter and not a few tears were the order of the day.

Derek shook Alex firmly by the hand and felt an immediate liking for the young man, which he sensed was reciprocated. They all crowded happily into the minibus, though Derek was still consumed with guilt about his secret. Unfortunately, it was not enough to conquer his fear of the possible consequences, should he come clean with Lara. He also thought there was a good chance that everything would be finished and she would throw him out, if she discovered his duplicity. He tried to push his darker thoughts to the back of his mind and enjoy the moment.

Lara saw them all settled into the apartment then she and Derek left, promising to return later for supper with them all. In Lara's book, everything was going swimmingly...

ꕥꕥ

A couple of days later Lara walked into the bedroom with a cup of coffee and woke her lover excitedly. "Derek, darling, look out of the window! Just look at this weather! It is so beautiful—look, look!"

He jumped out of bed and joined her by the window.

"Jesus! How fantastic! And that lot all fell overnight? I've never seen such snow. Wow! And just in time for Christmas!" He stood behind her with his hands around her waist and kissed her gently behind the ear. "What should we do with it?"

Lara suggested that they have a quick breakfast and call her car to drive to her favourite spot by the river, which would be deserted at that time. They could walk through the snow and give Derek his first taste of a real Russian winter.

An hour later, muffled and booted, they asked the driver to leave them on the forest road and come back in a couple of hours. Holding hands, they wandered slowly through the snowy pines, which were tranquil and silent. Snow was still falling but very lightly now—just a misty veil in front of their eyes. They followed a narrow path, which Lara often used, laughing and talking until they reached the edge of the mighty River Volga. They stopped and marvelled at the stunning view, gleaming in the pale sun. The enormous river was frozen for nearly a hundred metres from the bank—a pristine white expanse, marked only by the occasional animal track. Further out the great river looked black and brooding. The morning was windless and it was impossible to tell which way the river was flowing—just a vast expanse of white and black. Derek barely dared breathe at the majesty of it all—he couldn't remember ever having been so overwhelmed by a natural phenomenon in his life. Although Lara was renewing her acquaintance with a much-loved friend, the beauty of the scene never lost its magic for her. It was not easy to walk along the bank but they pushed through the deep snow for as long as they could.

"My love, I have arranged that we will go to a small party in a local restaurant tonight, to celebrate your English Christmas. It's all fixed, the children will be there and some other friends. I am sure you will enjoy our way of celebrating."

He smiled at her, "I'm sure I shall."

They were almost back to where they'd arranged to pick up the car when suddenly Derek had a funny five minutes, acting up like a small boy. He tripped Lara up, sending her tumbling into a snow drift. She spun round and grabbed his ankles, pulling him down into the snow too. They were both flailing about, laughing and screaming like children. He rolled towards her and tried to steal a kiss but she wriggled out of his arms and got to her feet, just out of his reach. She quickly seized a handful of snow and rubbed gently but deliberately in Derek's face. He stood still to let her do it then picked up a handful himself and with infinite care began to massage it gently onto her forehead. Tiny crackles of ice shone in her hair as he took her cheeks between his hands kissed her. Derek said, "What a beautiful, beautiful lady you are. You look like a real snow princess now." Brushing the snow away from her face he looked into her eyes and kissed her again, "Lara, I do love you so much."

ᏋᏋ

The restaurant was full. There seemed to be several celebrations going on. Lara's party was in the middle of the room and most of her guests were already seated, chattering noisily together and beginning to let their hair down already. Derek was sitting between Lara and Alex, thinking how much more sedate and dull a similar party in England would be. The table was groaning with food, salad, sliced meat, sausage, smoked fish, little meatballs, tiny pasta pies, black and red caviar on little pancakes—all of it new to him. There also appeared to be unlimited alcohol, Champagne, red and white Georgian wine, brandy and the mandatory iced vodka. As soon as a bottle was empty another materialised to replace it. There was no order to proceedings—the guests took whatever food or drink they fancied at the time. It was all so spontaneous and light-hearted. Derek looked around the table and felt a pang of regret that nobody from his own family had been prepared to come with him. It would have been fun to have someone to talk to, although those with any English at all, and especially Alex, made an effort to include him whenever possible. He also noticed that the whole company had gone to great trouble to dress up for the occasion, so different from the UK, where casual wear was more normal. Lara had insisted that he put on his best bib and tucker and he was very pleased that he had taken her advice.

Derek, rather guiltily used the opportunity to get to know Alex a little better, and they chatted together about life in Sweden and England. As guest of honour, Derek was happy to make the first of several toasts raising a glass of champagne to his newfound friends.

"Dear friends, thank you for coming to celebrate Christmas and a very special time for Lara and me. I am proud and happy to tell you that Lara has agreed to be my wife."

All the guests and even diners at other tables burst into spontaneous applause and Derek took a sip of Champagne, before bending to kiss his fiancée, to cheers around the table.

Uniformed waitresses appeared and replaced the cold courses with delicious plates of hot food, grilled sturgeon, chicken and pork, roast duck, venison and pots of vegetables. Lara had worried about the portions size in

England, but Derek had never seen so much food on one table. He couldn't resist, however and everything he tasted was fresh and delicious. A band began to play and instantly everyone was dancing. Derek held Lara close and they seemed to dance all night.

It was well past midnight when they arrived back at the apartment, tired and more than a little merry after such a good party. The children came to the apartment with them for a cup of after party tea. Michael already was sleepy and just waited for the rest of them to go to the flat for the night. But Lara and Oleva settled on the sofa with some coffee. Derek suggested that he and Alex retire to the kitchen for a nightcap. He desperately wanted to talk with Alex alone and establish a rapport with him. They began to chat about trivial things, Derek showing an interest in Alex's studies and telling him in return about his own small business. As they talked about the future, Alex warmed to his new friend and thought Derek could only be good for his mother.

"You know, Alex, after our marriage, I want your mother to help me run the business. She seems happy with the idea and it would be a shame not to use her abilities. She's a brilliant 'people person' and we both know how much energy she puts into her job here. It would be good for me too, to have somebody around that I can trust. Share the load, half the stress.'

"It's a big weight off my mind to hear you talk like this, I have to admit, I was a little worried when I heard about mother possibly moving to England. I wish you both every happiness and who knows, maybe after my doctorate, I might look to settle in England too—it would be better if we could all be together in one country, wouldn't it?

"Of course! That would be terrific! I'm sure your mother would be thrilled at the prospect and you know the rules of a happy marriage?" He smiled, "If your wife is happy then you will be happy too!"

Derek added, "Do think about the prospect of the UK seriously, I'm sure there are plenty of jobs in your field there, and if there's anything I can do to help, you have only to ask. When we're settled, why not come and stay with us. We have plenty of room and we can show you around the country. Bring a girlfriend if you like—the more the merrier."

"Sure, I'll bear it in mind. I am doing some pretty wild research just now, and need funding to develop a prototype machine. I can't finance it on my own at the moment and any sort of loan would be prohibitively expensive. As a business man, do you know of anyone who might be willing to take a chance and lend me some money long term? It's going to be pretty big deal, I can promise you."

Derek couldn't believe his luck—talk about handed on a plate!

"This is very interesting, Alex. How much do you think you'll need? I know quite a lot of guys with spare cash floating around, I might be even able to help you myself. Tell me a bit more about what you're working on."

"Wow! That would be fantastic. Someone in the family, so to speak, that I could trust, would solve a lot of problems. I am really grateful, even for the suggestion."

"Right. Straight after Christmas I must go the Far East of Russia on business. There's an opening there—an opportunity to expand my business into Russia so…" Derek began to rub his hands together gleefully. "Maybe we'll all become filthy rich and live the high life. We can always hope. When I get back, I'll contact you and see if we can fix something up with the money."

Alex said, "Oleva, Michael and I will be leaving soon.

We are going to visit grandmother's grave and flying back from there to Stockholm. I'll wait for your call."

ᘓᘐᘓᘐ

After the New Year celebrations Lara was feeling sad that her children were both leaving. She was helping Oleva to pack when her daughter suddenly said, "Mum, I've been meaning to ask you, does Derek know anyone in Moscow? Maybe he has friends there?"

"No, I don't think so. If he had, I'm sure he would have told me. Why?"

"Well, I thought I saw him at the airport when we arrived in Moscow. Of course, I'd not met him then, but I'm certain I saw a man who looked very like him coming out of arrivals. He was met by another man and they left the airport together."

"Really? It can't have been him, I'm sure he'd have mentioned it. Perhaps he has a Russian double." She laughed.

"I'm not sure, mum, I might have been mistaken, but…but just be careful. You are so trusting with people. I love you, mum and I want you to be happy with Derek, but do be really sure before you commit yourself. Anyway, enough of this nonsense—I was probably seeing things—we must go or we'll miss our flight."

Sometimes Lara couldn't believe that her children were grown up—at the airport she was fussing around like a mother hen. "Now take care on your way back, and make sure you wrap up well. It's very cold and the weather forecast says is going to get worse. Don't forget to phone when you get to Moscow, and when you're safely back in Stockholm."

Oleva rather resignedly said, "Yes mum, we're big boys and girls now, so do stop fretting. We'll be fine."

ജ്ജ

When Derek returned from the East, he took a taxi from the airport, as it was quite late at night and the roads were very icy. In the East of Russia, it had been far colder than anything he had ever come across before, but even here in Saratov, it was minus 10 C with heavy snow and a sharp north wind. He had had to haggle with the taxi driver, as the roads were so bad, and had finally agreed to pay double the normal fare. The cab was very old and frosty inside, despite the heater going full blast, but Derek was comfortably wrapped up in the fur coat he had bought for his trip east. He was also now sporting a very Russian fur hat with ear pieces that had been given to him by the boss man at the factory in Komsomolsk.

His trip had been a great success. There had been some very useful meetings and a deal was agreed, bar the shouting. The powers that be at the factory had been very happy with the samples he had shown them. But he need to return a second time to meet the higher echelon of managers to sign contracts. It made him exited to think about it.

Derek now had a cast iron reason for his travel back and fore to Russia. Of course, Lara knew all about this, she just didn't have any idea how it had all been organised in the first place. That he would keep very close to his chest. He hoped the FSB gorillas would be pleased when they heard that he was proposing to help Alex with money, which would put him under an obligation to his new stepfather.

It was almost midnight when Derek arrived at Lara's flat—he was so happy to see her again. Although she had waited up for him, she was almost asleep on the sofa when he let himself into the flat.

"Hi Hon, sorry I'm so late. The plane was delayed half an hour, and it took ages to get a taxi. I hope you haven't changed your mind about the wedding," he said. He smiled. "Tomorrow morning, we go to the Registry Office first thing to fix it all up." He swung her off the couch and twirled her round. She screamed that he was making her dizzy, but laughed and agreed that indeed they would be off in the morning to arrange the date. She stood away from him admiringly. You look so smart and elegant in your Russian clothes, I almost fancy you!"

The next morning, the ceremony was booked for two months' time. With sleight apprehension in her voice, Lara said, "I know it seems a long time to you, my dear, but we have much to arrange and it is really a very short time for me to think about leaving my Russia for ever—but not so much time to be frightened."

"Please don't worry, my love. You will be in good hands. We are going to share a wonderful life together, and you know I will do everything I can to look after you and make you happy."

Chapter 11

The tall, dark haired young man took his keys from the receptionist and walked to the lift. He was exhausted after his long journey and needed to rest, but he felt good about the forthcoming conference.

When Alex found his room, he opened the door and drew back the curtains. He was greeted with an astonishing view, which quite took his breath away. The room had a small balcony, beyond which was a spectacular panorama of the coast, with tiny islands dotted about in the deep blue Adriatic. There were little white sailing boats everywhere. A race must have been just finishing, as there was a small fleet of yachts sailing into the harbour, their multi-coloured spinnakers, shining in the late afternoon light. As he watched, the sun sank slowly, setting the sky alight in a blaze of red and gold. On the way from the Split airport, he had been impressed by the pretty city, which nestled between the mountains and the sea, but nothing had prepared him for the dramatic view before him now. It's no wonder that the roman Emperor Diocletian chose this spot in Croatia to build his beautiful retirement Palace.

Alex thoughts returned to real things—how wonderful it would be to own a property on one of these islands. "Who knows? If my research proves successful, one day it might just be a possibility." At least, for now, he had the view and the dream. He turned back to his unpacking, feeling very content with his lot in life.

After putting his clothes away, Alex took a long hot shower, letting the tensions of the day evaporate like the steam around him. He dried himself and lay on the bed, letting his breathing slow right down and his mind empty in total relaxation—something he a learned from his Japanese karate master back in Russia. His quiet meditation was disturbed by a sudden knock on the door. A young chambermaid smiled at him and gave him a small sealed envelope with his name written in beautiful script. Alex thanked her, and was surprised to find that is was an invitation from one of the conference plenary session speakers, a well-known Japanese professor of nuclear physics. He was asking if they might meet in the hotel bar after dinner for a drink. Alex knew the gentleman by reputation, but had never met him. He also had no idea why he might have been singled out, but was flattered by the invitation, and very interested to meet such an eminent person in his field. First, however, he needed to eat.

The dining room was almost empty as it was still a little early, but he took a table by the big picture window and was soon tucking hungrily into a truly delicious meal. When he had finished his coffee, he set off for the bar to find the professor.

As Alex walked in, he saw an elderly Japanese, who immediately stood up as he approached. The gentleman was immaculately dressed and smiled at Alex, stretching out his hand in greeting. "I'm Professor Akayama. I'm delighted to meet you, Alex."

"My pleasure." Alex replied, "but how do you know me, we haven't met before, have we?"

"No, we haven't, but let me get you a drink—what

would you like?"

"Just an orange juice, please, if that's OK."

The professor motioned to the waiter, who was hovering in the background, and ordered a juice and lager for himself.

The bar was full of young people, mostly delegates. Alex had already noted that there were several Russians on the conference list, but there were no obviously Slavic faces to be seen. *Still, plenty of time to find them later,* he thought. *It'll be nice to have a chat in my own language for a change.*

When the waiter had brought their drinks, the professor said, "Let me explain who I am and why I invited you here. Your supervisor in Sweden, Professor Yakomoto, is an old good friend and colleague of mine. When I visit Europe on business, I always make an effort to call and see him if possible, during my trip. I'm actually going to Sweden immediately after this conference finishes."

"Do give him my regards." said Alex. "He's a wonderful supervisor and a lovely man. Luckily, I will be staying on here for about a week after the conference. I have a Croatian friend, who skippers a large sailing boat, which he is free to use when it's not chartered. He's invited me to go sailing with him. Should be perfect, especially if the weather stays like this. Did Professor Yakomoto mention something about me to you?"

"Yes." The professor replied. "That's the reason I wanted to talk to you." He paused a little, then went on, "I have a proposition for you, Alex. When you finish in Sweden, I would like you to join me in Japan and continue your work at our top scientific research institute in Kyoto. It would be a terrific opportunity for you to make a name for yourself."

Alex was completely stunned by this invitation—he

still had not completed his doctorate and he was being invited to work at one of the most prestigious nuclear research establishments on the planet!

"Really Professor? That's quite a shock, but, thank you... But why me? There must be thousands of other more highly qualified students, who would give a right arm for such an opportunity."

"Well, Alex," the Professor replied, "You have an excellent recommendation from Professor Yakomoto and we are actively searching for highly talented young people from all over the world. Judging by what my friend says, you will fit the bill perfectly. Energy and Atomic research are becoming ever more important and I see you playing a part in this future.

"Do give it some thought, Alex. If you agree, we can talk again and I will tell you more about our Institute and the direction of our research."

The professor stood up, the interview over.

"Goodbye for now Alex—I'm sure we shall talk further." He gave a formal bow, turned on his heel, and was gone.

The following morning, there was a crush of delegates in the entrance hall of the Conference Center. People were queueing to register or simply milling around, looking for friends and waiting for the main hall to open. Alex overheard two young men, who were speaking Russian. He had seen their photographs on the conference documents and introduced himself.

"Hi guys, my name is Alex Petrov- I'm originally from Balakovo, but I'm presently studying at Stockholm University."

They introduced themselves with handshakes all

round. "Hi. I'm Peter and this is my colleague Sergei, we're both from the Moscow Institute." As he spoke, a third, rather older man, whom Alex didn't recognise, suddenly joined them. He also spoke perfect Russian and introduced himself as Vladislav Mikhailovitch. He said he had joined the conference at the last minute so his personal details were not in the prospectus. At that moment, the main doors were opened and the delegates were called into the main hall. Alex and his new friends sat together near the back.

The conference hall went quiet as a tall, grey haired man, wearing a very smart grey suit walked across the stage to the lectern.

"Ladies and Gentlemen. I declare the Tenth Conference of the Study of World Energy and Development open. This year we have speakers and delegates from fifteen different countries, and I'm sure we shall have an interesting and thought-provoking time."

He then introduced the first speaker and the hall settled back attentively.

Alex was sitting next to Vladislav, who proved to be a fun companion. As soon as there was any sort of break in the proceedings, he began talking about his research and Alex, being a bit of a boffin himself, was delighted to have someone with whom he could discuss his favourite subject, and in his native language.

That evening, Alex and the Swedish delegates were invited for a drink in the bar by the Russian party. The Russians soon got to work on the vodka, and there was lots of laughter and joke telling. Alex was not much of a drinker and was pleased to find that his new friend, Vladislav, was not too keen either. He told them all rather sheepishly how his father had managed to drink himself to death by the age of forty. The evening rocked on and despite the language problems, much fun was had by all. Even the normally staid Swedes let their hair down and they all eventually rolled out into the night the best of friends.

The next day, when the conference proceedings were over, Alex met his Croatian friend Roslav in one of the multitude of little cafés on the famous "The Riva" seafront promenade, one of the finest in Europe. It was good to see him again and within minutes they were happily reminiscing about the last time they met—the sailing, the nights out, the girls they had met. They were both looking forward to their coming trip. Roslav said that this year the winter had been very mild, ideal sailing weather, plenty of breeze, but calm seas. The forecast for the coming week was apparently very good and they planned be off the morning after the conference ended. Roslav said that they would sail along the coast for about thirty miles, then out around two particularly beautiful islands, where they would moor for the night, then back the following day. Roslav mentioned that he had also invited a couple of his friends and their girlfriends, and if Alex wanted to bring someone there was a spare cabin in the forepeak. Alex, unfortunately, didn't know any girls there, but said that he had become quite friendly with one of the Russian delegates, who was obviously pretty sporty and might be a good guy to have along.

Roslav readily agreed and suggested that they all meet up the following night for supper. When Alex mentioned the possible sailing to Vladislav the next day at the conference, he was very excited at the prospect.

"I've done a bit of offshore racing in the Black Sea," he said. "I'll probably be a bit rusty, but it's like riding a bike, you never really forget."

ꕥꕥ

"Of course, I shall, Comrade. I have befriended him, but have found nothing of interest so far. He is a very quiet and reserved young man and is reluctant to talk about his work. I've managed to search his room every morning, but there was nothing of interest there. I'm sure he suspects nothing—he would hardly have invited me sailing if it was otherwise."

Vladislav's interlocutor said, "After the cruise, you are to stay close to him for the remainder of his stay in Croatia—after that our Swedish Agent will take over. Do nothing, repeat nothing, to cause him to be suspicious."

"Yes sir, I understand fully."

ઌઌ

The sea was dead calm and the yacht was gliding along smoothly, only the hum of the engine to be heard. The sun was shining in a clear blue sky and it was unusually warm for the time of year. Alex was feeling sleepy, he needed to relax after all the excitement of the conference. He made his way to the bow, where he stretched out on small chair. He put his hands behind his head and drank in the stunning scenery. The Croatian coast was spectacularly green, hills with small rocky outcrops and pretty white houses with terracotta roofs dotted around everywhere. His mind slowly drifted back his life 10 years previously when he was still an undergrad at Sebastopol Military University. It had been an interesting time, but very tough with rigorous studying and very strict discipline. There had been enormous competition for places and he knew that if he didn't obey orders and keep up with all the work, he would be out on his ear. At that time, military authorities in Russia didn't take any prisoners!

Alex was vaguely aware of laughter and voices below, but he was happily ensconced in a world of his own, remembering his university years.

Left, Right, Left, Right. Atten—Shun! By the right. Quick march!

For all of his time there it had been never-ending—march here, march there, lectures, eating and sleeping. Very little opportunity to let one's hair down or have any fun. University students in the West would never believe how hard it was. And always under threat of being chucked out if you fell behind. Arriving straight from school, a little more than a slightly spoilt child, he had undergone five years of hard discipline, obeying every order from his superiors without question. Beds made just so, rooms and corridors kept spotlessly clean, lights out at midnight. Alex was often up at 5.30 to get an hour's work in before breakfast. The first three years were the worst, but after that things loosened up slightly, students were allowed to move into rented apartments, where at least they had some space and privacy. The teachers and professors had been marvellous though, passionately interested in their subjects and anxious to encourage the very best from each of their charges. Alex fondly remembered his mother's words. "Try to do something positive every day. Learn from others and try not to make their mistakes."

Looking back now, he realised that it had been a good training for life and a very stimulating experience. Without it, he certainly wouldn't have been lazing on a yacht in Croatia. *Pretty damn good* he mused.

The sun was already sinking and the temperature dropped abruptly. Alex shivered and did up his coat. He fell back into his reverie.

He was five or six years old and feeling very cold. His family lived in the Far East of Russia, where both his parents worked in ship building. They fitted electronic equipment and computers into ships and submarines. It was interesting work, but the weather there was very inhospitable—unbearably hot in the summer and bitterly cold in wintertime. He mistily remembered being taken with his sister to the kindergarten each day. One winter's day both children were crying from the cold and when they reached the nursery, their tears had frozen to their cheeks. His mother later told him that it had been minus 45 C that morning! Alex also recalled the summers, with school often cancelled because of the blackfly and mosquitos and daily fires in the surrounding taiga casting a gloomy pall over the city.

Alex was aroused from his daydreaming by Roslav with a welcome cup of tea.

ꕥꕥ

Alex stepped down into the salon. "Hi, Vlad, how's things?"

"Wow, brilliant, thanks. Shame we haven't had a bit more wind, motoring is a bit dull and I'll bet this baby would really shift in a good breeze. But I'm still having a great time, perfect to relax after the conference. Are you staying on in Croatia when we get back?"

"No, I'm going straight to Stockholm. Why?"

"I'm also going to visit friends in Sweden as soon as we're back in Split."

Interested, Alex asked, "Have you booked your tickets yet? We could try and fly back together."

"No, it was a spur of the moment thing as I was already this far. If you like, we can sort it out in Split on Monday."

Alex got himself a can of beer and a book and lay down in his cabin. He read for a while, but was quickly bored with his silly page-turner. He closed his eyes and thought about his research. He had already decided that while he was still in Sweden, he would attempt to make a working prototype of his invention. The work which would attract less attention there than in Russia, where the components might also be difficult to obtain.

He had money that Derek had lent him, and had investigated various possible suppliers, buying everything from the same firm might cause unwelcome interest. He should also probably have to tell his professor what was going on as he would need the laboratory facilities to build his apparatus.

Alex suddenly thought about Vladislav, who was spending a lot of time below deck and not getting any fresh air. Although he seemed a very pleasant guy on the surface, there was something not quite right about him, which Alex couldn't put his finger on. *And now he wants to travel back to Sweden with me?! Hm-mm.*

Suddenly Alex's phone rang, "Oh, hi mum, how're things? Good, yes, I'm with Roslav on the boat. No there are no problems, no one has fallen in and we're all behaving ourselves, sort of. No—the sea is actually very cold—much too cold to swim, brr, the weather is marvellous, really quite warm. We stopped off for the night on a very beautiful island. Terrific scenery—quite unlike anywhere I've seen before. Oh, by the way, are you still lovey-dovey with your Derek? What! Wedding in one months?! That's wonderful news. Mom. Jeez, you don't hang about do you? Anyway, massive congratulations. Yes, of course I'll come, I hope. Yes, and Oleva, I'm sure. That's really great news—brilliant. Yeah, take care, see you soon."

The next day, as they were mooring up in Split harbour, Alex went down to his cabin to collect his belongings. The door was slightly ajar and he was surprised and very angry to find Vladislav in his cabin, rummaging through his travel bag. “What the hell are you doing in my cabin.”

Vladislav looked embarrassed, “I-I was looking for a clock to check the time—my watch has stopped.”

“That’s bullshit—you were searching my things, you devious bastard. Who the devil are you anyway?” Alex was so angry, he couldn’t help himself. He leapt across the cabin and smashed Vladislav in the face. He fell back, blood streaming from his nose. As he struggled to stand, Alex automatically adopted his karate defence position. At that moment Roslav, alerted by the shouting, ran into the cabin and grabbed Alex from behind. Vladislav saw his chance and kicked Alex hard in the crotch. But Alex was no mug when it came to a roughhouse. He easily threw Roslav off and started in earnest to deal with Vladislav. A straight hammer blow to the solar plexus followed by a chop to the neck left him gasping on the floor. As Alex moved in to finish him, he was brought to an abrupt halt by the silver Biretta that appeared in Vladislav’s right hand, pointed straight at his stomach. Alex put his hands out in a conciliatory gesture.

“Ok, ok, let’s just take it easy, shall we?” Vladislav, with blood still streaming from his nose, snarled at them both.

“Just keep very still. You will sit on the bed and keep quiet while I get off the yacht. One squeak from either of you and I will shoot the first person I see, whoever it is.” He motioned to Alex.

“Give me your keys. I’m going to lock you both in here, where you will stay until I have left the boat. Don’t get any clever ideas—you have no idea what you are dealing with here.” Breathing heavily, he pushed past them and left, locking the door behind him.

The friends looked at each other helplessly. “I’m really

sorry about that, Roslav, he seemed such a nice guy." Although Alex protested that he had no idea what it had all been about, he knew now that he was part of a very dangerous game. In future, he would have to be very, very careful.

ȻɅȻɅ

A couple of days later, two smartly dressed men were sitting in the departures hall at Split airport. One wore dark glasses, which failed to cover significant bruising and abrasions on his face. "So, comrade. Your turn now. He will be arriving any minute. Remember, he is quite a dangerous individual and very useful with his fists.

"Don't make my mistakes—good luck."

Chapter 12

The beautiful 19th century troika sped along the forest road, pulled by three plumed white horses. In the back, wrapped snugly in a thick fur blanket, Lara and Derek were cuddling each other and laughing together on their way to the Registry Office in the local town. Tiny snowflakes swirled around the carriage and stuck to Lara's white ermine hat. Her long white wedding gown was hidden, not only by the blanket, but by her full length white fur coat, which had belonged to her Grandmother. Derek's immaculate new suit was also covered with a heavy fur coat, bought specially for the occasion. Two black limousines, carrying the best man and the most important wedding guests, followed behind, struggling to keep up on the icy road. It was a fairytale picture and one which the happy couple would remember forever. Lara had engaged a wedding agency from the local town to organize every aspect of the ceremony so that nothing could interfere with their special day. It had been expensive, but Derek, whose business was now thriving, had paid for most of it. Lara turned and waved at her children and friends in the cars behind. She looked sparklingly beautiful and very happy. Derek sat quietly enjoying the moment. The entourage pulled up outside a large, imposing building, which housed all the civic

offices of the town. They still had plenty of time before the ceremony so Derek and Lara remained in the carriage while the two photographers, hired for the occasion, were setting up their equipment.
Lara whispered in her lover's ear, "Do you have any doubts about becoming my husband?"

He smiled at her and answered, "I'm afraid it's too late to ask me that now." He gave her a merry wink. "I'm certainly not changing out of this expensive wedding suit. You're just going to have to put up with me, whatever."

She laughed. "You're right—no regrets, no doubts, just...I'll love you forever."

Photographs over for the time being, the couple entered the Ceremonial Registration Hall to the strains of Mendelssohn's famous Wedding March.

The splendid, high ceilinged room, was brimming with flowers and lit by dozens of candles. There were loud cheers from the guests, who were already seated, awaiting the arrival of the happy couple. Many of Lara's work colleagues were present and Derek felt a twinge of sadness that no one from England had been able to make the journey. Lara's long-standing friend, Vladimir, a local Notary, had had to be seconded in as 'best man.'

They reached their allotted place and stood before the Registrar, a tiny grey-haired lady, who seemed weighed down by her ceremonial robes.

"Derek, a citizen of the United Kingdom and Lara, a citizen of the Russian Federation have made known their wish to be joined in marriage…" She continued with the official form of the service in a strong clear voice, which belied her slight stature. At the end, she announced, "In the name of the laws of this country, I now proclaim you man and wife. Please exchange rings."

With shaking hands, Derek put the ring on Lara's right hand, according to Russian tradition and she did the same for him. "You may now kiss." As they embraced to a ripple of applause, the Registrar opened the book for them both to sign.

They then kissed again and, looking in her eyes, Derek said with great seriousness, "I love you darling. I will care for and look after you for the rest of my life."

Lara, with eyes full of tears of joy echoed, "I love you too, my wonderful Derek."

ᏟᏍᏟᏍ

Later that evening, with the street lights gleaming on the snow, a group of about ten happy people were waiting on the pavement outside the best restaurant in the town to welcome Derek and Lara. A large BMW saloon, decked with white ribbons pulled up, and the happy couple climbed out into the arms of their friends and family. Lara was flushed with excitement and looked ten years younger than her true age. Derek stood tall and elegant in his beautifully tailored suit. Despite neither of them being in the first flush of youth, they made a quite stunning couple standing in the snowy street.

When they made their way to lead everyone into the restaurant, their way was blocked by some of the younger guests, who had decided to play a Russian wedding game. One of them said to Vladimir, "How much will you pay us to give them free passage to the wedding table?"

The best man, who was standing with Derek and Lara said, "I think 10 dollars is all they're worth."

"Ten miserable dollars? For such a handsome new married couple? What sort of offer is that? They're worth far more."

"How about fifty dollars then?"

"Still not enough. Look how beautiful the bride is."

"OK! I will pay you one hundred dollars, but not a penny more!" Vladimir winked at Derek.

"That is much better! We accept. But we want cash, no cheques, please! Welcome to your wedding, friends."

Derek and Lara waited while the laughing, giggling company filed into the restaurant and lined up either side of the door. As the couple walked in they were showered with confetti and fresh rose petals, which had been specially flown in from the South. Then each guest offered their personal congratulations and a large bunch of flowers. In time honored tradition, many of the guests also gave envelopes containing money. Derek whispered with a smile.

"With all this money, I'll probably be able to give up working."

They were in a large private room in the restaurant, which had been beautifully decorated with flowers. Soft light from three big chandeliers picked out the white napery and silver cutlery on the tables, which were set around a small dance floor.

The Master of Ceremonies, a young professional wedding organizer, took his place and rang a little hand bell for attention.

"Can I call upon Derek and the lovely Lara to open proceedings with the first dance?"

A little band played some slow romantic music as Derek nervously led his new bride onto the dance floor. As they began to dance, the rest of the guests formed a circle around them, swaying together in time with the music. Two by two they joined in the dancing, and soon everyone was crowding the tiny dance floor. Derek was in seventh heaven—so proud of his gorgeous new wife, who had organized everything so spectacularly well while he was still in England. He put all his troubles with the Russian Security Service behind him and simply reveled in pleasure of the moment. He was interested to see how different this was from the normal stuffy English wedding. The tables were groaning with wonderful food, but the guests were already dancing and singing along with the music. Really very good Russian Champagne was flowing freely, accompanied by excellent Georgian wine. Judging from previous gatherings that he had been to in Russia, Derek didn't think it would be long before the vodka and the toasts started.

These guys really know how to have a good time. he thought.

He turned to Lara. "Are you sure there aren't two weddings going on together—there's certainly enough food for two." She laughed and said that it had hardly started yet—there were still all the hot dishes to come and loads of desserts. Suddenly her face became serious. "Darling, look here what happened." She pointed under the table. "Look, look, one of my shoes has been stolen. How can I dance and enjoy my wedding? You must find it and buy it back from the thief—I can't move."

Derek was on the ball and realized immediately that this was another of the wedding games, which Lara had warned him about. He was expecting something of the sort and had a wallet full of cash just in case. He would normally have found all this a bit childish, but he was enjoying himself so much that he happily joined in the fun.

Alina, another of Lara's friends, an English school teacher, saw the bride's feigned distress and minced over to her table. She was a rather beautiful, statuesque girl, with masses of auburn hair which cascaded over her shoulders. She was wearing a black silk gown, split to the thigh and impossibly high heels. She with Vladimir began negotiations with a guest Stephan, one of the Lara's business associate, for the return of the shoe.

"I bid fifty dollars," said Vladimir

Stephan tossed his head and gave a derisive laugh. "Fifty dollars? Absurd! Surely Lara's husband is not so mean!"

By now, the other guests had crowded around the table, watching the fun.

"Ok seventy bucks and not a penny more." said Vladimir.

There were groans of disapproval around the table. Vladimir went into a huddle with Derek.

"We also have an excellent bottle of malt whisky, which Derek brought over from Scotland."

"Still not enough for such a nice, expensive shoe. However, as he's a poor Englishman, I'll be generous. seventy dollars, the whisky and...you, Vladimir, must do a gypsy dance with Alina!"

This suggestion met with a roar of approval from the guests. Vladimir was, amongst other things, the town's notary and was a serious, revered figure.

He winked at Alina and bowed. "May I have the pleasure...?" he requested.

The band began to play a gypsy dancing melody as Vladimir and his partner took to the floor. He twirled her round and round as the music got faster and faster. Everyone stood up, clapping and cheering—the normally sedate lawyer was really letting his hair down. As the music came to a climax, he lifted Alina above his head and then lowered her down gently to the floor as he dropped onto one knee in a gesture of submission. The place erupted, people were laughing and shouting, embracing Alina and patting Vladimir on the back.

Derek and Lara were loving every moment. Suddenly, Stephan jumped up and shouted. "My wine is very bitter—I must have some sweetness from Derek and Lara. Gorko!" This expression, which means "bitter," is a feature of all Russian weddings. The bride and groom have to stand and kiss in order to make the wine, or whatever is being drunk at the time, regain its "sweetness." The rest of the company immediately joined in, "Gor-KO, Gor-KO, Gor-KO" until Derek and Lara were on their feet happily giving in to tradition.

After this impromptu show, the guests returned to their tables and attacked the food and wine with a vengeance. Everyone ate, drank, danced, and sang until the small hours. The evening finally wound down with the newlyweds dancing slowly together, their arms tightly around each other, as they moved together to the gentle, romantic music.

It was a very tired, but very happy couple that emerged from the lift on Lara's floor. Derek was suddenly embarrassed. "I know that traditionally I should carry you over the doorstep, but I'm afraid my back is killing me after all the dancing, and I'll probably end up in hospital if I try."

"Don't worry, darling, the thought was there, which is all that matters. And I wouldn't like our married life to start with me pushing you around in a wheelchair!"

The flat was overflowing with flowers. Lara busied herself trying to find vases and jugs for them all, while she calmed down after all the excitement of the day. Alex and Oleva had been offered somewhere to stay by one of Lara's friends so that the newlyweds would have the flat to themselves on their wedding night.

They were both so tired after the long day that they collapsed into bed and managed a quick cuddle before Derek turned over and crashed out, within seconds, he was snoring quietly. Lara's head was still spinning with the emotions of the moment. She didn't want to disturb her new husband, so got up quietly and made herself a honey and lemon. This quickly did the trick and soon she was back under the covers, sleeping like a baby.

The next afternoon, Alex and Oleva came around with Volodya and Katya, the friends, who had put them up. Within minutes there was a cloth on the table and caviar, blinis and other food were awaiting their attentions, along with the inevitable cognac and vodka. Volodya had a fine baritone voice and after a bit of vodka, was quickly into the Russian folk songs. Everyone, even Derek, joined in, and a merry couple of hours were had by all. Lara was surprised and rather glad that there were no complaints from her neighbors! When things finally quietened down, Volodya went onto the balcony to smoke, where he promptly fell asleep. The ladies repaired to the kitchen to clear up, while Derek and Alex were in the sitting room drinking coffee and talking about Alex's work.

The next day Derek waited for Lara in the Regional Office of Employment. Lara went to talk to her boss, as she had requested an interview with the regional director to discuss her retirement.

Across his huge walnut desk, Lara's boss eyed her disbelievingly. He steeple his fingers.

"Are you quite out of your mind? After twenty years, you come in here on a whim and give me this resignation." He waved the typed note at her angrily. "What are you thinking about? In four months, you will receive your full pension. If you leave now, you will get nothing and we'll be in a deep hole trying to find a replacement for you with no notice. I have to say that marriage or no marriage, it is extremely inconsiderate of you. And what if it doesn't work out? What then? You will be back in Russia, with no job, no pension and no money. Is that rational behavior?" He glowered down at the paper again. "Is this fellow of yours a millionaire?"

Lara sighed deeply. "No boss, he's not a millionaire, but he has adequate money and I'm sure he loves me and will look after me. I just don't want to risk losing him by hanging on here. You know we're already married, I cannot let him go back to England on his own for four months, it's just not fair."

Her chief looked at her resignedly. "Ok ok, I know you well enough by now and know how stubborn you can be when you want something badly enough. I still think you're making a big mistake, but I'll sign you release papers and you will be free to go."

He quickly signed a couple of forms and handed them to Lara. "So! How do you feel now?"

"Honestly, Sir, I'm scared half to death. I've always had a good job, especially since I've been here. I know how much you rely on me and I'm genuinely sorry to let you down like this, but I love him and want to be with him always. I could not bear for us to be apart for four more months."

Her boss relaxed slightly and smiled at her. "Lara, I sincerely hope you have made the right choice and that you will be happy. I wish you all the best with your Englishman, he is certainly a lucky man to have caught you. And remember, we will always be pleased to see you here, and if you ever need help, don't hesitate to call me. Incidentally, I will arrange it so you can keep your car and driver until you leave for England, it will be useful to have transportation, especially for getting your stuff to the airport."

He reached into a drawer in his desk and took out a beautiful, gilt framed icon. "This belonged to my great-grandmother and I would like you to have it as a blessing on your marriage. Good luck!"

Much to his surprise, Lara ran round the desk with tears in her eyes. She kissed him on the cheek. “Thank you so, so much, Sergei Ivanovich. You must be the best boss in the world. I’ll never forget you.”

As she left the office, Derek was standing waiting for her. “Hey, hey, sweetheart, no tears now. Everything will be fine. We’ll have plenty of money for both of us. In a few months, you’ll have forgotten all about this place.”

“No, Derek, I will never forget them. I’m not worried about my pension, but they have been wonderful friends, and my boss, for almost twenty years. I know I will very miss them.”

ॐ

Lara could not help but muse over the friends that she would be leaving behind. Her thoughts turned to Zhannet, whom she had not seen since the unfortunate incident with the cut internet and phone cables in her flat. Zhannet had been such a good and close friend for so many years, that Lara just couldn’t face going to England, without at least contacting her and trying to clear the air.

A couple of days later, she phoned her old friend and invited her to lunch to meet her new husband. Zhannet had been quite cool on the phone, still upset at not having been invited to the wedding, but after an apology and some persuasion, she agreed to meet them both.

That Friday, Lara and Derek met with Zhannet and took her to the swankiest restaurant in town. The atmosphere between them was very strained, with Zhannet being barely polite to them both. Derek was his usual suave self, where ladies were concerned and during a long lunch, with a good bottle of wine, relations began to thaw, and Zhannet became more of her old self.

"So, Zhannet, how're things going with your business—still managing to keep the wolf from the door?" Lara looked at her.

"Really very well," Zhannet replied. "My son and his family are involved, so we now have three offices and the Chapel of Rest for the funeral business and three flats in the city, which we rent out. All in all, I can't complain. And people do keep dying." She added with a mischievous smile.

"I know you were not too keen on private businesses, always working for the government, but it has provided a very good living for me and my family. It is such a shame that we fell out..." Zannet smiled sadly. "But I hope you will not both disappear forever. If you come back to Russia, you'll be very welcome to stay with me."

Finishing dinner Lara embraced her old friend, with tears in her eyes.

"I'm so pleased that you have met Derek and that we have forgotten our differences. When we are settled in England, I will write you an invitation, and, perhaps, you can come and visit us. We would be so pleased to show you some of England, wouldn't we darling?"

"Of course." Derek agreed. "Absolutely any time, just give us a ring."

Time was getting on and Lara and Derek still had masses to do before their move. They let Zhannet go by her private car with driver and were relaxing in the car on the way home.

Derek was going over the meeting with Lara' friend. "I'm afraid, darling, I didn't really like Zhannet very much." he said.

"She didn't look like a happy person—I think the funeral business must be rubbing off on her. She obviously has plenty of money, but it seemed not to be giving her much in the way of contentment. Not my sort at all, I'm afraid, but if you want to invite her, darling, I'll be my usual charming self, so don't worry."

They continued on their way, with Lara lying her head contentedly on her husband's shoulder and Derek staring straight ahead, troubled by his imminent visit to Siberia, and what problems that might throw up.

❦❦

Their remaining time in Russia was very hectic. As Alex and Oleva prepared to leave for their flights back to Sweden, Derek took Lara's son aside and asked him about a possible visit to England.

"I'll try," Alex said, "but I can't make any promises. My work is at a critical period just now and I'm proposing to use the money you lent me to construct a prototype machine on which to check all my results and to be sure the process will actually work. Of course, you and mum could always come over to Sweden for a week or so. It's a fabulous country, I'm sure you would both have a great time."

It was left like that, and they all went to the airport to see the youngsters off. At the departure gate, there were hugs and kisses and not a few tears on Lara's part as she said her goodbyes to her beloved children. Derek put a comforting arm around her and they walked slowly back to the waiting car.

Two days later, they had to fly to Moscow to visit the UK consulate and arrange Lara's visa, so that she had permission to remain in England. She would have to live in England for five years before she could apply for dual nationality. Business with the Consulates never seemed to be straightforward and it took them four days before it was all satisfactorily sorted. Lara then went back to Balakovo to finish her packing while Derek flew on to the Far East, hoping to arrange further contracts. Lara was still slightly mystified as to how her husband had managed to obtain all his contacts in the Far East of Russia, but she put any doubts behind her and prepared happily for her new life in the UK.

As Derek was waiting to board his plane to the East, his mobile rang. A harshly accented Russian voice, which he did not recognize, told him to expect to be met in Komsomolsk, and to be ready for a thorough de-briefing on his progress so far. By now, Derek was getting used to Russians popping out of the woodwork at every turn, and was much more relaxed about it all. They also seemed very generous with their money—he had already had business payments up front. Derek decided that he could string things out a bit, and was also determined to ask if his new "friends" would cover the money he had lent to Alex.

"After all, it had been at their insistence," he thought, "why should I pay it?"

ꕤ

Back in Balakovo, Lara was unable to sleep without Derek by her side. She was still slightly worried about the finality of giving up her job, although she was clear in her mind that it had been a necessary step. If she and Derek were to make a success of their marriage, they had to do things together.

As she was tossing and turning she began to think of him in Komsomolsk and her mind drifted back to times when she was a young wife of her first husband, living in an industrial city on the banks of the mighty river Amur, in the Far East of Russia.

ꕤ

It was a windy, cold autumn night. Several men, who were engineers from the shipyard, were standing on the bank of the huge river. They nervously were looking around and then again starring somewhere in darkness of the great Amur which was two miles wide with very speedy water.

Many of the men from that city and villages around had a lucrative sideline, making and using as food and selling red caviar from Siberian salmon bought from poachers.

They had already bought ten salmon which was only half of their usual haul from one lot of poachers and were standing on the bank of the huge river, chatting together nervously, as they waited for another.

Finally, they heard the faint drum of an outboard engine and a small boat appeared in the distance, heading their way. As they watched, there was a sharp gunshot and a police launch, with lights blazing, burst out of the reeds and a loud hail was heard demanding that they stop. The men on the bank watched in fear and desperation as the police boarded the boat, handcuffed the occupants and transferred them to the launch. They then poured gasoline into the little boat and unceremoniously set it alight. Within minutes, it had sunk without trace and the police launch turned and headed back to base.

The group on the bank breathed a sigh of relief as the police vanished into the mist. It was a danger for the men hidden on the bank too. If the river police would have stopped here at the mooring they would have been arrested. The Siberian salmon from this region is highly valued and protected accordingly.

The men had already completed a similar trip last autumn, “engineer’s fishing” they called it, which had been very successful. So they decided to wait a bit to increase their haul of fish.

They knew how this game worked on the river—it's like a little war between the fishermen whose life and family depend on the fish from this river—and the authorities—river police, inspectors who try to stop fishermen from taking out all the big fish which are rapidly moving to the west. The fish all on their own mission, ascending the river to release their orange miracle eggs, the legendary Red Caviar.

"Aleksandr, how long we are going be waiting here for another boat," a man from the group asked.

"Shall we wait another hour, we need more fish. Don't we?" Three men nodded along in agreement.

"I know, guys, everybody needs to sleep because tomorrow morning we have an early start at work. I will be seriously busy tomorrow at the shipyard, two new pieces of electronic equipment will be arriving from the South and I will be responsible for the installation in the submarine,"

"Shhh, look a boat is coming."

A boat was quietly moving along the bank and moored in the bay where the men were hiding.

A man the from boat jumped onto the dry bank, carefully looked around, and whispered, -

"Is anybody here?"

The hidden men scurried out of the bushes heading to the poacher.

They started to negotiate the price,

"Ok!" the poacher said, "One bottle of Vodka for each fish without eggs and 15 rubles for each with eggs. Guys, we are in hurry, so quickly take the fish."

More fishermen in the boat started to throw fish one after another onto the bank counting. "One, Two…Twelve…is that enough?"

The boat with poachers quickly disappeared and the "engineer fishers" started quickly loading their two cars which were concealed nearby.

"Good morning, dear," Aleksandr kissed Lara.

"Our fishing trip was very successful, I brought home six very big fish, I will tell you everything about our adventure in the evening but now I am in a hurry to get to the shipyard. But you, Lara, have a big day today to sort out all the fish. I can't wait for your freshly made red caviar and those other dishes that you make. We'll eat like kings for the next few months!"

He smiled and left for work.

Lara prepared their two children for school, dressed, prepared breakfast, and walked with them to the bus stop. As always it took a while for the bus to arrive, and after an uneventful journey, was then a ten-minute walk with her son, three, and daughter, five, to their kindergarten. Lara hoped the nursery nurses had made the building warm as it was a bitterly cold day.

"So, shall I start," she murmured to herself. *How many fish here…a-ha, six, this could take all day, but we will have a lot of caviar and fish for several months,* she thought,

"It will be good to finish before Aleksandr comes back from work and then we will go straight to bring the children back home."

Lara cleaned up the big table, and laid out the first fish. Siberian salmon are big, red, meaty, and long fish. So Lara used all her strength to split the fish's stomach lengthwise to empty the guts and pulled out two orange skeins full of fish eggs.

M-mm, this looks really nice, she thought, *now I will try to separate the eggs from the sacks, this is the tricky bit.* She continued to separate the eggs from their membranes, egg by egg with a fork. Then she put all the collected eggs into a very thin white muslin bag and tightened it up.

Lara also prepared a bucket of cold water, she put in a fresh potato and added salt. She began to stir the water and salt until the potato floated to the surface. That's it! The brine is ready for the eggs. She lowered it slowly into the brine watching the time. "Ok, 15 minutes, that is enough." Lara took out the fabric with the eggs inside and hung it up, allowing the brine to drip slowly from the bag. Tomorrow the dripping will have stopped. Then she will put them into sterilized jugs which would go straight into their fridge. That will be proper red caviar. The rest of caviar would be salted a bit longer, which would then keep until Spring.

After that, Lara went to the shed to prepare. She scrubbed out a big oak barrel where she was going to salt down the fish, to preserve it for the long winter months.

ᘓᘓ

Lara was suddenly woken from her reverie by the insistent ringing of the phone. She scrambled out of bed, thinking that it could only be Derek at that time of night. "Ello! Oh. No, I'm afraid he's not here. Who's speaking, please?" Whoever was on the other end immediately hung up. Lara tried to think who it might have been. He sounded English to her, but then so did anyone speaking English, she thought. A little nervously, she checked all the windows and doors and went back to bed.

ᘓᘓ

Derek took his luggage and hurried to make his check in. Once he got through and onto the plane with everyone else, a stewardess started to speak over the loud speakers welcoming them on board and giving them the information about the flight to the biggest airport in the Far East.

A woman sitting next to Derek, suddenly turned head towards him saying.

"Hi, Derek."

"Hi, do I know you, or how do you know my name?" Derek was astonished and genuinely surprised.

"It's my job to know a lot about people who claimed to be our friends."

She said softly, leaning towards him and whispering. He even smelled a nice perfume.

"But, please, don't be concerned, I will take very good care of you—and your trip."

She put her hand on his hand looking suggestively at him—"I will be accompanying you on your business trip as your assistant.

"My name is Elena, I hope you like my name." She raised an eyebrow and looked at him quizzically.

"I will be ready to do anything, I mean it…that you might want."

She slightly squeezed his hand. "I shall take very good care of you."

My God! Thought Derek anxiously. *Just what the hell have I got myself into? They will not leave me alone even for a split second.*

Chapter 13

That summer morning was quiet and warm. The pink and yellow first beams of light shimmered through the tree branches. Not a single leaf swayed on the trees and shrubs in the pine forest. An old reindeer nibbled the fresh green grass, still damp with morning dew. As it hungrily devoured the best grass, it wandered towards an old wooden fence where the deer regularly visited as part of their morning routine. Behind this fence were buildings where occasionally people would bring food to the deer who would gratefully accept the treats without fear.

The old deer raised his head and looked towards those human buildings.

Alex strolled out onto his small but beautifully maintained green garden and admired the green view towards the fence and forest behind it. He gently yawned then did several stretching exercises. As he turned, he noticed his old friend the deer peering over the fence and smiled.

"Just wait my friend!" thought Alex as he returned to his flat, took some bread from the cupboard and returned to the garden.

"Take this, do not be afraid," he quietly whispered as he slowly approached the deer and stretched out his hand with the bread. The deer, a little cautious at first, sniffed the food, then took the bread and began to chew slowly, with visible enjoyment on his face.

Alex was walking down familiar university corridors heading to his next lecture, which would be given by his favorite professor. Today he was cheerful, acknowledging his fellow students who were standing in groups, chatting or busily reviewing their notes in the noisy hallways. Turning a corner, he recognized his friend Michael and shook his hand with a firm grip.

"Is today a special day for you?" Michael asked.

"Hmm, who knows…maybe, ask me later,"…Alex smiled in reply and continued.

"What if we tomorrow will go for a drink and…and for the weekend you can come with me to a party. Maybe we could meet some nice girls."

"It sounds good for me but I did not tell you that I have a new girlfriend? Yes, yes and I adore her. So if we go then I'll bring her and I am not interested, Alex, in any other girls any more," Michael merrily replied.

"Well, well, I am glad for you my friend, we could go in her company and Shawn possibly…. I will call you. Sorry, now I am hurry to my lecture. Cheers."

Alex almost had to run in to the lecture hall where his professor had just started.

When all his lectures were finished Alex visited professor Yakomoto in his office.

"Hello again, professor, can I ask you for permission to work late in the laboratory this evening?"

"Hi Alex, nice to see you, did you understand my subject in today's lecture? It was a difficult topic and I could see some of you were struggling. It was hard work today." He admitted.

"Yes, professor, I understood and really enjoy your lecture, I took a lot from it. And for me it's really interesting that Great Britain and Russia did not submit their application yet to participate in the international competition for the best invention in renewable energies."

"Yes, Alex, I think too, it's strange. There is still time yet, several months, so we will see.

"Ok, Alex, you can use the laboratory in the evenings for your research. How are things progressing? Do you have already some tangible results of your research?" The professor smiled.

"Not yet, but I think we will see some progress soon," Alex said mysteriously, grinned and waved good bye.

Oh yes, today could be a very special day for me, thought Alex departing the professor's office. *I might possibly finalize my device because I have everything I need already in the laboratory. Great!*

But before that, Alex decided to go and say goodbye to some of his friends in the classrooms. He waited until the university was almost empty and then—he was aching to start his experimentation in his laboratory in the evening solitude—just him and his invention. And today, tonight, he possibly could actually test his device, innocently concealed in a sort of suitcase.

The case was a small ordinary one—the kind a businessman would usually carry on a short trip. Alex thought that the best place to test it for real would be in his flat—tonight.

"Well, friends, I'm going to be busy this evening, so bye, see you tomorrow. Michael, can I have a word with you privately?"

"Yes, Alex."

"If I need help from you tonight, can you help me? Possibly not just from you, maybe from Shawn too. I already asked him. I hope you have his phone number."

"What do you need?"

"I will explain it to you later if it's really needed. Ok?"

ഗ്ഗ

The FSB agent was sitting in a grey car, partially distracted by a game on his smart phone.

He was regularly glancing at the entrance of the university every time he spotted someone leaving. His interest was in only one person—that young student, Alex.

He had been on this assignment for a long time but nothing unusual had happened and there was nothing which indicated that the young inventor had either progressed to the prototype stage or where he was hiding his crucial files, on the memory stick. His reports to headquarters were uneventful, and his General was becoming increasingly critical of his performance in Sweden.

The next report may be different though. Over the past two weeks his “client’s” routine had changed. Now he arrived at the university with not one, but two bags. Possibly its means nothing—but who knows, possibly his “client” was up to something.

The agent yawned and continued to play games, wishing that Alex would leave the building and cut short today’s shift.

ഗ്ഗ

The main physics laboratory at the university was full of equipment, different kinds of glassware, and electronic machines. The windows were shuttered by blinds to provide a level of security from prying eyes.

Alex had been leaning over his device for several hours already and with a very concentrated stare he did something with a box, then connected together several more boxes and wires. A strong smell of solder hung in the air. He joined together everything he wanted, and returned to his research notes again to read and check. He was satisfied with how the hydrogen was contained, and recent changes to his design had improved the efficiency of the chemical used to facilitate the electrical energy transfer.

"That is it! It's actually working. Oh-h-h." Releived Alex wiped his forehead, stood up straight and looked down with pride at his device.

"Ten kilowatts in just this small device? That is great, I'm sure it can be scaled up to provide electricity for a plant, enterprise, city. Everybody could buy it, for different purposes and have constant electricity for years. I cannot believe how great it is...well done me!" He smiled for himself.

"Well, calm down, calm down for now. I should test it further before celebrating my success.

"But now I deserve a cup of tea with lemon. Where is my lemon? No lemon, it's a pity."

Alex went to the corner of the room where he boiled the kettle and made a nice cup of tea to celebrate and returned to his computer to check again.

"So, it seems, as if I've created a mini reactor without any radioactive waste—and without any carbon dioxide emissions. I think humanity has a new safe and constant source of energy. Hooray!" Alex sighed deeply and took a fresh long breath.

"What I can do now with this ultimate new technology device?" That was the one million dollar question for himself.

He started to worry about the ramifications of his invention. It was clear to him that there would be many people who would want to take his case from him. Maybe he would be in personal danger also.

Nervously, Alex got up and ran to the window and discreetly peeked through the blinds.

"Of course, here they are! They are waiting for me.

The grey car with the suspiciously loitering man in a suit looked like some sort of government clerk…but Alex knew who was there.

I need to get my case home for further testing. It's not safe to leave it here unattended. It looks like a suitcase, hopefully my rudimentary disguise will avoid too many suspicions '

Alex hid his computer stick and papers in a secret place in the laboratory. He put his device case in the sport bag which looked old and tatty enough not to be suspicious which he brought it here in advance.

"Allo, taxi office! I need a taxi at the university entrance in 5 minutes? Excellent! Thanks!"

He sighed deeply and started to plan. If the suspicious man in the car continues to watch him at his flat. "Well, I will call my friends to help, I think this evening they both will be at home. So, now off I go…"

Alex took his case, switched off the lights and hurried down the corridors and into the lift down to the entrance.

In the entrance hall he flashed his permission slip to the duty officer and stopped to wait for his taxi inside of the building. He found a spot where he could watch through the windows for his taxi and avoid being seen by the car.

Alex spotted the arrival of the taxi, the usual mid-size family car he had used before when working late. He took a deep breath, flung open the front door and sprinted down the steps. The taxi driver jumped with surprise as Alex swung open the rear door, dived in and slammed it shut in one quick move.

"Move, move. That grey car should not catch us and see where we go. My address is… Can you see that car behind us? Yes, that grey one, I need you to get some distance from it.

"Please, quicker, more, more." Alex shouted at the driver.

It was a crazy race, the light was going down over the city and the roads were not busy but there was enough traffic on the road to be dangerous. The taxi driver was obviously enjoying his role in the excitement. Turning left onto a main road just as the traffic lights turned red meant that Alex and his rescuer managed to gain the advantage as they accelerated along the straight road out of sight of his pursuer. Alex looked into the twilight behind him and could see some cars in the distance but in this light and at this distance he had no idea if the grey car was still in pursuit. He asked the driver to pull off the main road and take a route back to the apartment via some back streets. After 15 minutes, they arrived at their destination and Alex left the vehicle as quickly as he had entered, flinging three or four banknotes toward the driver. He ran into his flat, locking the deadbolt on the front door. After checking the balcony doors were secure he carefully placed his precious black case on the table and went to make a drink and to plan his next move, now that the immediate danger seemed to have passed.

"Allo-Allo, do you hear me? I need to report an incident with my surveillance subject.

"He tried to escape from my car tonight. He was at the university late and then took a taxi. He got away from me as the traffic lights changed—I couldn't follow closely enough without blowing my cover.

"He was carrying a sports bag, his behavior was suspicious tonight—it's clear he has realized we are interested in him. What are your orders?

"Yes comrade captain, I will."

The FSB agent was excited by the car chase after so many months of watching and waiting, but it has been a long day and sleep was becoming a priority. But orders are orders and his losing sight of his subject would not have been welcomed by his superiors. He parked his car in a position where he could watch the only door of Alex's block building entrance. As the adrenaline began to wear off, he took out his snack and thermos with coffee. *It will be a long night,* he thought.

Deep in thought, Alex sipped his tea and paced his small flat from corner to corner, slowly rubbing his chin. Recurring worried thoughts kept forcing their way into his mind, he was sure by now his follower would be parked outside, or maybe even standing outside his door, listening. He pushed the thoughts back to the recesses of his mind as he tried to formulate his plan.

He took his prized black case and grabbed a little torch from the chest of drawers in the living room and brought them to the corridor where his electricity fuse box was located in a tiny cupboard. With trembling fingers and damp sweat sticking his shirt to his back he pulled out the main circuit breaker, isolating his flat from the electricity grid. Immediately he was plunged into darkness.

With the small torch held in his mouth, Alex connected two thick cords from his device, clipping them onto the exposed terminals in the fuse box.

The flat again became awash with light and Alex sunk down against the opposite wall, legs outstretched. Half from the sudden tiredness he felt and half from excitement.

"Thank you God! I did it! I did it... It works!"

He smiled, and jumped up on his strong legs. "I will repeat it again…to be sure."

Alex repeated his actions again with the fuse box…and the flat was lit again, now he knew this wasn't just a miscalculation or a badly designed experiment in the lab. It works for real, his small flat was being powered by his device but he knew it would be capable of so much more.

"I did it, well done to me!"...His thoughts were swimming in his head.

"Now calm down, let's get back to the immediate issue, the Russian FSB are watching me and at this exact moment of time they are outside of this building waiting to ambush me or worse."

But I will not allow them to get their hands on it, this is too important. Take that you bastards! He gesticulated towards the windows a rude figure with two fingers.

"Hello Michael, I'm so glad you are at home and not asleep yet. Listen, my friend, I really need your help right now—I already called Shawn," Alex spoke with excitement, "I've already told him the plan, I need to tell you the same.

"I need urgently to hide a box in the railway station luggage lockers but I have a suspicion that a man in a grey car is watching me. I do not want him to follow me and see where I will put my box. I cannot tell you exactly what it is, in that box, but it relates to my research at the university and at the moment I need to keep this as a secret. One day you and Shawn will be the first who will know about this. Listen, Michael, take a taxi straight here after we finish talking. Collect Shawn on the way to the railway station. Shawn will tell you the further details. After arriving at the station give me a call.

"After that, I will come to the station, also by taxi, and you should watch carefully for my arrival and see who is watching and following me.

"Do we agree? I will pay for all the taxis involved. Ok great! Then I'll see you soon."

Alex understood that it would take an hour before his friends would arrive at the station.

He'd explained to Shawn that their task would be to stop the men chasing him—one or two FSB agents. Their mission should be to stop them well before the entrance of the main railway station building. Alex wanted to win enough time to reach the automatic left-luggage area and to lock away his black case, and then disappear into the crowds. With so many lockers, there was no way they could search them all.

Michael sat next to Shawn in the back seat of a taxi and in low whispers they discussed their plan for how to stop Alex's pursuers.

On their arrival at the station Michael paid and asked the driver to wait for them around the corner on the next street. The rendezvous point was not too far from where they were now but was not visible from here.

"Alex, are you OK there? We arrived and we're ready. Yes, we have a plan. I hope everything will be alright. So we'll wait for you and take our positions. Stop your taxi exactly opposite the station's main entrance.

You will see us, we will stand there, not far from the entrance but on both sides of the path leading to the entrance. We'll see you soon."

Alex ran to the taxi which was close to the door of his building then dropped into the rear seat with his heavy sports bag and commanded the driver to go, and with maximum speed yet again. His face was serious and anxious. Turning his head back he saw the grey car which appeared from around a corner and started to follow them very closely.

"Quickly, go, go," Alex shouted to the driver with urgency in his voice. "Get some distance between us and that car behind."

The taxi driver was wondering what he had got himself into. "Ok, I will but there is a speed limit!"

"I will pay extra, and I'll pay for any fines if you get them. Push on that pedal, please!" pleaded Alex.

"Look, look, the grey car is still tailing us, accelerate!" Alex turned to driver. "Listen, drop me at the station—exactly opposite the entrance. Wait for me on the corner of that street near the student café. I'll pay you now and for the waiting time too. In half an hour I should come back. If not, off you go and forget me. Do we agree? You know that your silence is your protection." Alex, heavily breathing, looked at driver eyes which were expressively strict.

"Yes, agreed," the driver said weakly and thought it better not to ask what was going on. A drug deal, a criminal on the run, a disagreement between gangsters—better to just keep quiet and take the money.

The same grey car continued to tail them and Alex was disappointed to see he only had a head start of a few hundred meters, much less than he planned. He would only have a matter of seconds to complete his task and dissolve into the waiting passengers in the very late hours of the Swedish rail station.

The agent who was relaxing in the car until a few short moments ago was caught off guard when Alex darted out of his home and jumped in the car. He wasn't expecting another taxi chase. He just was preparing to spend another quiet night, listening to music, and playing games. But quickly everything changed and he went immediately into high alert state, ready to see what the subject was up to.

His car was plain looking but well upgraded and it was a pleasure to drive. Alex had almost disappeared on this most empty night road. But this road lead to the railway station, he thought Alex must be catching a train and he would catch up with him on the platforms.

He pushed the gas pedal down further and the car eased forward with a satisfying roar, his eyes concentrating on keeping Alex's vehicle in sight while using the other cars on the road as cover.

A couple of minutes later, just outside the station main's entrance he saw that Alex with his clearly heavy bag had jumped out of the car and shot into to entrance of the grand station building and successfully disappeared.

"What a nimble client I have, he is making me work hard today."

With thought vexing him before he stopped the car opposite the entrance of the station and jumped from his car too.

ꕥꕥ

Michael and Shawn stood on different sides of the sidewalk leading to the station entrance and carefully monitored all the arriving cars. They were ready to start their hastily agreed play.

It was easy to notice Alex arrive, he was in a taxi like many others dropping off passengers at the station but whereas everyone else was taking their time unloading their luggage, Alex shot out of the taxi like a sprinter. He glanced over to see his friends in the agreed location.

There were quite a few people wondering around the square outside of the station, but less than Alex would have hoped, understandable given the late hour. There were only a few more trains due to depart this evening.

Michael noticed the grey car speeding up to the station entrance, unusual as there was only a single occupant. He prepared himself mentally to act, looking over to Shawn and nodded towards the grey car. Shawn nodded back, indicating he had noticed it too.

Just as the driver left the grey car and started to run towards the station entrance too, Michael stepped forward straight into his path and deliberately threw himself to the ground, rolling theatrically for good measure.

This was not the plan, the agent was clearly confused about what has happening but he instinctively made an attempt to help Michael to stand on his feet and didn't notice big and tall Shawn come running up behind him until he heard the words "You hit my friend!" As he turned toward the voice he noticed too late Shawn lunging towards him and unsuccessfully tried to avoid the incoming left hook flying towards his face. He crumpled to the floor in pain, disoriented by the ferocity of the unexpected attack.

Michael quickly got up and ran towards the next street where he had earlier agreed to meet his taxi driver. He looked back and saw the agent was moving and try to get up but he was clearly still dazed and trying to regain his balance as he staggered to his feet. A few people had come to his assistance and were trying to help him up. At least there were no policemen which was a good news for Michael.

He heard Shawn's footsteps running behind him and soon they both disappeared around the corner.

The agent, finally back on his feet had started to realize what was going on and was desperately trying to clear his head and continue his mission. As he wiped the blood from his nose he turned to run to the entrance. He rushed into the station hall and stopped confused because this huge building would leave him little chance to find his student and he was too late to look for Alex.

He tried to work out which way Alex could have gone. He checked the different exits to the platforms, corridors, shops, and waiting areas. He checked the departure board for the next train to leave and headed onto the platform. There were a few people waiting with their families but no Alex.

The agent took a deep breath, wiped his face again and standing in front of the departure board once more was thinking what to do and what to report in FSB office.

"Allo, allo, comrade captain, I am reporting to you that after tailing our "client" all day, I lost him at the railway station. Now, I need backup for tomorrow to sort out this problem—he is in possession of some interesting luggage which possibly is what we're looking for.

"Yes, captain, understood. I will do it."

Still breathing heavily he headed back across the high ceilinged hall and back to his badly parked car, where the driver's door was still wide open just as he left it.

Chapter 14

Ten thousand meters above the vast Siberian plains, Derek was still wide awake in contrast to the rest of the passengers on his flight who were gently sleeping. Not even two glasses of wine helped him to unwind and join his fellow travelers in rest. Future plans for his business were developing in his mind, but also, he was wondering what to do about the biggest challenge. This woman sitting next to him, a Russian agent who had a grip on him, reminding him of the spy Mata Hari who famously liked to dance and she was able to do the famous Russian beryuska dance which he and Lara had seen at the concert. *Does this spy like to dance?*—He thought.

Signing a contract with this large Russian organization would transform his company, and completing this transaction was a priority for Derek, but he was thinking of what he might need to do in order to achieve it. Maybe things could develop in an intimate way, but Derek wanted to avoid complications and make progress quickly and return to more comfortable, and predictable surroundings as soon as possible.

His business was moderately successful in making plastic parts, mainly components for furniture or the automotive industry. It was a highly competitive industry though, and the chance to open up a new market in Russia could be highly lucrative and would certainly mean an expansion of his operations. He had been in this region already after his New Year's trip.

But then he was in contact with different people then showing them samples of his production. Now he was coming for a second time.

After such a long flight, landing in Khabarovsk of the Far East region and transferring to a much smaller plane for the one-hour journey to Derek's final destination was a relief. His fellow traveler Elena had been helpful and he felt ready for the challenges ahead of him.

Derek did not have to wait long. As he descended the steps from the plane at the small local airport, he was met by two men standing by a black Range Rover.

"Mister Harrison" said a tall, serious looking man who showed no signs of discomfort from the sub-zero temperatures, other than a slightly bluish tinge to his face.

"Oleg Ivanovich is my name" he stepped forward arm outstretched and shook Derek's hand firmly in a manner which matched his stony demeanor.

"I am deputy director of the company where you going to have business talks for next several days. As today is Saturday, all our top managers and directors are enjoying some male bonding at a sauna in the forest" He pointed his finger vaguely in the distance, "it's just 10 kilometers from the city. I was instructed to bring you to that dacha, to relax with us and then this evening, we will bring you to your room in our hotel. Does that sound acceptable?"

Derek had no choice but to agree and go with the flow he thought.

"But your lady assistant, unfortunately," he smiled at her, "we will deliver straight to she hotel."

"Don't you mind?"

Elena in her beautiful fur coat seemed disappointed. "Of course, I don't mind. I hope there is a nice place in your hotel where I can have drink and dinner."

"Yes, there is and I'm sure you will enjoy it. Sorry, but you will have plenty of time to speak with Mister Harrison about your business. Now we go. It's very cold."

The weather was something never experienced before for Derek. It was a snow storm, with gusting winds and low temperature, Derek guessed it at somewhere below -20c. Derek hid his gloved hands in his pockets, he was frozen by now and wanted nothing but food, rest, and most of all somewhere to warm up. A stiff drink might help with that, he thought.

After leaving Elena at the hotel they continued their way further into the forest. Derek was beginning to doubt the distance was really just ten kilometers, but after about an hour they arrived at a pretty building in the deep forest on the bank of a river. The dacha was beautiful, wooden and shaped in the Finnish style but several times larger. Parked outside the dacha were quite a few expensive cars, signifying the presence of important guests there.

"Unfortunately, Mister Harrison, the director and his friends and colleagues already went to the sauna several minutes ago. So now quickly we should go also. This lady will show your room upstairs"

Oleg Ivanovich nodded towards a young maid.

"You will have in your room everything you need for sauna. Change and in 5 minutes we will meet you here

"I'm going to change too."

Oleg disappeared somewhere, presumably to his room and Derek went to get changed. He as quickly as possible changed into a white soft robe and with a big luxurious towel on his shoulder hurried to meet Oleg, not wanting to make a bad impression with his future business partners.

"Ohh!, Our friend from England, come in Derek, you arrived just in time."

The director in his white hat, was looking very hot in the foggy sauna. His face was red and sweaty, with a towel around his big belly. He shook Derek's hand and invited him to join their cleansing ritual in the men's company.

"Now Derek, you will learn how to clean yourself in a Russian manner. Swedes have a dry sauna but Russian like wet sauna," he laughed.

"Do the same as we all do and you will feel yourself as a new born man again and, actually, with weight loss afterwards. I will introduce you with my friends later, after sauna. They are all very busy," he winked to Derek.

"Please, make yourself at home."

Some men were sitting on the top benches and were sweating to the degree that sweat was not dripping, but running down their bodies. They were suffering from the roasting hot air and scalding temperature, probably about 100 degrees or higher but they still had cheerful faces—like they knew this is all like a painful medicine that was worth suffering through for the results.

Derek sat on the middle bench but lower than the others in the slightly cooler air.

Some men were laying on the narrow, table-like benches, face-down with two more large men whipping them vigorously with birch leaf brooms. They continued this ritual of stroking, slapping and all sorts of strange and unusual movements, much to the enjoyment of those receiving the "treatment.". Then just as their backs turned an angry shade of red, they drenched themselves from head to toe in icy cold water from a wooden bucket.

"Aaahh!", they moaned and groaned.

"Derek, come on, lay down on this bench, I will show you a real massage."

The director took a broom from where it was soaking in hot water and started with long stokes down Derek's back then started whipping with gusto. To Derek's surprise it was a really invigorating feeling.

"You will never find a massage like that in England for any money!"

Derek kept silent in his agreement, enjoying the ecstatic feeling and started to groan just like the Russians, losing himself in the moment.

Suddenly a back door was thrown open and one by one, each man started to run outside.

Derek, now a firm believer in the benefits of a Russian sauna needed no persuasion to follow them. They all threw themselves down into the snow and rubbed themselves down with soft snow before running down a few more steps to the river. Each man jumping into a freshly prepared ice hole into the frosty dark water. Some remained there for just seconds, others proving their constitution by remaining for some minutes.

Derek was not quite ready for this commitment so he simply rubbed himself down with the powdery snow, feeling himself getting stronger and healthier before running back inside the sauna. This time, he headed straight for the highest bench. What was almost intolerably hot a few moments ago was now comfortably warm. Others returned in ones and twos, sitting on the benches around Derek to repeat the process once more.

After repeating the whole ritual twice more, everyone started to get dressed and the mood was very jovial.

"Now I would imagine, how my wife would be pleased to meet me after the sauna and seeing my crispy body be ready for the long talk," one man said with a smile.

"Are you sure that it will be that long?" another joker remarked and all the men burst into laughter.

Derek was sitting at the long oak table on a simple sturdy bench along with a few other men. As he sat in his travel outfit, observing the people around him in the luxurious hall, dinner was about to commence. The hall was well decorated with deer heads, stuffed animals, crystal, heavy curtains, it was a very impressive place and the table was now fully laden with different foods.

Derek noted there was enough alcohol on the table to satisfy a small army after a heavy battle. He decided to stick with red wine.

The sound of a heavy chair being pushed back drew Derek's attention away from the table and he watched the director stand up and make a toast.

"To health and long life for all of us."

They drank a first glass and the feast started to the accompaniment of quiet Russian music.

Two waitresses were rushing to and from the kitchen and although they were hurrying, it seems as if they were very accustomed to their duties.

"Comrades, I would like to introduce our guest today. This is Mister Harrison, Derek. So, I ask you respect and greet him," the director said.

"All being well, in a couple of days he will be our new business partner. So welcome Derek to our country! We look forward to your friendship and your high-quality plastic products!" The director toasted and everyone drunk.

The room was becoming noisy with laughter and talking, and Derek was enjoying the atmosphere. It was very different from the way business was done at home. The drinks were flowing and so was the conversation.

Derek's neighbour at the table, a man with a bald head and insightful eyes turned to him.

"Pleased to make your acquaintance Derek, I am Ivan Tarasovich. To your left is Misha."

Misha finished his drink of vodka and with a slow rolling tongue, turned to Derek and said, "You are honoured to speak to our best friend—the boss of our local FSB branch, so be careful, Derek," and winked at him in the exaggerated way only a drunken man can.

"Don't take any notice Derek," said Ivan.

"Our friend Misha, who by the way, is a good friend has made good progress here. With the power of his police department we have a low crime rate here."

"Derek, shall we drink another vodka?" said the Chief of Police, Misha, and without waiting for an answer Misha had already half-filled Derek's glass with vodka.

"To us! For friendship between Russia and England!" Misha led the next toast.

"Sorry Misha, I cannot drink anymore, I had enough wine," Derek protested.

"Are we not friends?! Take your glass, we will drink for friendship. Cheers!"

Misha stared at him with drunk eyes, waiting.

"Mister Harrison, if you are ready to leave I will take you to your hotel"

The director's deputy Oleg saved him from the awkward situation. Most of the guests were by now very inebriated and everybody was merry and relaxed. Only Oleg, was not influenced, visibly at least, by the alcohol.

Ivan Tarasovich, the chief of local FSB shook his hand on the door step. The chauffeurs of drunk guests started coming in and helping their bosses to go and change in nearby rooms and then bring them to the cars.

Derek was the first to leave the men's sauna party and again the black car drove them through the deep, dark forest towards the town on this cold night.

"Mr. Harrison, I am glad you survived! I hope you enjoyed the sauna with us. You see now that all guests there have their hearts in good state to tolerate that party. I hope yours is enough healthy for that too.

"My deputy will show you the draft of our contract today, and if you are in agreement we can sign it tomorrow. I received a report from my department where you were last time that the molding parts produced by your factory are of the highest quality and I'm keen to sign our first order. I think you and your factory will be very busy on your return to the UK. I hope you enjoy your evenings in our town, and yours pretty assistant also." The director smiled to Elena and shook their hands to conclude the meeting formally.

Derek left the director's office and outside Oleg was waiting with a thick bundle of contract paper work which he decided to read through in comfort back at the hotel room.

Later that evening Elena was complaining about being hungry and so they went together to a cozy restaurant. After the recent mix of excitement and new experiences, Derek was happy to relax a little in more familiar surroundings, with food and a few unhurried drinks. Derek was enjoying his usual red wine, but Elena was clearly enjoying her champagne and was already on her third glass as Derek finished his first.

The conversation was lazy and easy, Derek had to remind himself to keep to small talk, remembering his travel companion was a Russian agent sent to spy on him. Elena was young and charming though Derek kept thoughts of his wife, Lara, and his business at the front of his mind. It was quiet inside as they waited for their dinner to be served. Outside the snow storm was whipping up with snow drifting up against the windows. The contrast between the harsh weather outside and the cozy surroundings in the restaurant made Derek feel even more comfortable.

"My dear boss," Elena was looking attentively into Derek eyes. "What do you think if we will go to your room with a bottle of Champagne after dinner?"

"Ok, but after a little TV with Champagne I will accompany you to your room."

"Of course, boss" she smiled.

The dinner was taking a long time to arrive but Derek didn't feel like complaining. He felt Elena rub her red high heel shoe on his foot under the table and she looked back at him coyly. Derek moved his feet back under his chair and looked at her questioningly. "Elena, shall we," he started, but at this point the young waiter arrived with two steaming plates which they ate, mostly in silence.

After dinner, they walked slowly down the corridor and then around a couple of corners towards Derek room.

Derek switched on the TV, and set a couple of Champagne glasses on the small table opposite of the sofa. Elena was drunk but tried to hide it and he saw that she was planning something.

After the last sip of champagne Derek explained tomorrow's plans to Elena. After signing the contract, he wanted to go to the airport as soon as his business concluded, and he wanted to change his tickets for an earlier departure for Moscow.

He was tired and relaxed and suddenly, he caught himself observing Elena, her curves, white smooth skin, cascade of long dark brown hair. The alcohol was certainly making its effect felt on him he thought *she is bloody sexy*.

"My dear Derek," she said in her sweet voice. "Tomorrow afternoon we are going to go back to Moscow together and my mission will be accomplished."

"It's very rare that I meet on my duties such a charming client," she moved close to him on the sofa and angled her head towards Derek with her beautiful red lips pouting ready for a kiss.

God, what I am doing? was the last thought Derek remember that night.

He grabbed her and passionately started to kiss her all over.

Chapter 15

The Russian General of Intelligence was working late in his office, well past his usual working hours. He was half reclined in his green leather chair, strumming his fingers on the huge chestnut oak desk, pondering his next orders for the troublesome Swedish branch.

"Let us increase the number of officers there temporarily, we need to get things back under control and we should recall agent Nicolai to Moscow. We will discuss his serious errors of judgement—and maybe find a role more suited to his skills in the East, Egypt or so."

"We'll bolster our presence in Stockholm with two or three more experienced officers to keep watch on our 'student' and finally snatch the invention from his hands."

The General thumbed through a few more reports, and came to the conclusion that at least Nicolai's actions had not attracted the attention of the Swedish intelligence services 'MUST.'

"But do they know about the student, and his invention?" It was a question his reports could not yet answer. Hopefully the additional manpower would help to fill in the blanks on these crucial questions.

He returned to his computer, logged in to a database, and started to query through highly restricted pages some more names from the reports.

ᔕᔕ

The DJ was filling the large hall with music, and the partygoers were enjoying the carefree atmosphere, taking them away from the concerns of their day-to-day lives. All young people, dancing in distinctive styles, wearing fashionable clothes but all with their own flairs. They all felt the rhythm of the music, and danced closely in the nightclub.

Alex was making pirouettes with a long blonde-haired Swedish girl who was flinging herself towards, back and around Alex with laughter, clearly really enjoying their dance. Not too far from them, his friend Michael was dancing with his girlfriend and big Shawn with a curvy, beautiful young lady with long dark hair. Their dancing obviously impressed those around them as a little circle of space formed giving them more space to perform their dance.

Couple by couple they went to the bar for refreshments, a beer, or an additional glass of wine to keep their spirits high.

It was clear that Shawn was enjoying himself a little bit too much and he was looking quite drunk—and happy. It didn't seem to worry his dance partner though, and the others could tell she wanted to leave with him. Even in his inebriated state he picked up on the signals and suggested to his friends that it was time to head home with his new friend.

"Ok, Shawn, bye then. See you in few days!"

Michael and Alex stood aside from the girls and were talking about something funny because Alex was laughing loudly listening what his friend was saying to him.

"Well, Michael, I will never forget that you both helped me that night. Now everything is well and seems peaceful. I did not notice anybody watching me. Possibly it was an accident. I do not know."

Alex was a bit crafty, he still didn't want to tell his friend all about his invention.

"Sorry, Michael, please, keep the girls entertained—I'm going to visit the gents.'

Alex pushed himself through the very crowded dance floor, where the evening was at its height, he turned into the corridor.

Away from the dancing, he felt his head was heavy and thought maybe it was time to finish the evening and go to home alone. That girl is a good dancer but he did not want to invite her anywhere yet.

Let's take things slowly, we will see, he thought.

He moved towards the gents' room, slightly unsteady on his feet, through the crowded corridor past the smoking corner.

Washing his hands, he bent down to the tap trying to rinse his face, and suddenly felt a strong embrace from behind. He tried to turn around to see which of his friends he hadn't noticed sneak up behind him but he found he couldn't turn his head as a soft cloth with a powerful smell was held over his mouth by a large hand, and then he blacked out.

Two men, dressed indistinguishably from the rest of the revelers left the toilet, holding Alex from either side, semi-conscious by now. They moved back through the busy corridor asking the onlookers to clear some room. A couple of concerned clubbers asked if everything was alright and the men said they just needed to get their friend outside for some fresh air.

As they left the club, a large car was waiting for them outside. A group of young men outside the entrance took a break from their smoking and chatting to watch what was going on. They watched the men put Alex into the Saab and one of the men, who vaguely knew Michael and had saw him with Alex earlier, felt uneasy, feeling something in the way they put Alex into the car wasn't quite right. He decided to make a mental note of the registration number of the car and check with Michael that everything was ok.

"Hi friend,' he reached Michael, "Do you know that your friend, who was with you earlier this evening, just now was taken away in a big Saab?"

"What?!" Michael's head, in seconds, became absolutely clear.

"Yes, two guys carried him by his arms into a back Saab, I think. I remember the plate number. Here it is…" he spelled out the numbers.

"My sweet, I should leave you, sorry and sorry. Here is some money for the taxi to get home." Michael passed her some bank notes,

"I am in a hurry—I think Alex is in trouble. I need to help him."

He gave her a kiss and ran.

His girlfriend was a nice, quiet, intelligent girl, and she let him go without objection, seeing the worry on his face.

Michael ran around the corner of the big building which contained the night club, to the next building where luckily the district police station was conveniently located.

The officer on duty, behind a glass window watched as a young man in great distress rushed into the hall, and stepped towards the window.

"Sir, I would like your help! My friend was kidnapped! I know what kind of car and the number plate."

"Calm down, please." Said the policeman. "Shall we start again slowly. What is your name, address and your friend's."

Michael was on the edge of bursting into anger. He understood that formality here could kill Alex but realized he needed help, and didn't want to escalate the situation.

After understanding the seriousness of the situation, the cop made a call reporting to someone higher and he suggested Michael sit and wait while the police went straight into action to find Alex. He explained that they should be able to track the car using number plate recognition technology, recently installed around the capital and suggested that they may need to ask Michael some more questions so not to go far.

Michael stepped outside of the police station and called Shawn.

"Listen, we have a situation, Alex was kidnapped, and he is danger. Yes, and now I wait here until situation will be solved by cops. I did not say anything here about my presumptions but we can guess who did this to Alex.

"I am really, terribly worried about him. Ok, understood, tell her good night and I'll wait for you here in half an hour."

Two police cars with sirens blaring were speeding by empty roads heading to the Stockholm district where their electronic system led them. The hunt was on…

The big Saab slowed from its high speed to a crawl and turned into a dark corner of a back yard behind a high building.

Two men jumped out from the car and hurriedly opened the back doors. They pulled out a third man and started carrying him to entrance. Third man looked drunk or ill because was not able to stand on his feet.

Holding him under his arms, they punched in a code. The door opened and they took several steps to reach a ground floor flat.

"Quick, quick," Kostya said, "we'll sit him down on a chair in living room."

"Pass me that belt."

"Are you ready to 'talk' to him?"

Kostya looked at his colleague agent Vadim.

"I hope you realize that we have very little time to crack him. If somebody reports to the police they could start to search for us and be searching this area very soon. I'll watch the windows, and if they appear in the yard, then we run and lock the door. We'll leave him here and escape through the loft door and then go down to exit the front door of another building according our plan. Don't kill him, be moderate."

"Yes, I will do. Where's that liquid, give him to smell." Vadim nodded.

Alex opened his eyes, his heavy eye lids trying to return him to his comfortable sleepy state again, but he forced himself to keep his eyes open and to try to return to the real world and understand what was going on. Who are those two guys who are standing opposite him and staring at him with sarcastic smiles? And where he is right now—and why are his hands tied behind his back?!

"What the hell?!"

"Good m-morning-g-g mister Student! How was your sleep after your nice party?"

Vadim asked and winked to him

"Would you like a cup of coffee? Or maybe a water?" With a condescending tone Vadim continued.

"Now we should wake you up totally." He grabbed a jug of water from the table and splashed it over Alex body.

"Ouch! It's cold, isn't it? Now this is serious for you, Alex, shall we speak as gentlemen, before we make you very hot?"

Vadim face changed, "Could you put the iron on, there, there in that corner."

He pointed Kostya to the opposite corner of the dilapidated flat.

"So, Alex, by the way, we know everything about you and your family, mother, sister, everything. But there is something we do not know and, now we going to ask you, and we want to have that answer. We need from you your file, the information concerning your invention. Tell us where you hid it.

"You can guess who we are. Actually, I would remind you, we are citizens of the same great country, Alex, our Motherland of Russia.

"So here in Sweden, you and we are just guests. I hope you will understand and we will get from you that what we want without using force, and it's enough of playing the cat and mouse game.

"We are cats, big cats—even here, in Sweden. But you should stop being the mouse, we will help you. So, do we have a deal?"

Vadim started to breathe heavily and his face was visibly redder.

Alex began to think he was the star in an uncomfortable film scene and this was the first take. What would happen if there was a second take?

He became scared and his mind was swimming.

He felt fear, but also anger. No way would he give these goons his invention—whoever they are representing did not deserve it, he thought. He snapped back to the urgency of the situation, and was chaotically searching for something which would help him now.

"You bastard, do not play games with us, tell us where it is!" Vadim started shouting close to Alex's face as he was sitting on the chair in the middle of the room.

"I have no idea what you are talking about." Alex looked seriously at his interrogator.

"So, you did not understand me, eh?"

Vadim lost his patience and gave Alex a sharp left hook and then a matching one to the right side of Alex's face.

Alex sat stunned for some seconds and then lifted his face, complete with bloody nose and said, "If I would have had what you want from me, then I never would give it to you because now I hate you!"

Vadim strutted into the corner, picked up the already hot iron and stood close to Alex. He was angry and brutal in all his words and actions. He looked like an attacking animal who wanted to bite you to death.

"I will give you two minutes to remember. If you don't tell me then I will make you hot and iron up your chest." Vadim flashed a nasty smile, and Alex thought he was enjoying his job far too much.

"Vadim, Vadim, some cars have pulled into the yard, police I think, big BMWs…now we should leave," Kostya turned to Alex.

"Listen—today was just a warm up for you, we will meet again very soon.

"You have two days to think. After that we expect your cooperation and your invention should be passed to Russian government. If you will not do it, then remember this we will make you suffer very much—we know where your mother and your sister live.

"It's very simple. Now you sit here and wait for your rescuers. We will contact you in 48 hours, do you understand? I said it in clear Russian for you, bastard."

The two Russian agents sprang out through the apartment door and sprinted up to the top floor. They heard the sound of buzzers inside the other flats as the Swedish police were trying to reach any of the residents to buzz open the entrance door for them.

As the Russians reached the top of the stairs, they heard the entrance door swing open and crash against the wall, and what sounded like many policemen burst through.

The commotion woke up all the remaining residents of the building who managed to sleep through their buzzers ringing moments earlier. Some of them peeped out of half open doors, trying to see what was going on.

Several armed officers were staying glued to walls but one was shouting at each closed door then in silence listening through door if any sound from inside.

"Hey, help me, help me!" They heard a weak voice from inside. "I cannot open the door, break it!"

Then after several strong kicks, Alex saw several people, armed cops swarm inside pointing assault rifles at him. Alex quickly explained that he had been kidnapped and they wanted to torture him."

The man in charge, an inspector released Alex from the chair and snapped at his deputy to radio for an ambulance. Another officer poured Alex a glass of water from the sink and noticed the hot iron standing close by. Alex was pleased to see the rapid response of his rescuers. Five minutes later, medics arrived and gave him a thorough check over. More officers arrived, some in plainclothes who started photographing, fingerprinting and then conducting a full search.

"Mr. Petrov, my colleague will give you a lift home and tomorrow we need you to come down to the station for a more detailed interview which may take some time. You should call a friend to be with you tonight. I understand your friend is waiting for you at the police station, I'll have a message passed to him." The Inspector said

"Yes, thank you. I will meet with you in the morning. My face and jaw are in such pain and I am in shock from what happened to me this evening."

Alex arrived back at his flat and waited in the police car, while an officer entered first, checked on security, then waved Alex to come in and left him on his own.

"What a disastrous day today!" Alex looked at the mirror which reflected back to him a face which he never saw before—a black eye, red nose covered in plasters, and swollen lips.

"Those two Russians, especially the one who hit me, they were really evil nuts.

Well I should think now carefully about what to say to the police tomorrow, Alex thought,

"Possibly I will tell them they are Russian agents, but I will not tell them about my file, or my device, or give them any reason to suggest why they are chasing me. It would be best, I think."

He took phone and dialled Michael's mobile number.

The Chief Inspector of police was sitting in his comfortable chair and thinking what he should do next.

"That student Alex just left our office after recording everything about yesterday evening. And he has his suspicions at least, who his kidnappers were."

It was the first kidnapping case in his long career and certainly the first where, possibly, Russian spies were involved'

He thought he has dealt with every possible case in the last 35 years but this was new and exciting. Not very often such a complicated and interesting case drops into his hands, an experienced inspector, and he was treading new ground. He must solve this tricky case and his experience told him that the political nature of the case would need to be handled carefully.

Recognising he needed advice he reluctantly reached for his black book of contacts and flipped through for the number of the MUST intelligence services.

"Yes Sir! That is all we know about the incident. The mother and sister of Mr. Petrov could be in danger. Yes, I will..

"No," he said, "Alex said he has no idea why he has been caught up in this whirlwind."

"Yes, we already started an investigation, we have some finger prints in the flat, which was rented under a stolen passport, same story with the car. No, we were not able to catch them, they escaped through the roof space. The student is Ok, but…

"Yes, Sir, we will do that and pass all paper work to your department, it will there tomorrow morning."

"Mama, how are you? Do you like it there, is your husband good to you? How is Derek and his business?"

Alex was smiling as he listened to mother's cheerful voice. She usually hid her emotion well, but today she was in a bubbly mood.

"I am so glad for you, really. Mum, I miss you very much. Also, Derek invited me to visit you both in England, so I decided to visit you! I've booked a ticket for tomorrow on the Ferry to Southampton. I will send you an email with my arrival details.

"Ok-ok, mum, I see, you're glad too!

"I already finished my studies and wrote my exam research. So, in one month, I must come back to Stockholm for the presentation of my doctorate of science diploma and that is all…I'll have completely finished my studies.

"After that I'm going to search for a job in England straight after my arrival. As you remember, I borrowed money from your husband, so I'm going to start earning as soon as I can, I do not like to be in debt.

"Well, Mum, listen to me carefully. Are you alone now at home? That is good. Listen.

"Maybe you can pick me up from the port with Derek? I will have quite a lot of luggage. I would like you to take control of my luggage. Why? I do not want Derek to investigate my belongings. It's important! He must bring all my cases straight to my bedroom. Especially the biggest one, a sporty bag. Because I need to hide that bag somewhere, possibly in your house. But secretly from Derek, he should not know ever about our conversation. I have a plan, I will tell you later. Mum, trust me. Do we agree? We will manage it? Good.

"That's great, thanks mum.

"We will have time to speak about everything. Take care of yourself and regards to Derek."

Alex did not sleep that night, he was sitting, walking measuring his room, he was thinking, polishing his plans about what to do and when. When night met the morning and the outside blackness turned into grey light, Alex dropped his heavy head on the pillow and on the bed still fully clothed, he fell into a deep sleep.

Next day the same chief inspector received new instructions from his boss in headquarters even before he had chance to send the paper work to them.

"Yes, we know where Mister Petrov lives. We will establish surveillance immediately, yes, Sir. I'll take sure personally that everything is in place.

If the Russians continue to chase Alex we will have a chance to arrest them, we will organize an accident or so, and will bring them for interview where your colleagues from MUST can decide what to do with them. Yes, Sir, we will make sure it happens smoothly."

Next morning Alex spoke to Shaun and asked him to help him in his hasty exit plan. He must leave Stockholm today, and go by ferry to England where his mother and Derek would be waiting to bring him to their home.

But the trick was how to pick up his device from the railway station's left-luggage box while avoiding another confrontation with his Russian pursuers. He had a plan.

"Shaun, please, rent a cheap car and come to my flat. I"ll wait for you this afternoon at three p.m. I need to get to the ferry at six. Be ready for our rally. I hope you are not afraid. Good! See you later, friend."

Without any hesitation Alex took to the phone again.

"Allo, Chief Inspector? I need to call on you for your promise of help, I need your help today.

"I'm going to visit my Mum in England as you know. My problem is that I can see a suspicious car from my window. It's been there all day, with a guy who just sits waiting. It's possibly the same Russian guy. Maybe you can find a reason to check them out if they start to chase me again. Maybe I might have to break the speed limit a little to escape, and possibly you could turn a blind eye. I think this will help us both, I get away from here for a little while and you have some more time to come up with a plan. Thanks. Yes, I will leave about three p.m. That's great.

"Hoh-h," Alex sighed with relief and started to pack his things, clothes and most importantly he prepared the empty sports bag for his precious case which he would pick up from the station.

"Wake, up! Get ready! Look our student is leaving home with a lot of luggage and he is loading it in a white car—he has a lot—where he is going now?

Number one agent looked at his colleague, "be ready to race!"

"Go now, go, go, and keep visible distance."

Two cars, one white with Alex and Shawn, another grey with two Russian agents, were rushing through the streets at high speed. Both cars had some very near misses as they attempted to gain half a second over the other by taking a sharp, fast turn or accelerating through traffic lights that had long since turned red. Down one side street which should have provided a useful shortcut, there was a street market, Shawn tried to thread his car through the small gap between stalls but it was impossible. He clipped the corner of stall only by an inch or so. The momentum of the speeding car threw the whole lot up into the air, and the car pursuing then ran over the goods, leaving a mess of fruit and vegetables all over the road. The market sellers jumped out of the way and shouted after the cars in exasperation.

The sound of police sirens reached the agents ears.

"Allo, allo, number Three?" Number One agent held his phone in his sweaty palms, speaking quickly, with stress in his voice.

"We are approaching the railway station, you should be there in several minutes to take over the chase. You can see on your device where we are now. We should assume the student is going to leave the city, it could be airport or Ferry, I am very doubtful that it will happen by railway. Yes, yes…Listen, we could have now problems with Swedish police because of a few minor traffic offences.

"Do you understand? Be ready to travel. Follow him to the end of the Earth if you have to. Russia or England, it doesn't matter. Others have failed in this task, you have been brought it to make sure it succeeds—your task is to seize his suitcase, at any cost. Do it!"the agent shouted down the phone.

Two police cars reached the grey car, and briefly sounded their sirens. The passenger in the first police car pointed to the side of the road, ordering them to stop.

"Sirs, show me please your driving licence and identification."

The police officer took the documents and stepped back behind the car and made a call with a quiet voice reporting somewhere details about the occupants.

He came back to the grey car,

"Sir, I am instructed to impound your vehicle and insist you return with me to the police station."

Four men were sitting in an interview room at the police station, another two were covering the only exit doors.

"So Mr. Petrovskiy," police officer stared over the desk to number Two agent.

"Tell us again the reason, why you were speeding and why you are not registered at the address which you told us earlier?"

Sitting by the officer, another man was in silence scribbling notes in his notebook. He was slim, blond hair, in his fifties and with close interest was studying the eyes of the detainees.

"I've never dealt with an espionage case, but if I were a betting man I'd say we have here some Russian spies.

In that case, now we have 24 hours to investigate or release them with further observation and start preparation for court procedures.

"I will report immediately to my commanders and see what MUST can do to Russians who think they have the rights to use violence without regard to our laws."

ꕥ

Alex jumped out of the car and ran to the railway station. After some minutes, he appeared again at the entrance of the station and run back into the car where Shawn was waiting for him. Alex held a black case in his arms tightly which he put in his sports bag later.

"Now we are ready to board the Ferry." He winked with a cheeky face at Shawn,

"Go, go, my friend. Now keep to the speed limits, we have plenty of time and we can relax and enjoy the journey for a change."

But Alex in the excitement of the escape did not notice the eyes carefully monitoring the situation at the station entrance, and once Alex's car left the railway station a modest car gently pulled out and at a distance started following them.

Chapter 16

White and blue, looking like a big iceberg, the ferry was leaving the waters of Stockholm city bay towards the North Sea heading to Southampton.

Passengers hurried to find their seats and cabins, many hauling heavy bags. The initial rush of activity eventually died down as people spread across the ship and started to decide where to spend their evening. The cafes and restaurants were full of people and queues began to form. People were in a good mood and because everyone knew they would be on the ferry for a long time, the queues seemed to be part of the fun of the journey.

Alex made haste to the third deck where his cabin was located. It was not easy to push himself through the crowded deck reception area with several bags of luggage.

He slammed his cabin door behind him and took a glance around his tiny cabin before sitting down with big sigh. He took several gulps of water and then started to search for a place where he could stash his important bag.

"A-ha, maybe here." he spotted a small alcove under the bed, not ideal but the best he could do in such a cramped space.

Lying down on the bed, he started to calm down, recalling what happened over the last two days, regrouping his thoughts and trying to make a plan what to do now while travelling on this fabulous ship. But it was a difficult task at that moment because in his head he still held the memories and emotions of what happened to him just yesterday and today.

I am lucky to have real reliable friends, without them. he thought,

I would be in real trouble, thank God also for help. Alex felt a rumble of hunger in his stomach, followed by his eyelids feeling heavy. Before he had time to think about which feeling, his tiredness or his hunger was more pressing his eyes suddenly closed firmly and he went into a deep sleep.

Alex opened his eyes with a start, staring up at the white ceiling of the cabin. For a brief moment not understanding where he is. A few moments later, as his consciousness returned him to reality he remembered he was on the ferry. A second later he heard the sound of the old diesel engines fire up which confirmed it. Sounds of happy people chatting as they passed through the narrow corridor outside his cabin made him think of exploring the ship for something to eat.

He put his feet on the floor, shook his head a little and glanced at his watch. *One hour! I thought I just closed my eyes for one minute. Ok, quickly I'll wash my face and go to find food.* the thought of a quiet relaxing meal bringing him fully awake.

Alex changed his shirt, put a fashionable jacket on and then was struck by a thought. “Hang on, how I can leave my case in the cabin? No, I'd better not.”.

He took his case from the sports bag, looked in the mirror and he liked what he saw, despite the trials of the last few days he looked like a presentable young businessman with a black briefcase. He bent his lips into a smile. “Its ok for now, I will not give you to anyone,” he tapped his case with one hand. *Now we go for food and even a good drink or two,* he thought as he locked the door of his cabin.

The very fresh night breeze finally completed Alex's return to consciousness when he stepped outside onto the deck. Alex walked slowly along the deck with one hand lightly holding the rail, swaying gently with the ship, stopping now and then to peer into the blackness of the night which he found strangely relaxing.

The ferry was getting lively, Alex could hear faint muffled music and laughter from some distant areas, and probably restaurants or bars, he thought. Passengers had their late evening meals in restaurants or watching TV on big screens. But outside, the deck promenades were mostly empty. Only a few people were enjoying the crisp, fresh air.

Alex soon reached a restaurant and peered inside, from what he could see, there was not a single table free. But a young man, the maître d', saw his opportunity to keep his restaurant busy and asked Alex to wait a few minutes while some of the diners were finishing their meal. It had very nice interior and a musician played a quiet sweet melody, so he waited.

True to his word, the maître d' found him a table in a nice position near the big window so he could enjoy the night sea view and there was a convenient place to put his case on the floor, out of the way of passing diners.

Seated comfortably, he started to study the menu. *Oh-h, here is a nice steak, just what I need!* he thought, *and lemon cheese cake, what could be better.* He swallowed the saliva which he realised had gathered in his hungry mouth.

While sipping his red wine and waiting for the food he noticed that the waiter was talking to a good-looking young woman. She was blonde with a long hair style, a very nice figure with a tiny waist but she also looking a bit athletic. She wore an elegant black dress with high heeled red shoes and a red pendant on her chest. The waiter walked towards Alex's table and she followed towards him.

Oh, no, Alex thought to himself, trying to avoid eye contact.

"Excuse me, sir, do you mind if this lady will be seated at your table? It seems a shame to waste a large table for four people, while many people are waiting for a free table?"

"Of course, I don't, welcome to my table," Alex brought up a friendly look and sent a smile to his newly arrived dining partner.

Alex was torn, as he had planned a relaxing evening in his own company, but the woman was beautiful with smoky green eyes, a nice lip line, and an excellent slim body. As she was taking her place, she took a little mirror and expertly checked her lipstick, eyes, and face. Then satisfied with her look, closed her red, expensive looking handbag and neutrally smiled at Alex.

"Sorry to disturb you here but it seems I have no choice."

"It's ok, it's nice to have company," he responded, unsure if he was telling the truth or not.

"Because we are two strangers whom fate forced to eat together, may I introduce myself? My name is Alex, possibly better to say, Hungry Alex." He smiled widely at her.

"Pleased to meet you, Alex, and I would say you are lucky to meet me, because I am Hungry Nataliya too," she laughed in reply.

"Very good Nataliya, so I am waiting for my meal already so please take my menu."

When the waiter left her, they started with polite small talk. The conversation meandered between how nice the ferry was, how beautiful the weather was at this time of night and each asked questions about each other, finding out more about the person sitting opposite them.

Alex was intrigued to understand why this beauty was traveling on her own and why she come for dinner so late. She seemed to be very open and naïve, and was happy to answer his questions.

As he, after a glass of wine, became more relaxed and open.

"Here is your meal, sir."

"Thank you!" Alex bowed his head down to the plate, inhaled and his face indicated he was happy with his choice.

"This smells delicious, Nataliya. But I would like to wait until you get your plate before I start my meal."

"No Alex, please, start to eat—bon appetite." She answered.

"Ah-a, here is my plate as well. Mmm this looks and smells as good as yours!"

Alex snuck a few glances towards Nataliya during the meal and he liked her style. She was eating quickly but not rushed, and she had a certain air about her.

"Nataliya, can I ask you what is your profession?"

"I finished secondary school and became a professional nurse."

"That sounds very good. So, with you I should not be afraid if I were to get injured!" He smiled to Nataliya.

"Oh no," she answered, "I know the human body very well, I know how to help."

"I can't recognize your accent, Nataliya, it seems like somewhere from Eastern Europe?"

"Well spotted, Alex, I have family ties to Latvia, my parents were born there."

They finish dinner with a pudding and continue talking about different things as two friends already. Sometimes they stopped talking and stared through the window where powerful waves were putting on a magical performance, as if it was specially arranged just for them.

The musician started to play a gentle melody which was sweet and they felt in the mood to dance. Another two couples were already moving towards the dance floor.

“Would you like to dance, Nataliya?”

“Why not?! It would be my pleasure. I’m sure that after that I will go to sleep with blissful memories that I was at a wonderful party where I met a nice man.” She gave him a speaking glance.”

They danced slowly and in silence, cheek to cheek. She bent both of her hands around his neck. Alex tenderly embraced her, putting his hand on her waist and back, inhaling her sweet perfume and savoured the moment.

Nataliya rested her head on his shoulder and was happy to hide her thoughts from Alex, “So, I see now, it will be difficult for me to take his case from him. I should be careful with him as my number One agent told me. It seems as he believed everything I told him but he is smart, and possibly he has created this illusion of me. As long as I keep him here, it’s better for my plans,” she deliberately sighed deeply.

“What is that, Nataliya, such a big sigh, are you tired or troubled?”

“No, no, it’s just some tough memories came to mind. Sorry. I like our dance.”

She pulled back and gazed into his eyes. “Alex, do you know you are good looking man.”

“Oh, yes, a lot of girls told me this,”, he laughed, “but thank you for this precious compliment.”

“We could have a glass of champagne, would you like that Alex?” She asked in a low voice.

“Yes. I would like and I will treat you,” was the smiling answer from Alex

“Thank you.”

“I am really tired and starting to dream about bed,” Alex said in a neutral voice, watching some couples slow dance nearby.

Nataliya looked at him with a raised eyebrow, smiled at him tenderly, almost cheekily.

“I thought a young man like you could dream about something better,” she looked him straight in his eyes with a flirty expression.

“Possibly I can come up with a better idea after I finish my champagne,” he answered with an awakening look, “Here is our champagne, cheers, my beautiful stranger, for us,” they touched their goblets together as a stream of tiny bubbles raced up the side of the glasses.

This is getting interesting, thought Alex sipping his champagne and at the same time tried to clear his head. *So, it looks like this nice young lady wants to seduce me but now is not the time for adventure, nor the right place. I must return to my own cabin before my emotions get the better of me*.

He started to think how to nicely say goodnight to Nataliya without looking rude and keep his dignity. Alex had a feeling that maybe she is not such a soft, innocent woman as a modest nurse, returning from Sweden to England after a heart-breaking divorce, should be. He started to think there was something more, something secretive about her, hidden more deeply than he noticed on first appearances. She suggested to him that they could meet each other later in the UK. Was she proposing a date?

"No-no-no. I am not ready for her, and I have to concentrate on safety and making a success of my invention," he allowed himself a cautious glance over to the case.

Nataliya turned to him, "I think we should get some fresh air now and then if you wish you may accompany me to my cabin," she looked at him with questioning eyes.

"Good idea, Nataliya, shall we go?" he lifted his case and walked over to the small desk in the corner of the restaurant to settle the bill. A waiter was busy stacking menus as only a handful of people were left eating, or ending their meal with a final coffee. It was well past midnight.

"Alex, why did you not leave your case in the cabin? It looks quite heavy."

"Erm, I thought it would be safer with me. Once my case was stolen from a ferry cabin and I lost a lot of important things, it completely ruined my trip. So now I am worried about this and keep anything of value for me, with me." Alex lied to her without any hesitations.

A Russian agent with the nickname "number 3," Nataliya, heard what Alex said about the case. But she did not believe him. And with growing excitement she understood that the prototype of his invention already existed and right now was in Alex's hand less than a meter away. She would steal the device at any cost, no question of that. It was her job, but more than that, it was the challenge that excited her.

Ok, calm down, she thought, *I must act this evening because tomorrow he will disappear and maybe I will never see him again. One of my colleagues surely will, but my career is dependent on this. If I could get him to his cabin I could make him ill, but that plan seems to be slipping away, so I should act quickly.*

They stayed on the outside deck staring into the shipping channel. The dark sea behind the ferry, was alive with movement, as huge angry white waves rolled into each other, pushing each other with a violent hissing noise. The perfectly round bright Moon created a beautiful twinkled reflection like a brightly lit motorway stretching out into the sea. There is some shelter from the strong cold wind on the stern but they could not even think about sitting there, on a bench, because they were not wearing coats and were both starting to shiver.

"Well, Nataliya, shall I accompany you to your cabin and then I straight go to mine."

He said it as he if he meant it.

"Ok, my dear stranger, this way," she pointed her hand vaguely to the right. There are steps which lead us to my cabin, two decks lower—it's not far."

Once they reached the steep stairs Alex led with Nataliya closely behind.

"Do it now!" A voice screamed inside of her. She half bent and reached down to grab her shoe, lifting it high above her head.

Alex had only taken a few steps when he felt a crushing blow to the back of his head.

"Argh!" screamed Alex involuntarily from the pain. His legs gave way beneath him as he lost his balance and tumbled down the rest of the steps, landing in an awkward position on the floor of the deck below.

He lost his grip on his case while he was falling, and it landed a few meters from him, shortly after he did.

He did not lose consciousness but was shocked and disoriented as he tried to figure out what happened to him.

He was stunned to see that Nataliya, his beautiful and innocent dinner companion just seconds ago was now stalking him like a tiger. She jumped down the last couple of steps and he watched her draw back her one shoed foot, before swinging it towards his face. Instinctively, he grabbed her foot, feeling a sharp pain in his palm as her high heel tore through his flesh. Somehow, he pulled her foot towards him and she dropped down with a soft thud, flat on her back. She immediately sprung back onto her feet like an acrobat and they both lunged towards Alex's case at the same time. She used a karate chop on Alex's arm with which he was using to grab the handle of the case, and his reflexes caused his hand to let go of the case. Alex, now understanding who she is and what she wanted him gave her a strong right hook. He made contact somewhere around her shoulder, fighting for his life, and his invention. Not a word was spoken, but it was perfectly clear to each what the intention of the other was.

Nataliya lost her balance stepping back, and staggered leaning on the rail at the side of the deck. Then she started to open her red bag, and reached in with one hand while looking directly at him. Alex knew what was coming next, he jumped on her and tried to grab the small gun she had produced as if from nowhere. Struggling for the gun, Nataliya took a step or two up the railing to get away from Alex's advance, using the strength in her legs to pull away from Alex. With both hands on the gun, Nataliya was in an unstable position, but she kept pulling with a strength with seemed impossible. With one hand on the gun, Alex used his other hand to strike her again reaching upwards he just made contact with her chin. As he did so, the gun slipped out of his other hand, the sweat caused by the exertion weakening his grip. Nataliya was still pulling with every ounce of energy she had left. Before Alex could react, she fell backwards over the railing, her legs flying up in the air before following her, and the gun overboard and down into the dark water below.

It was quite a drop down to the water, but Alex heard the faint splash in the night. He leaned over the rail and looked down and saw Nataliya splashing in the cold water, already over fifty metres towards the stern of the ship. The huge ferry continued her way to the English coast as if nothing had happened.

Alex, breathing hard, nervously looked right and left. Nobody.

He was in panic but tried to keep his nerves controlled, he picked up his case, looked around and checked the floor. He quickly grabbed the red bag and the one remaining shoe and tossed them overboard. He found a napkin in his pocket and quickly wiped down the barrier and stair rails, looked around again—nobody. Just the quietness of midnight on the open water. Then he ran.

Lara and Derek were standing on the pier awaiting the arrival of the ferry. Mother was awaiting her son with excitement and looked forward to telling him how much she missed him and loved him.

Derek was excited too. Now he had a chance to repay his debt to the Russian FSB who were anxiously waiting for him to complete a miracle to release him from the snare. Hopefully with his business, money, and most importantly his life intact.

He was hoping to see Alex, and also whatever it was that Alex had that the FSB needed. He respected Alex because he is the son of his beloved wife, but also because he held the key, some kind of paperwork or prototype device—he did not know what. But he remembered that he'd lent Alex a lot money to move forward his research.

"Lara, can you see, Alex is there on the walkway."

"Yes, I see, I see," she happily waved towards her son. "Shall we go closer to help him, look, he has several bags."

While Derek was driving the car home Alex was telling them about his life over the last few months, about exams and friends. Lara normally liked to have a nap in the car during long distance drives but today she was listening with admiration to her son and asking him a lot of questions.

"How is Oleva there?"

"She is Ok, mum, but something has changed in her relationship. I hope nothing serious. Please, mum, don't tell her that I told you."

"Ok, dear don't worry. I will find my way to find out what is going on."

Derek was silently driving car but Alex asked him, "How was your trip to Russia, did you like it there?"

"Of course, I liked it! How couldn't I? I have experienced the Russian sauna in winter following by bathing in a freezing lake. A great meal with songs afterwards."

"O-o, Derek, you saw a lot then, glad to hear that you liked it. Is business better now?"

"Yes, it is very good now, your mother can tell you, also I will speak with you later when we take a break from driving. Would you like to stop at the services to stretch our legs and find something to nibble?"

"It's a good idea," said Lara, "we can always eat my prepared Russian dishes later."

"Oh, mother, I can't wait to taste your food, I will keep telling you to open a restaurant and you will be successful."

Alex was smiling to Lara.

Next day Alex woke up after a good lie in. He lazily gazed around the bed room where he stayed and liked what he saw. It was light and airy, very clean with a good taste in decoration. It was clear to him straightaway, that his mother lived here and had put her stamp on everything. He went to the window which overlooked a forest. The detached property was on the edge of a large forest and a field attached to it. It was a wonderful view. He admired the beautiful scenery, on the field with fresh green grass were several horses, that were peacefully feeding and one of them had a little one, newly born, which was suckling milk from its mother. Alex smiled and turned to be ready for this new day and possibly for a new life in England.

He took a quick wash and headed downstairs where mother was waiting for him for breakfast.

"Good morning, my dear! Did you sleep well in our house?"

"Yes, Mum, very well, thank you. O-o! We have English breakfast! Excellent, thank you, mum. Very tasty and a lot of calories. I heard from experts!"

"Come on, darling, eat up,"she said smiling.

"Mum, when do you expect Derek back for lunch?"

"He will come home in around three hours, we will have lunch then, if you wish, in the evening Derek can take us to a restaurant."

"I don't mind. Mum. Now I would like you to help me. As I said before I need to hide one of my cases. I thought about your loft. I need to do it before Derek comes back home. I do not want anybody, besides me and you to know about this case, where it is. I do not want Derek know about it as well."

"Of course, my son, I will do exactly as you ask."

"Mum, tell me, who and when someone visited the loft last time? I mean, does Derek has any interest there in any way?"

"No. As far as I know, no interest at all. I knew that he was there last time when his mother died he put there some of his mother's furniture, and maybe some sentimental things. But it was 10 years ago. That big loft is surely covered in dust by now.

"So, I thought I would organize a major cleaning operation. I think there are some corners where you can hide your case, don't breathe in too much dust, son."

"Ok, sounds good. So we can now start a hiding operation, lock the door, mum." he said seriously. "It would be better, mum if you were to stay here, downstairs. You just show me how to open your loft and the rest I will do myself, ok?"

"Son, one question for you. Yesterday I noticed that you were very nervous, not calm, a little anxious, you can't hide it from me. What was wrong? Is something troubling you?"

"No, everything is fine, mum. I've been studying for many months, preparing my diploma, lots of things going on at once," he lied to his mother, feeling guilty.

Lara started to cook lunch and was deep in her thoughts. She realised how happy a mother she was, also how lucky she was married to Derek. He behaved sometimes very strangely but she had not yet found out why. Their relationship was great, they still had a tender romantic attitude to each other and she cherished it.

Alex stood in the center of a big loft full of various old furniture, boxes, all totally covered by thick dust. He gave a good look around then decided to dig carefully in a deep corner where he thought nobody could easily stumble across anything. He slid in a big plastic bag with his case inside and then camouflaged it with other old things taking care not to disturb the dust too much. So, nobody would guess that he'd been here.

"Oh, mum, that is a nice smell, what are you cooking for lunch?" Alex with fun and laughter started to speak with mother about food, cooking, recalling their kitchen in Russia.

Then he changed the topic and said seriously. "Mum, after our lunch I would like to do something with Derek. Please, do not ask me and not interrupt me while I'm saying or doing this, just think and act if everything is ok and normal. But I will tell you, I going to make a production of hiding my bag in the secure storage in the city railway station. And Derek will help me. Please do not ask him anything about it or say anything if he tries to talk about it. Mum, do you understand? Will you follow my instructions?"

"Yes, my son, but it seems like part of a detective story. Be sure, I will do as you asked me." She smiled at him winking.

"Derek, can you give me a lift to the railway station in your car?" Alex asked

"No, problem, when?"

"If you are free after lunch that would be ideal," said Alex

"Are you going to buy a train ticket?"

"No, I going to put my bag in a secure place at the railway station. Just some of my research things."

Derek in wonder raised his brow. "Do you think at home, here, will not be secure enough?"

"Don't be offended Derek, I already decided to do this back in Sweden. It will give me peace of mind." Alex gave him a confused smile.

Alex took his sports bag which he'd prepared in advance to look the right shape and with many stones for weight and went downstairs.

At the main railway station, they stopped opposite the entrance and Alex asked Derek to wait for him in the car. “I’ll only be a few minutes. Wait for me here please.” And he disappeared through the wide automatic door into the station.

Derek drove some yards further and parked. He sighed deeply and started to look around. While driving to the station he noticed that a car was tailing him but he did not notice when it first started following them. He had already thought that with Alex arriving, the FSB will be on full alert and they would not leave him alone. And possibly they already know that Alex is here, in the UK. He observed again all the cars nearby, it very possible that the blue car is watching me. Damn them! Now they will force me to search through Alex’s brain for the locker code or break all the cameras in the railway station.

The man in the blue car was dark haired and about thirty years old, he had a handsomely shaped face and lips and his eyes were covered by expensive looking sunglasses. He saw that Derek’s car had stopped near the central entrance and Alex quickly left the car with a big sports bag and rushed into the station.

The Russian agent did not follow Alex because he thought he would blow his cover and gain nothing. He dialled a Swedish number on his mobile.

Chapter 17

Evening was turning into night, and Alex could hear nothing but the occasional bark of a distant dog. He sat in a spare room, decorated as a study and idly stared out through a large window at the full moon. It was a warm night, and the moonlight bathed the garden with an eerie grey light. Alex thought that he could see a lot of stars tonight, the air was crisp and clear. The house was silent, his mother and Derek had gone to their bedroom over an hour ago.

Sitting at an old wooden desk, he stretched out his long legs, and put his hands behind his head before letting out a yawn. Maybe it was time for bed, but Alex still had a few last-minute things he needed to research in preparation for his job interview tomorrow.

Alex was extremely keen to get the job. A world-famous energy company would be a great place to work, but not just that. It would be a great reason to settle in the UK—or at least to visit a lot more regularly and see his mother more often. Alex felt good. He was quietly confident—he had already made it through the first round of interviews, picked from thousands of applicants from across the world. He already knew of some great applicants who were not invited back for an interview, so clearly, he was being considered seriously for the role.

His mind drifted from the matters at hand to recalling his narrow escape from Sweden. He felt a pang of worry as he remembered events on the ferry and how he had caused the Russian agent to tumble over the side to certain death in the cold waters. He did what he had to do—but what if the police were to come knocking on the door? How would he explain himself?

Logic took over. The Russian agent surely would be travelling on a false passport, even if a body was to be discovered, there was nothing to link her back to him. He allowed himself to search a few news sites on the internet, but there was nothing.

Alex managed to push the worry to the back of his mind. He couldn't do anything about the ferry, or the Russian agent but he could focus on his important day tomorrow. There would be time later to think more deeply about the ferry, but the priority now was preparing for the interview.

He read a few more recent news articles about new projects on the energy company website, made a few notes and shut down his laptop before heading to bed.

"Mum, today is an important day! Remember that job I told you about a while ago—for the nuclear energy company? I've got an interview later this morning. I've arranged a hired car—wish me luck!"

"Ah yes, of course I remember son. I will keep my fingers crossed for you. I'm sure you will do well, it would be great if you got the job. We would all be back together in the same country finally! I have some news too, Derek and I, we are off for a short golfing trip—up near Aberdeen in a place called Cruder Bay. We've had it planned for a while, and although the timing isn't great I'm sure you will be fine here on your own for a week?"

She warmly smiled at Alex. “I will leave you some money so you don’t have to worry about cooking. Remember there is the pub nearby and the carvery is excellent.”

“No problem Mum, I have plenty to do!” Alex became more cheerful. “This is the final stage of interviews, and if I’m chosen then I’ll be heading to the headquarters in Paris for a few weeks training. But I’ll still be here when you get back and I have plenty of studying to catch up on. Also, Mum, soon I will have to return to Sweden to get my diploma and tie up a few loose ends. I need to arrange to send the rest of my belongings to wherever it is that I’ll be living. Hopefully the UK!

While you are away, Mum, I thought I’d relocate my secret object, then even you will not know where it is.” Alex grinned cheekily at his mum.

“Well, my dear, I am very glad for you. You have big plans and, I think you deserve it. So, Forward and Higher, every day, that what I am repeating to you from your school days. This motto I would like you to remember always, every day, every week and year. It will help you, trust my words’

“Yes, mum, I remember it, you have the art to give wise advice. Thank you’

“Do you know that on the way to golf course we going to drive through the Highland Mountains? I am very excited to see them. Derek told me, its beautiful scenery. I saw Scotland just in pictures and documentary films and it is a very fascinating place to me.

There we will stay to rest for one night in a B&B. And also, it will be exciting for me to visit his friend—we’re going to stay there for a night on the way back.

His friend is a widower who is a member of the same golf club and he lives somewhere remote in Scotland in a mansion surrounded by gardens. He had a very rich landlord grandfather who passed him a substantial inheritance. So, he is very rich, Derek told me. And his late wife had Ukrainian roots. As you see, son, we have big plans for this week too. Its pity that you cannot come with us."

Lara picked up her phone to make another call to Derek at the factory. He was just supposed to be popping back for a brief meeting to ensure everything was in hand before they went on their trip. An hour at most Derek had said—four hours ago. Lara grew increasingly concerned as they should have started their journey by now. Their well-made plans were already starting to unravel.

Again, and again she stared at her mobile, no answer. With disappointment visible on her face, she sat down on the chair in the big conservatory next to all the packed luggage. She turned on the television, more to keep her mind occupied rather than out of any sort of real interest.

On the news channel, the presenter was part way through a piece about a person who vanished from a ferry between Sweden and the UK. Nobody has claimed any missing person who fits the description and no-one is sure what has happened. Lara made a mental note to ask Alex if this might have been the ferry he travelled on. The trill ringing of her mobile quickly broke her train of thought and she grabbed the phone and answered it within a couple of rings.

"Darling, where are you? We were planning to leave the house many hours ago. Ok! Hurry please!"

Derek gave his last instructions to John, who would be managing the factory in his absence. He made sure to stop by and see all the workers to say his "bye-byes" and strode out of the office towards his car.

Two men in fashionable suits, one noticeably shorter than the other were talking to each other, leaning up against a black Ranger Rover.

Once they noticed Derek they stepped towards him.

"Hello Derek!" the smaller man shouted. "Surprise, surprise! I don't think you expected to see us again did you?" The taller man curved his lips in a smile.

"As you can imagine we need to talk…but not on the door step of your factory. Would you like to sit in our car and we will take you to a nice pub, not too far from here."

The tall one, staring intently into Derek eyes told him that this was a command and not a question.

"The thing is, gentlemen that I am very much in a hurry right now and I must go home where my wife is waiting for me to go on a trip. So, maybe we could talk when I'm back in a week?" Derek nervously asked. The begging tone of his voice showing that he already knew the answer.

"Mr. Harrison," the taller agent opened the door of the Range Rover, "Get in, please!" he said in a steely uncompromising voice.

They were driving towards the area of "Outstanding beauty," it's a huge area of land covered by dense pine forest, not too far from Derek's place. He was sitting in the back of the car, next to the tall agent and wondering what the intentions of the agents were. The angry look on his face did not indicate a friendly conclusion to their little trip.

They got me, the bastards! They continue to watch me and now they know, obviously, that Alex is in our house. I did not realise that this will happen so quickly. Now again they will grill me with questions…but I am not ready for this talk yet."

They made several turns on the forest roads and stopped at a forest tea room, which Derek knew to be a popular place. It was an old-fashioned place, looking a bit like an old English pub with all sorts of tasty homemade food and pastries.

"Well, Derek, we do not play games with you," started the tall agent after they ordered tea and sat at the outside tables. In different circumstances, Derek would have quite enjoyed the location. A quiet table in a nice corner right by the forest's edge.

"You have business with us, and you know it. You signed up! There is no way back from the choice you made. You are our informant and paid agent, a paid *Russian* agent.

"You know what will happen to you if your country's authorities will find out about it.

"I'm sure I don't need to scare you, you know all this already. And what about your lovely wife? If she were to receive some compromising photos of you Derek? You and our agent in Komsomolsk on your trip to Far East of Russia. Passionate photos, I'm sure you don't want that to happen Derek?

"Anyway, how rude of me. My name is Victor, maybe now we are acquainted you will find it easier to answer my questions." Victor did not remove his eyes from Derek, even for a second while he sipped his tea. Derek felt the terror wash over him. He felt beads of sweat begin to form on his forehead and his cheeks begin to blush. Derek did not want to know their names, he wanted them to disappear forever and let him live his life.

"I understand your threats and what I need to do for you. I have no choice, I will find that invention from my stepson Alex."

Derek paused and slowly wiped his face with a napkin from the table.

"Alex is staying with us right now as a guest. He's here for a job interview, I don't know where. He still had many things back in Sweden, but if he did bring the invention with him I can tell you for sure that he's hidden it in a locker at the main railway station. I drove him there, and he told me he needed somewhere safe to store something."

Derek tried to talk with confidence.

"I ask you, do not push me hard now, and give me a little time. I will find out more and tell you. How valuable can that invention be, if it even really exists? Is it worth all this fuss?"

Victor listened carefully, looking at Derek with suspicious eyes. He seemed as though he was thinking, then let out a deep sigh, and twisted his lips from side to side,

"Listen, Derek, in two weeks we should have a result from you. Let me be clear on the success criteria for this little mission. You will pass us that device or you will tell us exactly where we can take it from. As simple as that.

"Is it clear, Mister Harrison!?" He raised his voice. He stood up sharply and walked away towards the car.

"Derek, I gave you two weeks, I am generous with you today. You know our phone number if there is anything urgent. But do not worry I will call you."

"Darling, Darling, sorry for the delay. I was at an urgent meeting which I had not planned—it just happened unexpectedly," Derek was hurrying from the car to Lara. He kissed her, "I apologize very much," Derek tried not to look into her eyes.

"Ok, my dear, you are forgiven! Shall we prepare the car?"

"Yes, sweetheart we should hurry now, I am hungry. We can stop for a snack on the motorway somewhere."

Lara helped Derek fill the car with golf equipment and luggage, she did not forget to take with them a picnic basket which she enjoyed making every time they travel long distance.

If you wish to see unspeakably beautiful scenery then you should visit the Scottish Highland Mountains. That is what Lara thought as they were driving on a rural road between two massive mountains covered in some places by pine forests which were planted in straight rows. She stared out of the window mesmerised by the beauty of nature. Ancient pine forest intermingled with patches of new growth. She was impressed that the country must look after the fauna very well to prevent the mountains from becoming bare and dusty.

Lara spotted many sheep on the sides of mountains and even some at the edge of the road, bravely munching the grass as occasionally cars roared past. It looks surreally beautiful.

“Darling could you stop at that point, not too far from the sheep? I would like to touch them,” she smiled merrily, “I would like to talk to them. . Also, we could have a nice picnic.”

Throughout the next several days, Derek was very busy with golf. He met his old friends, gentlemen from various parts of the country. They all enjoyed competitions, and also the practising. Most golfers came with their other halves. Some of the wives liked to accompany their husband to the golf course, to walk from one hole to the next, enjoying the fresh air, beautiful green surroundings, relaxing atmosphere and meeting new people.

Other wives were exploring the surrounding villages and chasing interesting items in the local shops. But Lara brought her paints with her, and an easel stand for drawing. She desperately wanted to try to paint a landscape. Their hotel room was overlooking the ocean. Dunes, very wide and long, about three miles of beach where the tide periodically played with the vast expanse of the sands. Lara was inspired by that scenery so sitting in front of the big bay window in their room she was absorbed in her painting for several hours every day. When Derek finished his day of golf, they would go together for a meal or drive to the nearest fishing village for the freshest fish and chips straight from local fishermen. There were so many amazing locations close-by, they made sure to take in the very best of the northeast of Scotland.

They had their last dinner in a cosy restaurant on the beach side with an ocean view and were privileged to see a great sunset. Tomorrow morning, they were prepared to leave the golf course and travel down to England, towards home.

"Sweetheart, unfortunately tomorrow we must leave this wonderful place. But as you know we are going to stop for a night with my Scottish friend Mr. McCouat at his house."

Derek paused in thought for a second or two, "Or rather his mansion! My love, you will enjoy that visit, believe me,"

Derek tiredly smiled to her and continued. "Jim's late wife had Ukrainian roots—Oksana. Her father, back when he was a young man, moved to England after the Second World War. He, like a lot of other young men from different countries, was released by the advancing forces of the Soviet Army from a labor camp in the west of Germany. So many of them moved across the channel as quick as they could. Of course, they settled, started jobs, visited dance halls, it was there, where her father met an English rose. So, Oksana was born, and grew into a beautiful woman.

"My friend Jim, who is from a famously rich Scottish family, got an impressive inheritance from his father which included a mansion. But he is very educated and a very smart guy. I look forward to introducing him to you."

"Darling, I see that you are getting tired." Lara interrupted him. "It's a very interesting story but possibly we return to our hotel to rest?"

"You are right, Lara, we'll leave in a few minutes," he stretched his leg under the table and sat more comfortably.

"So once on a business trip to England he somehow met Oksana and fell in love at first sight. After three months, they married and he brought her to his mansion. Since then they were together until her death five years ago—it was very sad for us and he was grieving for long time—now he is returning to his old self, I think.

"Oksana was very beautiful, full of energy, full figured, long dark brown hair which she wore in a classy style.

"With my late wife, we visited them a long time ago. We enjoyed staying there and their generous hospitality. Jim now lives on his own, with only a part-time cook and a servant to help him run the house. Tomorrow, I'm hoping our visit will bring him a lot of happiness. Well, sweetheart, shall we go?"

"Just a second, darling, how did she die?"

"It was very tragic, it was a cancer of her brain. The variety of cancers these days is taking people of all ages without concern for age or anything else."

Next day Derek turned through the big black and gold metal gates framed by tall imposing stone posts. The long road with mature oak trees on both sides led the car towards an impressive stone mansion, maybe from the 18th century.

A tall, silver haired man stood on the stone steps outside the grand entrance door. He was surrounded by an ornate wooden arch which must have provided some shelter from the Scottish winters.

"Hello Derek!" he greeted them from a distance, as he descended a handful of steps and made his way to the car.

Derek introduced Lara to Jim. He gave her a welcoming smile, took then her hand for a kiss.

"Pleased to meet you Lara, I have heard a lot from Derek about his beautiful wife"

Jim looked warmly at her. Then he turned to Derek, "Tell me, my friend, where is that place on Earth where you found such a beautiful wife? I would like to fly there tomorrow!"

Derek merrily laughed in answer, "Jim, I will tell you later, without Lara and maybe after a glass of your vintage whisky."

"Ok-ok, gentlemen, enough please, and thank you for the compliments. Shall we head inside for a drink? It's been a long journey."

"Sorry, Lara, too many jokes, welcome to my little 'fazenda.' Come in!"

He winked at them both and took a travel bag from the car to help Derek.

Entering the huge building Lara from the first steps was surprised by the interior. She admired the space, the quality of the finishing, and the antique furniture. She stood in the center of the entrance hall, looked around at the wide stairs which lead upstairs, and then turned to Jim.

"Your 'fazenda' reminds me of a castle from a movie. I could only imagine, how much energy and strength you need just to keep it warm and clean."

"You are right, Lara, it does. But happily, I can manage it. As for warmness, you know, only a warm person who loves you can give a home true warmth," he said seriously, a shadow flashed over his face but in a moment, it disappeared.

"So, my friends, I will show you your bedroom, you can refresh yourselves there. Then in an hour I'll wait for you at the entrance and I'll show you my gardens. I know, Derek, you saw it already and are not interested now, but, I think Lara, would enjoy seeing them.

"Also, later I will give Lara a tour around my home, if you don't mind Derek. And finally, we will have a nice dinner. My cook will try to demonstrate his best skills for you both today. Agree?"

"Great plan, thank you Jim," they replied happily as they headed up the grand staircase to their bedroom.

Lara put on a long red v-cut dress, and a diamond necklace which had been a present from Derek. From her waist, the dress fell nicely in drapes and the silky heavy material emphasized her fine figure with its sexy curves. Her shoulders were covered by her long dark brown hair which completed the beautiful look.

"My sweetheart, your great looks could strike Jim—careful my darling! I would be jealous," he murmured as he kissed her neck from behind, "maybe we could have an early night?"

"Why not? If you can avoid overeating or drinking too much my sweet Derek, then everything is possible," she turned face to face with him and her lips touched his.

Lara visibly enjoyed their evening meal by candlelight. The dining room was also lit by a big crystal chandelier hanging from the high ceiling directly above the center of a long wooden table for twelve. But they all sat in the one corner closest to the log fireplace and had a nice slow conversation during the meal. Jim was a very generous host, he brought from his cellar two vintage wines, alongside champagne, Russian cognac and whiskey. His cook showed first class skills with tasty dishes all round.

The evening was already in full flow, and taken by the mood, Derek decided to taste all the drinks before eating properly. With predictable results, he was totally drunk mid-way through the meal and was barely able to communicate at all. Slurring his words, he could just say

"Help me get to bed darling, bed, please, love you, want to kiss you."

It was a very disappointing situation for Lara, she raised her brows and with a confused voice asked,

"Jim, sorry, I've never seen Derek like this before now, he is not a drunkard but today," she shrugged her shoulders, "could you help me put my husband to bed, please?"

"Of course, we will do it now. Don't be ashamed, Lara, sometimes it happens with men. As for me I don't like drinking so much and especially I don't like to mix my drinks, that was Derek's downfall this evening, unfortunately."

Lara thanked Jim for the help and they both continued to stand for a minute by the bed where Derek now was laying and already sleeping like a baby.

"Lara, would you like to keep me company over a cup of coffee?"

"With great pleasure, Jim. I think Derek does not want coffee at the moment," she smiled cheekily.

"I'll wait for you downstairs in the great hall at the fireplace."

They were sitting in front of a great roaring log fire, in a black marble fireplace and what looked to be an original ornamental fire screen. The hall was lit only by candles, so it was half dark. Lara wore a poncho over her shoulders, sitting in an old, high-backed chair sipping her coffee and was listening and answering Jim's questions. Because she was wary about the tragic events in Jim's past, and she was tired she wasn't asking Jim many questions. But Jim asked her about her life in Russia, how she met Derek, her children, and about her feelings about this country. She got the impression that Jim was really interested in who and what she was and is.

The reflected light from the log fire was dancing across their faces. While he was talking she turned her head to look at him and caught herself in a thought that she liked this proud, graceful face with its silver head of hair. She felt a flash of attraction for him which enveloped her. She had a feeling as if she had known this man for a long time. In her eyes he was a very attractive and intelligent man.

That is what alcohol is doing to my mind—I should drink less too, with these thoughts she rubbed her fore head with her diamante sparkled finger and decided to finish this evening in the ever so pleasant company of the owner of this beautiful home.

Jim caught her long look at him,

"Lara, I think you have already heard from many men that you have beautiful twinkling eyes," he said softly smiling at her.

"Oh, thank you, I will try to believe that at my age I'm still attractive.

"Jim, could I ask you something? Are you content with your life now, are you going to move on with life?" He turned his face to her and looked in her eyes with a serious expression,

"No, Lara, my life is empty now and despite my big house, stability, and wealth my life is lifeless. I am going to change it but do not know yet with whom or how."

"Have you tried to have a new woman in your life?"

"I have not yet, Lara, but I have thought about it a lot."

"Thank you for an honest answer, maybe it was rude of me to pry," she murmured. "Well, Jim, I would like to say a big thank you for coffee, the meal, an enjoyable evening and I would like to leave you now for bed."

They stood up, Lara extended her hand, and he slowly took it and kissed it with a light touch of his warm lips, then looked deeply in her eyes said, "I would be happy, Lara, if you would visit me here again." He paused, "With Derek, of course. Just let me know any time."

Lara kept her eyes down towards the floor then shot him a glance with an unreadable facial expression, said in a low voice, "Good night, Jim," she turned and slowly ambled out of the hall.

The next day, Lara and her husband were up early to head home. In the car, Lara was sitting quietly, absorbed in her own thoughts. She was analysing the visit to Jim, and how much of a shame there was that such an amiable, attractive man was sitting alone in such a beautiful house. An idea came to her, she knew it was just a perfect idea."

Why couldn't she start her own business running a private marriage agency? She knew there was a market for single gentlemen who were looking for women to marry. Not just endless correspondence on websites, but she could actually accompany the men to Russia where they could meet a few different ladies to see if they get on. If all goes well, the men could invite the ladies to visit England, or maybe to take a holiday together somewhere. She would charge a fee, not a lot—enough to cover her costs and a little extra. But if they decided to marry, they would pay a larger amount and everyone will be happy.

Derek could help her set up the business, with the benefit of his experience and she could run it on a day to day basis while Derek managed the factory. Maybe with Derek's new business contacts in Russia they could both travel there together to develop their new business opportunities. She could help Jim, and many other similar men find happiness with new soulmates, and hopefully new wives.

"Darling, I feel you changed somehow after you returned from the Far East of Russia? You haven't mentioned anything about your business, and you seem to be very tired in the evenings before bed. Is everything ok? Did anything happen over there you want to tell me about?"

Lara decided to engage Derek in conversation because she knew on long drives he would get tired and start to lose concentration. On a previous trip he started to fall asleep and they narrowly avoided a serious accident so she thought engaging him in conversation would help to keep him focussed.

He responded in a slightly sleepy voice, "Yes Lara, my Russian customers ordered a lot of plastic parts. Components for cars and furniture mainly. I was very happy with how things went there, if it goes well, it will double the size of my business and allow me to hire another manager which will allow us to travel more. Just think, we could choose a different cruise four times a year, how does that sound to you? But first, I must fulfil their first order successfully. There is still a lot to do!"

"It sounds wonderful Derek, but maybe four times a year is too much. Maybe we could rent a villa on the Italian Amalfi coast for the summer. It would be fantastic for me. Sun, sea, plenty of swimming…"

She glanced at him,

"Darling, do not sleep, stop the car at the next lay-by and have a half-hour nap." She jerked his shoulder, put her hand in his hair and rubbed his head but she could see Derek was hardly was able to keep his eyes open.

"Here, here turn left, pull in over here." She said with worry in her voice.

They stopped in a bay and in one-minute Derek was snoring. Lara reclined her seat and closed her eyes too. The stress of driving long distances with Derek was tiring for her too.

ᏋᏋ

Alex sat in a large meeting room, with three people sat across the table from him. The two men and one woman, dressed smartly in business suits were all in their late forties, and took turns quizing Alex on his life, his studies, and his ambitions. One-by-one they would ask a question, alternating between HR, technical, and operations as they tapped away on their laptops.

Alex had been in the room for over an hour already. He was wondering how much longer the interview could go on but still they found new avenues of questioning. He had shown excellent results in the previous rounds of the process, and they were really pressing to be certain if he would be one of the twenty-five who would be chosen out of the thousand applicants who would soon join the company and have the opportunity to bring his skills and intelligence to move the company forward.

"Alex, have you taken part in any research projects during your university study?"

"Yes, I have. I'm currently researching a new renewable energy source."

The interviewing panellists exchanged glances, and Alex saw the technical interviewer smile as he typed his notes.

"Was it successful?"

Alex took a deep breath, smiled back and replied. "Yes, it was. I made a prototype of a device which will soon be patented."

The panellists thanked him for his time and promised to let him know the results as soon as they finished the rest of the interviews.

Alex got back in his car, feeling good after the gruelling session. He felt like he had responded well, and did his best. Now he just had to wait. But in the meantime, he had other matters to attend to. He hurried back to Derek's house. He'd made his mind up that he needed to meet with a local patent attorney to get some advice on how best to protect his invention. It was good that the interviewers had not asked any more detailed questions about his device before he had protected it, but he'd had a lucky escape. If he got the job, they would be sure to ask more, and he needed to ensure he didn't give too much away.

Once he had the advice he would start completing the patent application. He already had a lot of diagrams, formulae and technical notes so it should be pretty simple, he thought.

If it turned out that he needed to do some additional work, he thought he should find somewhere more secure for his prototype. He did not trust that place on the loft. It was good that his mother and Derek went on their trip, there was nothing to stop him completing his plan.

As he turned into the street where Derek lived, he noticed a suspicious looking car parked up in the road. Alex thought to himself how good he had become at spotting this sort of thing in the last few months. The street was quiet and most houses had their own large driveways. It was unusual for a car to be parked out on the road, especially with someone who sat inside for no obvious reason.

He pulled up his car a reasonable distance behind the other car and tried to think what to do. There was no movement in the other car so Alex sat and watched. He kept an eye in his mirrors just in case someone approached from the rear.

In the twilight, he could not make out much detail within the car, but he could see the driver tilt his rear-view mirror to get a better view. So, he too was being watched.

Alex left his car quickly, and slammed the door shut. He rushed into the house and sprinted upstairs. He went straight to the front bedroom and looked outside at the car in the street. The driver was still there.

He could feel his heart beating in his chest. If the agent came to the house, if could only be to take his prototype. He told himself he needed to calm down and think of a plan. He needed to buy himself some time to get the patent process underway before the Russians could steal his device. It was clearly only a matter of time now, and they were obviously desperate to get their hands on it. It wasn't safe in the house, they could break in and take it while he was out.

He relaxed, put the TV on, and found something tasty in the fridge. He thought fondly of his mother, she had left plenty of homemade food in the fridge. He waited for the twilight to turn to darkness. There was no moon outside, it was now pitch black as he looked through the kitchen window into the back garden.

He retrieved his secret bag from the loft and brought it down to the kitchen. He opened the back door and took a good look around while he eyes adjusted to the darkness. He saw the outline of an old brick building he'd noticed earlier while he was studying and daydreaming out of the window. It looked like an old coal storage shed which had been neglected and was very overgrown. Not the sort of place someone might suspect that something very valuable could be hidden.

After waiting a few minutes just to check that there was no-one watching, he grabbed the bag and made his way to the corner of the garden where the old building stood. He pushed open the wooden door which banged against some old timbers and rubbish inside. The door only opened halfway, and Alex hoped the noise hadn't been heard by anyone else. He listened for footsteps, but heard nothing suspicious and slipped inside. The brick shed looked like it was over a hundred years old, and by the state of the inside had been unused for half of that time. Alex used the dim light of his mobile phone to navigate around without attracting attention. The roof looked in need of repair and the windows although still intact were obscured by dust and the overgrown bushes outside. As he moved around, he foot banged into a thick iron ring in the floor. He knelt down and saw the outline of a hatch in the floorboards. He pushed some of the rubbish away and grabbed the iron ring and lifted. The hatch opened with difficulty and Alex held his breath as a cloud of coal dust moved around the small room.

The void below the floor was a couple of feet deep and there was still a lot of old coal down there. It was dirty, but could be the perfect place to stash his bag. He lowered it down, and closed the hatch. He pushed some of the dust into the small gaps around the hatch and then moved the timbers over the trapdoor and placed a bag of rubbish over the iron handle. He was confident that anyone casually exploring the shed would not be able to find anything. After checking outside, he moved back inside the house, washed his hands and checked to see the agent was still in the car outside. There was nothing more he could do, so he checked the locks on the doors and windows and went to bed.

Morning brought nice sunny weather. Alex opened his eyes, had a good stretch then recalled yesterday's events and jumped up to the window. *Oh, yes, the bastards are still on duty. I wonder if they had their breakfast yet?* he wondered, grinning to himself.

I'm going to enjoy my breakfast now, and then I'll play a game with them, he thought.

So, he went to the storage room and found a large box, about the same size as his case.

Then he wrapped it in paper, taped it up with packing tape and walked to his car. The Russian started his car, Alex was getting used to being followed by now.

Alex headed to the railway station again, keeping his eye on the rearview mirror. He saw the agent driving with one hand on the wheel as he was having an animated conversation on his mobile phone.

He jumped quickly from the car, ran inside with the box and rushed back to the room with the storage lockers. He glanced around the room, saw a CCTV camera and moved into the opposite corner of the room out of view of the camera. He stood between two rows of lockers, and jumped on the empty box, crushing it under his weight. He folded up the crushed cardboard and stuffed it into a bin. *Try and find that now, you bastards!* he thought, pleased with his plan.

He caught his breath, and left the storage area to head back to the car. He saw a man in a leather jacket leaning up against a wall, pretending to check the timetables, but he was clearly keeping an eye on the door to the storage room. *That'll be my Russian "friend,"* Alex thought, and tried to avoid eye contact.

That'll confuse them for a while, thought Alex as he turned the corner onto his street. As he started the make the turn, a black van with tinted windows shot out of the street and almost hit his car. He slammed on the brakes as the van narrowly avoided him and accelerated away.

They've searched the house!! Alex thought to himself in panic. The agent staking out his house, who followed him to the railway station, must have called in a search team while he was away. Alex screeched up to the driveway and ran to the front door to find that a small pane of glass had been broken. The house was a complete mess, they had obviously brought multiple agents to ransack the house, emptying every cupboard and turning over furniture to try and find the device. With his heart in his throat, Alex rushed to the shed and pushed the timbers away from the hatch. He hauled it open and jumped down into the void. The bag was still there!

Lara heard her mobile ringing unexpectedly, she picked it up

"Hi Mum, where are you now?"

"I am sitting in the car, we've had a lovely trip," she smiled.

"Sorry mum, I need to tell you some bad news."

"What happened son!?", She replied in panic.

"Mum, don't worry too much, please. The house has been broken into—and it's a real mess. Sorry to give you such news when you should be enjoying yourself but I don't want you and Derek to be shocked when you get home. I already called the police. When you come back we have some work to do to tidy up, but I'll make a start after the police have left and help you return the house to its glory."

Chapter 18

In an office, somewhere near the top of a skyscraper located in London, a serious looking man in his early fifties sat in an expensive looking stylish black chair. Rubbing his eyebrows, he took a break from the computer and swivelled around to face the floor to ceiling glass window and the breath-taking view of the city below him.

Leaning back with his hands behind his head, his eyes glazed over as his mind was deep in thought. Someone knocked on the office door twice. “Come in,” he barked.

The door slid open and a pleasant looking stocky middle-aged man hurried to his desk. “Mr. Smith, we have interesting news from our Swedish colleagues. It’s the Russians again. Here—I prepared a report for you about this young inventor, I mean—Russian inventor,” he slid the document across the desk towards his boss.

“Thanks, John. I’ll review this in detail right away. But first tell me now everything you know about this case in your own words.”

“So, this is what we know. There is an obviously talented student at Stockholm University. His name is Alex Petrov, he is a Russian citizen but for several years was studying in Sweden and soon, this summer, he possibly will get his Doctorate in nuclear science.

"We do not know yet why but for some reason, Russian intelligence have taken a keen interest in this chap."

The Chief of Secret Intelligence agency MI6 was listening with full attention, then asked,

"Why do we know about him, John, what is happened exactly that put him in our line of sight?"

"The first time his showed up on our radar was connected to that incident on-board the ferry. You remember the strange report from the local police where an unidentified woman disappeared from the ferry? She boarded in Sweden but did not arrive in England.

"Mr. Petrov's name was mentioned in the Swedish investigation report because he was on board the same crossing and he was noticed leaving the restaurant with her. But according to reports Alex came in for dinner on his own and the waiter put that woman at the table with Alex. There was some connection there, we do not know the details but the investigation found no evidence of his involvement in her disappearance and concluded she probably fell from the ferry after too much to drink.

"Now, we just received a routine background check request from an energy company as part of their security check of several candidates who are being considered to fill their vacancies in the UK. As far as I know, they going to take quite a lot, in one go, it's about twenty young professionals. Guess what, Mr. Petrov is one of the candidates.

"Today we got even more interesting information from our liaison in Swedish MUST. They informed us that this guy was kidnapped by Russian FSB agents from a party, in their capital, and was detained for some hours in a flat and underwent some "Heavy' questioning. He was rescued but the agents escaped. But before this young gentleman left for his trip to England he asked for police protection, an escort on way to the port, because some people, he said he did not know who they were, were monitoring him. The Swedes obliged and arrested two men. They were arrested for speeding but released as they could find no other evidence to detain them. The men were in Sweden under a temporary residence permit. The police now continue surveillance on them due to a risk to Alex's sister who is still living in Stockholm with the aim of getting enough evidence to deport them.

"So, you will find all the details in the report," John glanced toward the document on the Chief's desk.

"Ok, I agree we need to stay on top of developments here and see where it leads us. It seems the Russians will continue to keep us all in a job," he said with a subtle grin. "Have you come up with a plan yet John?"

"Yes, I've asked our friends at MI5 to start a surveillance operation after discussing with the team. Under the pretence of a request from Sweden to ensure his safety they agreed, but what I'm really interested in is what he has that the Russians are so interested in. If we do have any FSB agents on the ground in the UK and we can catch them in the act and have them expelled, then all the better. At the moment, Alex is staying with his mother Lara Petrova and her husband Derek Harrison, who is a local businessman with a plastics factory in the Midlands. A factory whose tax returns show business expanded to twice the size since he married that Russian lady. I am interested to know how and why he managed to land some big deals over in Russia so quickly."

"Very well, John, thank you for the detailed report. Let's bring in the MI5 team and meet back here this evening to put some details around the final planning. I'm going to read your report now, I'll see you later."

Mr. Smith nodded to his deputy John as he picked up the document and started reading.

A brand new white Peugeot was steadily ticking through the miles along the roads leading it towards its destination. It was heading towards the Midlands, where their person of interest was known to be staying. The two officers, Robert, who was driving the car and Steven, in the passenger seat re-reading the report issued by MI6, were both sipping coffee after their early briefing in London. It would be a long shift today as they were to be relieved by another two officers early tomorrow morning.

"Here comes the rain, we could do without this today, eh?" Steven remarked. It was already getting dark as they turned off the motorway towards their final destination. The rain went from a light drizzle to a heavy downpour as Robert turned up the speed of the windscreen wipers.

"Dark and rainy, not ideal conditions to start our operation," Steven commented again.

They turned into the cul-de-sac of Alex's mother's house, slowing right down to peer at the house numbers through the rain streaked windows of the car.

"Stop, stop there just under that big tree. It's just opposite the house where the student lives." Robert vaguely pointed his finger somewhere down the street. They sighed with relief, turned off the engine and stretched as best as they could in the cramped confines of the car. They started to observe the road, the houses and the rest of their surroundings in a well-practised routine. The house where Alex lived was in darkness, it seems nobody was at home. The detached, bigger than average house was located at the end of street in a nice corner plot adjacent to the edge of a massive pine forest. A couple of other cars slowly drove up the road and parked outside of their respective houses, and after they went inside to enjoy their evenings the officers could relax and start the waiting game.

It was a long drive for the two officers, and Steve decided to drink the last half cup of coffee from his thermos flask. Robert was still alert and continued scanning all four directions from his driver's seat. He flicked the windscreen wiper control manually, as often as he dared to in order to maintain a good view without attracting attention.

As he scanned the street again, he noticed a dim orange light in a car a few dozen meters down the street on the opposite side of the road. The dim glow of light from the cigarette grew slightly brighter as the smoker inhaled, providing just enough light for Robert to notice there were two men in the car. Robert pushed Steve's elbow.

"Look there, two houses down, can you see that black car? Two guys waiting for something, maybe we have company. Russians maybe?"

Steve squinted through the window, "Yes, they don't seem like a couple of lovers out for a romantic evening! Let's take a slow drive past for a closer look?"

"Ok, careful, just let me get my gun ready just in case."

The white Peugeot started rolling along the road towards the black car. When they drew level, it became clear to Robert that these were indeed Russian agents. He purposely met the eyes one of them, to check for a reaction and he saw how they opened wider with surprise. As the Peugeot continued past, the two adversaries maintained eye contact.

The two Russian agents were expecting to spend a quiet night watching Alex, not being watched themselves and they seemed panicked. The MI5 agents slowly did a U-turn at the end of the street before parking behind the Russians, with just one parked car between them.

"Now then, let's see what happens now!" said Robert, knowing they were in a great position to observe the Russians. They could see the driver in the black car regularly checking his rear-view mirror, and the two Russian agents seemed to be having an animated discussion. Robert smiled at the situation.

The stand-off continued for almost half an hour before the Russian agent's nerve broke first.

"Vladimir, let's get out of here, we're compromised. Let's make a move and see if they follow us. Head off into the forest roads, we can lose them in there," Peter command him.

"Oh, look Steve, the Russians are on the move, let's see where they are going!" Robert went into an excited, hunting mood.

The black Rover followed by the white car behind started to speed as they left the urban roads behind. The road was leading them straight into the deep pine forest, with plenty of smaller roads leading off to the left and right. Robert pushed his foot down on the accelerator, putting the Russians under pressure. Now, the street lights had disappeared and the rain was hammering down on the windscreen. With no space to slow down, Vladimir made a desperate attempt to make a sharp sliding turn and slip down one of the smaller side roads to get away. The tires lost their grip on a loose patch of gravel on the road and the rear wheels slid out from underneath the Russians. Vladimir tried to correct his steering, turning into the skid as the rear wheels regained their grip. Now the car was almost at right angles to the road, and he could do nothing as the momentum of the heavy, speeding Range Rover ploughed into an ancient pine tree at the side of the road.

In the white car behind, Steve shouted, "stop, stop!" as the Peugeot screeched to a halt just a few meters away from the crashed vehicle. Their headlights illuminated the billowing white clouds of steam pouring out from the hood of the Russians car.

The two MI5 agents looked at each other for a moment in shock before grabbing their pistols and throwing themselves out of the car. They ran up to either side of the smashed-up Range Rover, guns drawn but as they got closer they knew there would be nothing they could do to help. The front of the car was pushed in almost half a meter, and the windscreen was cracked and stained with blood from where the passengers, clearly not wearing their seat belts, had smashed against it.

The MI5 agents reached in through the shattered side windows and felt in vain for a pulse from the Russian agents.

"Damn them!" Robert said bitterly. "Who asked them to move from that street?! But now, as you see, we are involved in this accident, this was not the plan."

"Yes, it would have been better if they stayed alive and had to be deported. They were only doing their job, but now only their bodies will fly home." Steve agreed. The two men took a moment, contemplating the fate of their adversaries, in different circumstances they knew they could have shared the same fate.

"Well, now I will call the local police and let them to sort out this mess."

Robert reached into his inside pocket for his mobile phone.

Moscow headquarters. General Litvinov who was responsible for the success of operation Fulmination and for his agents in Sweden and England, was pacing his office with nervousness and rage. He was trying to cope with the anger which took over him after he received the bad news from Britain. Before he could think about how to get the operation back on track, he was thinking about the conversation he was about to have with his boss. He needed a cool head before breaking the unwelcome news. His boss, who reported directly to the president, had made it clear that the importance of this operation had come directly from the top, and failure would not be tolerated.

He would have to answer for the failure of the mission, and for this level of failure, punishments would be swift and certain.

The already ailing mission was now going from bad to worse. Two good officers killed in action on foreign soil.

His report to Captain Orlov who was personally overseeing his foreign operations still did not have any details on the "Whys'" or "How's" of the operation's failure. So far it said only that two Russian nationals were reported dead in a car accident in a forest in England. The information from the British foreign office was sparse, even more so than usual. Obviously, the police had been told to lock down the situation, and none of Orlov's sources had been able to glean any more details. Litvinov knew that he needed to have more information before briefing his boss—the first question he would ask would be was it an accident or were there any external influences resulting in this disaster.

A real pity, Vladimir and Peter, they were good men, the general thought, But now I must find replacement officers as soon as I can before we lose control of the situation. I should prepare the names before going to my boss, and the plans must be watertight. I won't get many more chances to close this operation.

The General reached his chair, with a very worried look on his face took out his personnel file, looking for the ideal person to complete this mission. After some time, the general leaned back on the chair and said to himself,

"Ok, I have a plan."

He thought that the operation with this inventor must be finished on a positive note. It would be his chance to retire with honour. Major Kosinskiy, was a distinguished officer, who had successfully completed every mission he had ever been assigned. Better still, he was already in Britain but was coming back to Moscow after six months. No problems with returning him to the UK again, and he could start work in hours. He would be the one to finish this operation—he could be trusted. His current role was important, but he was sure his boss would agree that he could be reassigned for such an important mission. A week or two to wrap things up might be all it needed and then he could return to his current task and everyone would be happy.

To help provide more input into the direction of the mission, the general had decided that some expert knowledge might come in handy. This could help to change the course of the mission, and if he could get this knowledge quickly, it would show his boss that he was considering all avenues.

"Aleksey, come in now, I have an urgent job for you," he barked through the open office door. "Get the head of the Moscow State University on the phone. Speak to the most senior person there and tell them—no, *order* them, to send over the best academics they have in the fields of physics, energy generation, anyone with a reputation of innovating within these fields. Make it clear that this request is of critical national importance and they must attend a meeting with me, at ten AM tomorrow."

Aleksey, who hadn't got any further than the doorway when the general started shouting his demands, was frozen in motion, repeating his orders again in his head so that he wouldn't forget anything.

"Yes, comrade, general!" Aleksey performed a perfect salute, turned on his heel and paced back towards his desk to start work.

The next morning, two elderly gentlemen sat alone in a large conference room, waiting to find out who, and why they had been taken away from their usual work of teaching and researching and sent to this imposing building at not much more than a moment's notice. Their faces were flushed and sweaty, and either they had hurried over from the university very quickly or they were more than a little worried.

Litvinov strode into the office, paused for a moment just inside the doorway and slowly closed the door until it clicked shut. He saw the two men with their concerned faces and smiled. He knew the reputation of this building but after years of working there he had become used to it.

"Please gentlemen, relax! Apologies for taking you away from your work but we have important matters to discuss. Firstly though, my assistant will be along very shortly to bring you coffee," said the grey haired general as Aleksey opened the office door with one hand while struggling with a tray in his other.

"If you would be so kind as to introduce yourselves please?"

The first scientist stuttered a little. "I am Petrov Ivan Ivanovich, senior Professor of renewable and nuclear energy faculty. He looked around at his colleague for support. "And I am Konev Sergey Petrovich, Professor of research into efficiency in energy generation. I work at Omsk University, but was visiting MSU for a conference, when they asked me to come here."

"Excellent, gentlemen. Your expertise will be very much appreciated as our subject of discussion today will be renewable energy," explained Litvinov.

The demeanour of the two eminent scientists changed immediately as they started to relax, and they looked pleased to be able to talk about their favourite subjects.

"Before we get into detail," said Litvinov leaning toward them slightly and lowering his voice for effect, "I ask you to never discuss with anybody the content of our meeting here today."

He continued, "My question to you. Is it possible that in our time, someone might harness a new source of energy, and possibly even build a prototype? How feasible would it be? Please, take a moment to think before you answer."

The General pressed a button on the phone, "Aleksey, bring us three coffees and a little cognac for us, thanks."

The professors explained in turn, and in great detail about their points of view, based on their knowledge and some presumptions. They talked for over an hour, taking the time to explain some of the more technical facts to the general. They discussed recent developments in the field, and that there were several interesting developments at the early theoretical stage, but the difficulty was making it work cost effectively.

"Gentlemen, I thank you again for sharing your knowledge with me. You are a credit to your institutions. To summarise our discussion, you both believe that we're nearing the point where a new development could revolutionise our energy generation. Both theoretically and practically, you both expect someone, somewhere to crack this major issue the world has been facing now for many years."

"Yes, that is a good summary." said Professor Petrov.

"Of course, the person or country that does it first will quickly become dominant in producing cheap, environmentally friendly power and what's more—will be able to licence the technology across the world. The income from this will surely propel that country into superpower status such is the demand for more power to feed the world economy."

The general looked excited. "You have been a tremendous help. Thank you, gentlemen, I'll let you get back to your research and I'll have my assistant send a letter of commendation to your universities for your work here today."

Back in London, MI6's Mr. Smith held an urgent meeting in his office with the MI5 operatives assigned to the active operation in the UK.

"I see from your initial report that things went badly during the initial stages of your surveillance operation, Robert, could you repeat in detail everything that happened? I need to ensure our written report doesn't have any gaps which could come back to us and cause an incident."

The chief of Intelligence already had read the written report on what happened and understood that the Russian FSB took this case with the student seriously and had now had at least two agents on British soil, both now dead. It is possible others were here, and if not then they soon would be.

"OK then, I agree your actions were appropriate and justified, if regrettable. It was a road accident and we have issued a D-Notice to the media to ensure only basic details will be published. The less news that get back to Moscow the better, and we can retain the advantage if they don't know we are onto them.

"Possibly later the Russian embassy will ask for an explanation of the circumstances of their death from British authorities. Nothing to worry there. We are clear. We should concentrate now on surveillance—extend the watch to the whole family, I want to know more about Mr. Harrison and his Russian wife Lara. We should know rather quickly what secret the Russians are trying to get from Alex. Also, what is the role there of his step father Derek.

"Possibly we might even consider direct contact with Alex, with the police helping us have a meeting under their roof. But let's leave that on hold for now. The local police also reported that somebody broke in to, and searched, Mr. Harrison's house, turned the place upside down by all accounts but I guess they didn't manage to find what they were looking for. But now we know who did this. If the Russians want to get something so important then we want it even more. But we will see, we will find the point where we will nail them, and then we'll embarrass them publically." With these thoughts Chief of MI6 called for John to come in to the office.

"John," the chief looked serious, "Now you should double your surveillance efforts to cover all the family members. Use all the resources we have to—make this quick and clean. We can be sure that those two dead Russians will be five live ones very shortly. We need to be careful before we're overrun with FSB agents. Let's take a trip over to the technical services division, and see if they have anything useful for our guys here."

Later that night a white car slowly approached Derek and Lara's street. Two young men in sporty clothes casually got out of the car and walked back down the street, talking to each other quietly. They stopped opposite Derek house not far from where his car was parked. The taller man took out his phone and pretended to make a call while the shorter one knelt down to tie his shoelace. Nobody would have noticed even if they had been watching closely that as he stood back up he stepped backwards and with his hand behind his back placed a small device in the wheel arch of Derek's car. The fake phone call was concluded and both men walked back to their car with a good view all the way up Derek's front yard to the front door.

Captain Orlov, the Russian agent brought in to replace the ones killed in the car accident had by now arrived. Before this mission he operated in another part of Britain. His first task was to scope out the area and see if there were any other surveillance teams in operation.

He drove up the road towards Alex's house, and noticed a car with two men inside. He wasn't sure who they were but was careful not to make eye contact. Thinking quickly, he parked a bit further down the street, outside a house which looked empty as there were no cars parked in the driveway. He took a blank piece of paper from his glovebox, folded it in half to look like an envelope and walked up the path confidently. He popped the "letter" through the letterbox before returning to his car and driving away. Again, he looked straight ahead and didn't give the two men any reason to suspect him. Orlov was an experienced field agent and didn't want to take the risk of confronting the other agents, if that's what they were until he knew more. He decided to change his tactics.

Orlov had reviewed maps of the area before his arrival and already had a plan B in place. He knew the house was at the foot of a forested hill which would make for a good distant vantage point where he could keep an eye on the comings and goings of the house. He drove up the hill and took out of his car's boot a small stool and a painter's easel. He set himself up as an artist out for the day to capture the beauty of the area. He started sketching while keeping a close view of the house.

The Russian agent knew that tomorrow was a big day for him. He would meet Derek at a local pub as agreed. If the two guys in the car were British agents then they would likely be unaware of Derek's involvement and would stay guarding the house keeping watch on Alex. It was difficult running this operation on his own but Orlov was confident he could keep things running smoothly until some back up was sent in from Russia to this area where he need most help.

ൡൡ

It was Robert's turn to keep watch on the house. He was sipping coffee while Steve took a short nap. Suddenly a shrill beep came from a plastic box on top of the dashboard. It was the control panel for the tracker attached to Derek's car. Steve woke up quickly.

"Steve! Start the car, the chase begins."

They followed Derek's car at a distance, knowing they could track him easily through the device attached to his car. It was a short trip, after just five or so minutes they arrived at a country pub. Rather than pull in straight behind Derek, they continued up the road for a minute or two before doubling back and parking at the far end of the car park.

Derek came to the pub much earlier than he was invited by the Russian agent because he wanted to prepare himself for the difficult conversation. He thought a nice half of local ale would steady his nerves.

He was in deep thought about what he should do, as he took a swig of his beer. Should he flat out refuse to help the agents because he could not get from Alex what they wanted? Should he ask again for more time? Alex was not a stupid young man, he had hidden his secret in a place Derek couldn't reach. Possibly the Russians were so brave that they would smash all the lockers in that station. He smiled inside at the thought.

He did not notice that two customers, two good looking men came in, deeper in a quite conversation and sat not far from him, just opposite the bar.

Orlov entered the pub, noticed that Derek was waiting for him with a glass and he moved straight to the bar, "One pint of Lager, please," he ordered in broken English, with a distinctly Russian accent. With beer in hand he dropped into an empty chair at Derek's table.

"Hello, Mr. Harrison! Did you not expect a new face?" His smile askew as he looked steely into Derek eyes.

"You can call me Michael. You are working for us, as you remember. The last time you had a meeting with my comrades you got a time limit to do the job for us," he sipped his beer. "So now your report to me, Derek, please."

Two British agents sitting at the table nearby clearly understood they were witnessing a meeting between an unknown Russian agent and Derek. The faces of the two men told them everything they needed to know. Derek looked miserable and scared but the Russian was full of confidence and impatience.

Robert immediately knew what they needed to do. "Steve, we need to put a tracking device on that Russian's car. I noticed him arrive though the window, it's the one with the plate ending XHB. Do it quick without attracting any attention," he whispered to Steve.

After Derek and the Russian agent separately left the pub, Robert made a call, "John, we have news for you and the boss. Surprise! Mr. Harrison is co-operating with the Russians...so we have now to update our action plans'…

Chapter 19

"Good morning my sister, what is the weather like in Sweden?"

Alex in a happy mood began to chat with his sister Oleva. "The weather is Ok, brother, but unfortunately I am not."

"Hey, what's wrong?"

"Well, things aren't going well with my husband and I am thinking of divorcing him."

The problem is that I don't feel that he needs me. He avoids planning our life together, he does not want a baby, a family house or to settle down. I need stability and security." She started sobbing.

"Come on, my dear, don't do it, you are breaking my heart," Alex replied with emotion in his voice.

"How I can help you? I should come and kick his face in if he does not care about you enough? But seriously I would like to advise you. Be patience with him as long as you can, be just kind and a good wife. Possibly he will come around. Do not judge a person for just one season, go through it all and then make your decision. Those were mum's words which she was always repeating for us, do you remember?"

"Yes, brother, I remember, I will try to keep us together, but if things continue like this I will leave him and possibly consider moving to the UK to establish my life there. Where I can be close to you and mum."

"Only as a last resort, then I agree. If you need my help I will be there for you, sister. Also, I would like to tell you that very soon I will come back to Sweden, to finally take my Doctorate confirmation orals, collect some of my possessions which were left with friends, and visit you both."

He heard Oleva's tone change, she sounded calmer, and started chatting more happily on the phone.

Alex interrupted her, "I will stay in a hotel in Stockholm for several days and let you know at some point when and how exactly I will meet with you. Big hug for you now."

Alex sighed, and with a long exhale tried to push aside his worry for his sister's problems.

He needed to prepare to make very important call. He picked up the phone.

"My name is Mr. Petrov, Alex, I would like to speak to the manager of the Energy and Climate Change Department, but I am not sure of his name."

In reply Alex heard the polite and sweet voice of a secretary, "Just a second, Mr. Petrov, I will connect you now."

After just a few seconds, a bright, energetic, and pleasant voice on the other end answered, "Hello Mr. Petrov, how I can help you."

Alex explained briefly what he wanted and asked the manager for a face to face meeting.

The manager of the government department regularly received this sort of call. Sometimes they were useful, often they were from crazy mad scientist types, but they were usually interesting meetings in one way or another and it made his job more interesting.

"Well, Mr. Petrov, you have certainly intrigued me, so shall we make an appointment next week? My secretary will help us to find a mutually acceptable time. She will call you back shortly. Please bring with you some evidence of your impressive claims that we discussed. Good to talking to you, soon we will talk in person."

ఴఴ

The deputy of the Director of British Intelligence, John, hurried into the office of his boss with urgent news. "Mr. Smith, I have something new to discuss with you urgently."

"John, you always come with something urgent, why you do not come to my office just for a nice chat, without any news?" He smiled at him tiredly, "Ok, I am listening, go on, what do you have for me?"

"Thanks to our technical colleagues, we are able now to listen to the Russians talk on the phone and we can also locate their car. At the moment, we can hear just one Russian agent—Michael. The very same agent who had the meeting in the pub with Mr. Harrison. So, he made his report by phone right after the meeting, to somewhere, presumably in Moscow. From that report its clear to us why the Russians are chasing Alex, Mr. Harrison's stepson." He stopped for a moment and looked around then stared at his boss with a winning expression. "As they understand it, Alex is an inventor of a revolutionary new renewable energy source. And, what's more, he made a prototype, a device which he is hiding here in the UK. Unsurprisingly, the Russians desperately want that invention!

"That is why they tried to get this invention from him in Sweden, evidently, without success, they attacked and even kidnapped him. Now they are on our territory continuing their operation.

"We did not hear all the details but the picture is clear, we are dealing with aggressive economic espionage from the Russian state on our territory and against our national interests. That young inventor is already on the shortlist of our main nuclear energy company to get a job here and he brought his invention in our country. And listen to this, Alex is going to Sweden shortly for his Doctorate certificate, he got his PhD at Stockholm University. Interestingly, that information about Alex and his visit to Sweden was passed to the Russians by his stepfather—Derek. What a great Stepfather! Eh!?" John nodded ironically. "His wife Lara would be furious at him if she discovered all her husband's games against her son.

"So, Mr. Smith, knowing how the Russians operate and that they are not averse to using undiplomatic tactics in these sorts of circumstances we must protect and secure Alex. They will be bringing in additional agents, as we speak, no doubt. We need to form a joint operations team with our Swedish colleagues to keep him safe over there and make sure we hand off surveillance and protection to MUST in a carefully orchestrated manner. If not, I fear for the safety of Alex, and his invention."

The Chief of Intelligence sat in silence for a moment with his eyes wide open, trying to digest all the information supplied by his deputy. Then he smiled. "It's certainly going to be a busy few weeks ahead of us. The Russians are turning up the heat quickly on this situation, we must protect this guy, and our national interest in connect to his invention."

"Well Boss," John moved himself closer to the table, "As time doesn't seem to be on our side here yet, lets formalise our plans, and get the right people working on this."

"Great. So, first things first, let's set the wheels in motion to guarantee the inventor's safely. But once he returns from Sweden, John,—I want you to make contact with him and arrange a meeting. We can work out later how we will achieve that and what we will discuss with him, but I want to be there too."

ଓଓ

Alex sat at the table in the corner of the cosy English pub. The black wooden beams on the ceiling were twisted and cracked with age but would probably be still there long after him, he thought to himself. The pub wasn't busy. The lunch time wave of diners had passed and the evening wave of drinkers hadn't yet arrived. He was deep in thought, occasionally interrupted by the quiet vibration of his latest iPhone as he exchanged text messages with a friend from Sweden.

So, the meeting with the manager from the government department was all set up. Before that though, Alex was thinking about what he still needed to arrange. He needed to get all his documents sorted out ready to send to the patent office. He needed to check to see if his prototype was still in working order after all the moving around it had done over the past weeks. It may need some minor repairs or readjustments. Alongside of making sure all the patent paperwork was in order and the prototype ready to go, Alex was thinking he should put some thought into a business plan so he can discuss it with the manager of the Energy department if, as he hoped, the meeting went well.

Alex put his phone on the table, and took a sip of his beer. He smiled inwardly, how surprised will their engineers from the British Fusion Energy Center be when they became aware of his invention? Alex knew they were working hard in search of new sources of energy. He read their reports and research papers and wondered how close exactly they were to his research. He wondered if they had stumbled across the same problems as he had done, and which direction they were heading in to solve them. He felt a sense of pride about what he had achieved. No doubt with time, they would change direction and catch up with his invention, but he was the first. Although Alex respected them deeply as fellow researchers, there is always competitive rivalry in such academic circles.

Alex had a deep fear about losing his device. The only way to move it from safe place to safe place was in his hands, and when it was being moved he knew he was vulnerable. A Russian agent could easily just snatch it from his hands, and although he could build another one, the secrets within the device would be lost. He hoped that he could send his invention to the patent office very soon.

"Mum, could you help me today?" Alex questioned, whilst having breakfast with Lara.

"Of course, my son! When and what?" She asked, puttering in the kitchen.

"I will be ready in one hour. Could you help me take some parcels to the post office? Mum, it is very important to me. I am going to send my invention to the Patent office but I do not want anybody to hinder me, or maybe even try to steal it from our hands. Your role is simple mum, you will carry another parcel, a fake box.

"I will keep the real box to send away, and we will go to the post office together. I will also be carrying in my hand a tiny alarm, which should scare off anyone if they should try to attack us. So, if you hear a loud noise like a police siren, do not be afraid—it's just my alarm. Ok?"

Sitting in the back seat, Lara glanced back and saw through the back window that a white car started to pull away just as they did. "Son, it looks like we have company," she said in low voice.

"Don't worry, mum, we will speak later," Alex glanced at the taxi driver and winked at him cheekily, "my mum is always very suspicious."

ᏋᏋ

Robert was reading his newspaper, regularly glancing at the front door or Harrison's property. A taxi arrived and parked outside the house, and after a short toot of the horn, Alex and his mother Lara hurried out of the front door. Each was carrying a large box, wrapped in brown paper and held together with copious amounts of packing tape.

"Steve, enough daydreaming—look there, Alex with his mother, get ready to follow them."

They followed the taxi to the post office, and watched as the two targets disappeared inside of the building.

Robert decided to leave the car and walked up to the post office door. After a quick glance through the glass door, he turned around and kept watch on the street outside.

Aha, there he is, thought Robert as he spotted a car slowly driving by down the street. The driver was looking sideways trying to catch sight of what was going on inside the building. As the Russian agent peered through the door from the slowly moving car, Robert purposely caught his eyes and smiled. The agent realised what was going on and accelerated away, recognising he had no chance of capturing Alex from inside the building.

That is Orlov! Robert thought to himself, *too late bastard, go to home while you still can,* Robert told him in his thoughts.

Alex was in a cheerful mood later that evening. Now the stress of worrying about the safety of his invention was off his mind and he felt like a new chapter of his life was beginning. He was happy in the UK and it seemed as though prosperity was just around the corner. Excitement too, but hopefully a different kind of excitement than what he had been experiencing in recent weeks. After a pleasant evening meal however, the mood turned sour. As Lara was clearing away the dishes, Derek leaned into Alex and whispered accusatively, “Lara told me you sent a big parcel to somewhere and she helped you. I hoped you would ask me to help you to arrange all these things here in the UK. I’m offended, Alex, you never seem to take me up on my offers.”

“Sorry Derek, I didn’t mean to be disrespectful, maybe next time?”

“So, what’s the big secret, where did you send the parcels?”

“I have sent my invention to the Patent office, tomorrow it will be there. I thought it would be best not to bother you with these things, Derek.”

Derek’s face changed, his faced flushed and Alex could tell he was trying to choose his words carefully.

“I’m disappointed in such a victorious moment you purposely ignored me! You made something, I believe, very important, using my money if you remember, you left me. Am I nobody to you?” Derek started to raise his voice. “How can you do it to me?!”

Lara returned from the kitchen, “Are you OK boys? Problems?”

“No, darling, no, we just talking.”

As Lara left dining room, Derek face turned nasty again as he moved even closer to Alex,

"Listen, Alex, I see that you do not trust me that is clear, and I can't live with someone who has such little respect for me. Find a place to live and move out. The sooner you do it the better it will be for both of us. I do not want your mother to know about our talk. It will be in your interest to keep things calm and civilised while you make your arrangements. Find a way to tell her that you are leaving us. I will happily give you some money to speed things up if that's the problem'

Derek stood up sharply, looked hatefully at Alex and stormed out of the room.

Alex sat frozen in shock, trying to work out why Derek had reacted so badly. As he calmed down, he collected a few glasses from the table and went to the kitchen to help his mother.

"Mum, tomorrow I am going to Sweden, I found a good deal on a nice hotel in Stockholm, I will stay there," he explained to Lara while drying the plates and pots with his mother, "I will come back after the Doctorate ceremony."

"Oh, darling, why you did not tell us in advance, I wanted terribly to be at the ceremony with you and Derek would be glad to go also. You should know, my son, how proud I am to be your mother. I still get tears in my eyes when I think about, what I missed, about that ceremony when you received your professional diploma in Sevastopol. I'll regret forever not being able to see your reward after all that hard work."

"Mum, I'm sorry. With everything that has been going on I have only just checked my emails and I almost missed it myself. So, do not be disappointed and sad now, the ceremony will be over very quickly. You do not need to arrange a whole trip with Derek just for this. One day we will go together to Stockholm and I will show this beautiful city, and we can take our time exploring the islands. OK?!? And, I will have a lot important events in my life yet which you will not miss." Alex embraced his mother and excused himself before heading to bed.

The next day Alex was already in the taxi heading for the airport. He still felt uneasy about the conversation with Derek, but glad he hadn't upset his mum by telling her about Derek's outburst. The timing of the trip was good, as it gave him an excuse to disappear for a while until he heard back about the result of his job interview and prepared for the meeting at the Energy Department. In the meantime, he had some things to sort out in Stockholm before he could cut his ties there and relocate to the UK for good. He began to worry that Derek was not the man everyone thought he was, and felt sorry for his mum. His reaction was way over the top, his anger was unexplainable, and what was he hiding?

He arrived in Stockholm to catch the tail end of a beautiful evening. There was almost no breeze as he watched the start of a pink and red sunset from the window of the bus transfer to his hotel. Out of habit, Alex glanced at the other passengers on the bus, and the cars following. Nothing suspicious.

He smiled inside that all seems good, his pursuers didn't notice where he was going. His last-minute plans giving him an advantage. But it doesn't matter anyway now, the invention is in safe hands.

He pulled his phone from his jacket pocket and thought which one of his friends he would call first, keen to meet them and catch up.

ꕥ

The Director of British Intelligence, Mr. Smith asked his secretary to connect him with his colleagues from MUST in Sweden,

"Mr. Anderson, I hope you are well and the weather is still good in your green country.

"The reason for my call is that the student Mr. Petrov we both have a mutual interest in is already back in your country. He arrived by plane in Stockholm today, a last-minute booking, as I understand it. It looks like a short-term trip, but I ask you to organise some protective surveillance for us, please. We know the Russians have an active operation in the UK and while we figure out the reason for their interest we would appreciate your support. We have not yet advised him of our surveillance, so a discreet operation would be preferable to us if you could oblige?

"Thank you, Mr. Anderson, it is always a pleasure and please do contact me directly if I can ever return the favor for you."

Cheerfully he finished the conversation, holding back some of the finer detail on their investigation. There would be time to fill in the blanks for the Swedes once Alex was back on British soil.

ↂↂ

With great excitement and a positive mood, Alex approached the main building of his University wistfully recalling where he'd just spent the best 5 years of his life. There were a lot of joyful events, interesting lectures, and long evenings in laboratories resulting in his own scientific research and successful experimentation. He was happy to walk through the familiar door and meet his professor.

Alex stepped in to the office, where his professor stood up and brought his hands towards Alex warmly, he took both hands, obviously glad to see Alex again.

"Hello, my favourite student," he smiled widely, "so you did not forget your old teacher? Forgive me, I should not call you student now, as I had to used, because, in fact, you have had your PhD confirmed and you are a doctor of scientific research in nuclear energy.

"Tell me, how you are and what your plans are for the future."

Alex slowly told him about his move to the UK, his good progress with his job search, only holding back on the story about his invention and his numerous run ins with the Russian FSB. Before he visited his professor, he had a hesitation, to tell him or not about his device. His keenness to share his good news with the professor was strong, as he knew how much it would mean to him. Alex was keen to share his ideas and discuss what he had achieved with someone who would truly understand the magnitude of his discovery but his head told him to wait just a little bit longer, until the idea was protected, and the Russians could not steal it.

No, better to wait. The professor would still be the first person he would share the details with, but later.

"Professor, I am so glad and proud to have had you as my teacher and mentor all these years. As result of your help and my research, I truly believe I'm close to something amazing!

"I know what you want to ask me…But I would ask you to wait a little longer, don't ask me anything yet, please. Soon, I will be returning to see you with all the details, because I need your expertise.

"At the moment, I'm waiting to hear about a job in an energy company in the UK. I have a big hope to start work there soon."

"Alex, if I or my friend from Japan would invite you to start working with us, what would you say?"

"I would say, that I made my choice, Professor, I will go with the job in the UK, I like that country, my mother settled there, there are a lot 'Pluses' which I have already considered."

"Ok, my dear boy, I wish you the best in your life. If you have anything to share or need any help from me, here it's my mobile, call any time."

The Professor with kind, tired eyes gave Alex his card and accompanied him to the door. "We will see you soon again at the ceremony in Town Hall, you will see it will be very interesting for you."

During the couple of next days Alex met his devoted friends, Michael and Shawn, together they visited different memorable places, the cinema, even to a concert, where Shawn was clearly bored trying to close his eyes. But Michael pushing his side, hissed at him to behave. They already knew their future jobs. Shawn would continue to work at the university, he wanted to reach the rank of professor, and Michael wanted just any job at the university, and would be happy with a position as a professor's assistant to start.

The friends showed Alex the place at the station where they "played" the man who was chasing him.

"Alex, can you tell us now, who were those people, who was chasing you?" Michael wondered.

"Friends," Alex looked at them merrily and paused, "I can tell you now," he looked as in conspiracy to the left then right, "It was Russians agents, spies."

Michael and Shawn started to laugh the first and then glanced on each other,

"Are you joking, Alex?"

"No, I am serious, boys. Listen, I'll tell you now. But let's not speak about this again.

"I was working and continue to work on an invention. This is of great interest for Russians for some reason. So they started and still continue to chase me to steal that invention from me. But they did not get it—with your help and I hope they will not. That became the principal concern for me and that is all! I cannot tell you more guys, at the moment. That is it!" He widely smiled for them.

He continued. "So, we are here together now, enjoying our times, but we should be careful because those agents could be watching us even now. Possibly they will try to kidnap me, I hope you will find some tricks to save me again, eh?" Alex, smiled at them then became serious.

"Friends, I will tell you about my scientific work later, when I am ready. Do not be offended, please, ok?"

They were laughing and decided to move on but his friends started nervously looking back periodically.

The next day Michael helped Alex send several parcels to his mother's address. After his very quick departure from Sweden, his friends took his private possessions and managed to return his council flat.

The great Stockholm Town Hall was lit up for the award ceremony for diplomas and PhD graduates. There are were parents, teachers, officials from the University and Authorities, all were gathering, waiting for the main events to start and then twenty-five graduates and Doctorates would appear in the hall and one by one ascend to the stage to get their well-deserved certificates. Each person was hoping that this would be the start of a long, successful career. Alex was standing on the stage in a black gown with a squared black hat, he was pleased to be receiving his PhD, but deep down was a bit sad, because his mother was not amongst the guests and his sister was not able to attend either.

He thought back to when he met his sister and her husband recently, they had a nice time for several hours, but there was a tension in the air during the meeting. It became obvious to Alex that something wasn't right between them. Alex tried not to get involved but Oleva created a situation where Alex felt he had to make a comment on their problem. They were a young couple, they both had no experience on how to live with someone beloved. It's not every day roses, even in a successful marriage. But they should learn every time from their mistakes, try not to offend each other even if they disagree, they should compromise and be ready to step back if its needed," Alex had read some psychologist's book about relationships, about marriage, its good in theory but in practice, it's difficult to apply but he was sure, it would be worth it.

Then Alex got a thought, if he ever would meet his love and marry, would he follow all this advice? He satisfied himself that he would, because all that advice given to his sister came from his heart.

He hoped that Oleva will work to overcome their differences and happily continue their life together.

The next day Alex was on a flight back to the UK.

There was not enough time to sleep on the plane, but Alex was enjoying the view. Soaring over the top of clouds, the dramatic blue sky met on the horizon by a solid white blanket of clouds. He found it easy to imagine it as white, endless fields covered by snow and ice. It could be a scene from a film about the Arctic. He finished his imagination with thoughts that it would nice to go and see the Arctic or Antarctic one day.

When he snapped back to reality, back to his plane, back to his seat, he became aware of a nice young lady about his age seated nearby. She looked like a professional, with a laptop on which she continuously tapped away. Her outfit was accordingly, strict and elegant on her slim body, Her long blondie hair and pretty face impressed him.

"Excuse me?!" Alex said to her, "Do you know what time we arrive in London?"

She looked at him seriously then she cheekily smiled back, "Yes, I know, in two hours' time," then after a bit of thinking she added, "My name is Marie."

Alex returned a polite smile, "I am Alex, pleased to meet you."

The rest of flight they talked without pause. Alex felt that between him and Marie was a spark, a chemistry starting to work. He knew now that she was on business trip and she was the deputy of a manager, she led a human resources team in a French company. So, she was from Paris where her company was based. But the time had come to finish their talk, as the plane started to descend and Alex returned to his thoughts again.

He did not want to lose this chance in life, so he asked her for her contact details, in case he might be in Paris. Marie, deep down, did not want to lose the connection with this pleasant young man either. They gladly exchanged phones numbers.

Alex in his high mood rushed through corridors, escalators, down the steps towards the exit, into the queue to the passport control gates.

The customs officer took his passport, looked at Alex intently, checked his computer, and then asked, "Mr. Petrov, what is your reason for visiting the United Kingdom?"

"Erm, I'm visiting my mother who settled here." Alex stared back at the officer.

"How long are you intending to stay?"

Alex raised and lowered his shoulder, "I've not really thought about it, maybe until my visa expires."

"Mr. Petrov, we would like to check your documents and the information you provided more closely. Please follow me through that door," the officer pointed behind him.

Alex was astonished. What was this? Was it some sort of trick or something more serious, maybe they know about the ferry? His heart skipped a beat, *we will soon see*, he thought.

He was invited to a room where two men were already waiting. They had friendly faces, wore good suits, and seemed confident.

"A-ha, Mr. Petrov, here. Sit down please. I would like to explain something. It's nothing to do with your passport, it's all to do with you.

"Alex, we are not your enemies, we are not going to harm or hurt you. We are working for a secret organisation representing British national interests, and we would like to protect you.

"When we say "protect you", this means that we know something about you, about the troubles you involved in. We even know everything that just happened to you in Sweden. But to give you this protection we would like you tell us all the truth about yourself and what are you doing."

The man stopped, poured a glass of water for everybody and took a sip himself, "Bye the way, Alex, my name is Mr. Smith, and here is my deputy, you can call him John," he smiled at John.

"So, Alex, shall we speak openly about everything."

Chapter 20

Derek, wearing his thick luxurious bath robe and favourite slippers walked up behind Lara and gently massaged her shoulders as she sat at her dressing table. As she prepared herself for bed, she smiled at him in the mirror in front of her. She whispered jokingly, "Derek, what are you up to?"

"Nothing, I just want to tell you how proud I am to have you as my wife, and how much I love you. Listen, darling, I was thinking about my birthday and I have a great idea."

"Tell me, my love?" She turned to him and put her arms around his waist, looking up, her eyes met his.

"Maybe a bit of a party? We could bring both families along and a few friends?"

Lara sprayed a little perfume on her neck looking excited. "That sounds like a great idea darling. I would love to help you organise your party."

She followed Derek to the bed and slid in next to him. She snuggled under his arm, kissed him on the side of his head and spoke quietly. "Lets organise your party tomorrow. For now, let us talk about something even more interesting!" she giggled.

Derek awoke early the next morning, sitting with a pen and paper, noting down the beginnings of his guest list. Starting with his brothers and sisters he asked Lara if she would mind making some calls to invite people.

"We can finalise the time and place later, let's just let people know for now. I mentioned the idea of a party to Jim, you remember him—from Scotland. He has already agreed. I think I'll find a hotel somewhere nearby so people can relax and not have to worry about having a drink and finding their way home."

Lara nodded in agreement as Derek continued thinking aloud.

"You can invite your daughter Oleva, I hope she is able to visit us and of course Alex will be here. I will invite my daughters myself, they can be quite difficult sometimes as you are aware. I'm sorry they have not been nice to you in the past, maybe this is an opportunity to build bridges, we will see. Now, enough chatting, I need to get to work!"

After Derek left the room, Lara walked purposefully to her wardrobe. She opened it, and took a step back, thinking deeply about what she would wear for her husband's party.

She felt herself trembling with excitement and sat down on the bed. She thought to herself, what was making her feel this way? Was it the party itself? The guests? His daughters? No. Then she realised that it was Derek's mention of Jim. The possible presence of Jim at the party had got her excited, she admitted to herself. Lara was surprised at herself and went to the bathroom to splash some cold water on her face.

"Mr. Harrison, I would like to speak to you in person." Said the nice, deep, accented voice on the other end of the phone.

"Do I know you?" Derek replied. He played along, but immediately understood what this call would be about, even if he didn't know the caller.

"No, you don't. As I have never seen you. But I intend to conclude some business with you and I know a lot about you. Where and when can we meet—your choice? You can call me Ivan Ivanovich."

"I understood you. There is nothing really to talk about. So, I would suggest meeting in a week or so. Maybe the day after my birthday."

"Can I speak frankly, Derek? I think we have problem with the 'when,' I cannot wait that long to meet with you, I have other matters to attend to.

"Shall I suggest to you that our meeting will be two days before your birthday in the same place as the last meeting."

Derek sighed deeply. He wanted to prolong the waiting game with them, knowing there was nothing he can do now for the Russian FSB, it's too late.

He knew there would be consequences to him, and didn't want to think what they might be. His business? His family? The happy thoughts of planning his party had become a distant memory in just a few seconds.

"Yes, I know that place, but I think delaying the meeting would be better for both of us, maybe between then and now I will be able to get some useful information for you?"

"No, Mr. Harrison. That is my last word on this matter. Two days before your birthday, at two pm, in that place. And be aware, if you don't come with information, I will ensure you receive a personal present from me on your big day." The tone of the caller's voice changed. Derek could hear the impatience was for real. The sound of the receiver at the far end of the call being slammed down acted like a punctuation mark to end the sentence.

What a sweltering day! Derek wiped his face with a white handkerchief from his pocket. Lara always make sure he had one in the same pocket when she ironed his clothes, just how he liked it. He decided that he had done enough for the Russians, he had tried his best and what more could he do? He would not attend the meeting and be pushed around anymore. He was regretting the whole business deal, what had started as an exciting new avenue for him had gotten quickly out of control. If he hadn't accepted their help in expanding his business into Siberia, he never would have ended up spending the night with that Russian agent either. Maybe the time had come to call on the British authorities and accept whatever damage the Russians would cause to his business just to end the madness. With the police involved, surely the Russians would disappear back underground as quickly as they had appeared.

"Hi, my darling, my Jane. Is my little boy good and healthy? Are you both ok?"

Derek started talking to his daughter.

After exchanging news from both sides, Derek invited his daughter for his birthday party and was glad she accepted, and would bring her son whom Derek loved immensely. He confirmed again to his daughter that he will continue to pay his private school fees and when they came he would buy some nice clothes for them. Derek offered that Lara could take them shopping because she has good taste in clothes, she would help them to make the right choices."

"Why would your Lara need to go with us to make a choice?" Jane raised her voice,

"Father, I do not want her to come with us at all. I already made it clear to you that your marriage to this Russian woman is a betrayal to our mother. If she wasn't dead, she would be ashamed of you," she started sobbing in anger.

"Come on, darling, I am happy with my wife Lara. I ask you to accept this fact and get on with your life too. I'm sure your mother is looking down on me and she would be pleased that I am sincerely happy."

"Father, you said your business is now growing well. I would like to know what would happen to all your assets if suddenly you were…gone. You know I wish you to live for the next hundred years, of course."

"It may be difficult for you to understand but, listen, my dear, I will protect the woman who is committed to me and to share with me the autumn and winter years of my life. Also, I will give my children a start for a better life if I can. Do you understand me?

"Good, I've already made the will—I will leave the house to my wife, for Lara. The business I leave for my daughters, I mean for you too, Jane. But it is on the condition that every month Lara will receive a percentage from the business's profits. So, I hope everybody will be happy. I think that should be fair?"

Jane's voice became low and hoarse, "What sort of percentage, father?"

Derek picked up on Jane's tone and started to become angry. "My dear, you will find that out soon enough, do not be rude with me!"

"Well, well, father, it seems to me that this woman has bewitched you. You have lost the plot! Do you realise what you have done?!"

Now she was getting angry and started to shout at him. "Well, thank you at least for telling me in advance father. Now I can tell you the truth that I won't be coming to your party and don't want to speak to you again!"

"Tread carefully, daughter, remember that I still pay for the private school for your son."

Derek was in shock after hearing his daughter's callous words. He bit his tongue, holding back a little rather than saying what he wanted to.

"It was your idea, as I recall, to put my boy in private school, you started, so now you can bloody well finish," she screamed hysterically.

ଓଓ

"Darling, what a nice interior this restaurant has, its a lovely atmosphere," Lara remarked, as they walked through the doorway.

Within a couple of steps, Derek knew that he would enjoy having his party at this location. Lara had done a great job in selecting it.

A young waitress showed them through to a big, grand looking room, with an exposed timber frame roof. Derek, busy staring at the ancient ceiling then glanced down to see all his friends in the room already. Everyone laughed at Derek's surprised look and then broke into a raucous rendition of the Happy Birthday song. As Derek started working his way around the table to greet his guests he now realised why Lara was so slow to get ready this evening, she wanted to make sure all the guests were at the party already. Even though he knew he was having a party, Lara had obviously wanted to make it special for him, he smiled. Even Oleva had managed to make it, Derek spotted her sitting with Alex, deep in conversation.

People began to settle down and those standing around the large oval table started to take their seats. Derek felt the white tablecloth and was surprised how thick it was. As he took a more detailed look at the furnishings of the room it was clear that it had been decorated very expensively. That is a good sign, he mused, and hopefully they will have taken as much care with the food!

Derek's brothers and sisters seemed in a good mood, all sat next to their other halves. Some of Derek's old business associates were sitting opposite Lara, and Jim was with them, looking like he was enjoying himself. Next to Jim were Lara's children.

Lara noticed that all the women were in skirts or dresses, which surprised her. She had observed that most English women seem to be always dressed in trousers, but obviously everyone has wanted to make the effort for this special occasion. Lara was pleased that people had dressed up for the day. She spotted a couple of the wives get up to leave the table to gossip and smoke outside the front doors. Lara could never get used to seeing women smoking. She had never smoked in her life and it wasn't a popular thing with women in her life back in Russia. Lara was enjoying watching how people were interacting around the table. Derek wandered over, gave Lara a big hug and excused himself to go outside and talk to the ladies.

As Derek left the room, one of his brothers raised his voice across the table, noticing Lara alone.

"Lara, you are a brave woman!".

"Why?" she asked.

"Because you married our brother!"

"How do you mean?" she replied quizzically, but they turned it into a joke and changed the topic. The sound of sweet music appeared from nowhere as a signal that it was time to dance. From around the table, there was the sound of chairs being slid backwards across the wooden floor as the braver couples immediately rushed to dance cheek by cheek. Brothers went out to call their wives. Jim, who was sitting opposite to Lara at the table, circumnavigated the table and invited Lara to dance.

"How are you, Lara?" Jim led her in dance keeping one of Lara's hands on the heart side of his chest. With his other hand, he held her with tenderness by her back.

"You see now I am happy and merry today," she smiled at him,

Jim gave her a long deep look straight into her green eyes. It was a serious look which told Lara something, but she decided not to comment and continue bubbling with him merrily.

Deep down she was afraid to accept that this man has something serious in his soul to offer her.

"Your husband did not stay with you this evening...he is here, there, everywhere."

Jim started to smile too, "I would not leave a lady like you, alone at any party. I would be afraid that some man could steal you from me."

"Jim, I am glad that you are in a good mood today. And I am enjoying our dance." She glanced at him cheekily. "Look, my husband is already at the table and wants to finish a bottle, shall we go."

"Lara," he looked in her eyes again, "Remember what I said to you, if you need me, my help, anything from me, just make a call."

Derek was sitting at the table and talking to his two business friends. He wanted to discuss an idea with them, to suggest they to merge their three businesses into one, creating a big factory, and the three of them could have equal shares…His friends were listening to him with great interest and voicing their opinions to him. He was deep in this conversation but managed to keep an eye on Lara dancing, she looks beautiful, his gorgeous wife.

But suddenly he felt as through a spike went through his heart, was Jim interested in her?

Or maybe the other way around? His mind started to churn with worries like black clouds before a storm, why had he invited Jim, it was a mistake, he thought, he should have guessed that Jim was a lonely man looking for love of course he would have difficulty to pass by a woman who he liked, and it could be my Lara. No, no, never again, Jim had been a good friend but maybe now was time to put a bit of distance between him and Lara.

Derek's mind became aware of the real source of his anxiety. He had enjoyed his party, but soon it would be time to leave. Time to return home possibly and find the Russians on his doorstep… What, or who would be waiting for him when he got home? They promised a present. He was having second thoughts about missing the meeting, his previous bravado had all but disappeared now. Derek decided to stop stressing himself out, nothing had happened so far, maybe the Russian have finally realised that he can't help them.

Derek approached Lara and asked for a dance. He embraced her closely in dance and, whispered, "Sweetheart, I have had a fantastic evening, but I'm exhausted—shall we go home?"

"Yes, my dear, I am tired too, we will go. Oleva and Alex mentioned making a night of it and are heading to another pub afterwards to talk and relax'

"Ok, that's fine, we'll say our goodbyes to the guests and leave."

Lara entered the house first, taking off her shoes as she entered. She noticed a big envelope on the floor. "Look at this, while we were at the party we got some mail, maybe another present for you!"

"Possibly nothing important, let's leave it for tomorrow." Derek approached her and kissing the side of her head he tried to take the envelope in his hand. But she, pulled her hand back jokingly.

"Ok, darling, shall we quickly see what we got and then have a tea before bed?"

She winked at him merrily and started to open the envelope. Derek was petrified about what might be in there, should he stop her? What if there was something that would hurt her? He couldn't move, he just stared at Lara with wide eyes.

She took out a pile of large A4 size photos, she developed a frown as she looked at the first, and then second, and third, then threw all of them towards Derek.

"Derek, what is this?" she demanded.

He didn't need to pick up the photos. He could see from the floor what they contained. So, this was the present from the Russians, delivered as promised on his birthday! They got him! Totally!

Derek sat on the sofa and rested his face in his palms. Saying nothing he kept his silence because he knew he had nothing to say which could excuse him for this betrayal. He was ashamed to look into the eyes of his beloved woman who trusted and loved him.

They sat for some minutes without a word then Lara stood up, went over to the window in silence then sharply turned to her husband,

"Is that what you promised me on our wedding day?" She looked at him with a combination of sadness and disgust on her face.

"What do you think I should do now after receiving all those dirty photographs?

"That is why you come back from Russia very tired! Tired from what? You found a prostitute and worked hard with her?!

"Did you even think that you could bring illness to me?! Or did I accidently marry a man without brains? If I would know that you, in your age, so weak. I would think ten times before changing my life for you."

She turned again to window and was crying helpless with shuddering shoulders.

Derek was still lost for words but he knew he needed to say something,

"Lara, please, let me say. I know I am guilty! It happened when I was on my trip in Siberia.

"I was very drunk one evening and was missing you very much. But a woman started to talk with me kindly and we ended up in bed, the next day when I realized what I'd done I could not forgive myself. I am so sorry, darling. It's not about my soul or heart. It's about my bloody drunk instinct which I deeply regret. But now, you see, somebody wants to harm me, us, my business, so that is why you able to see these sins now. Forgive me, please, if you can. I do not want any talk about divorce. Please, calm down and we will talk about it with cool heads."

Derek could not tell her yet all the story about his involvement with the Russians. She would not accept it now.

He stepped towards her and touched her shoulder, but she moved away,

"I do not want to talk to you now and I do not know if I will be able to forgive you. I'm so humiliated, offended. I think it's better for you now to leave for a few days. Because my children are here now and I can't behave as though things are normal with them and with you like nothing has happened. I do not want them to know this shame you brought into our lives. But what I really want to do right now is to slap you in the face," she raised her voice and looked hysterically angry. "You should go," she hissed at him.

He turned to the entrance door and before opening it, he sent her a long, despairing look,

"Lara, you know that I loved and still love you, forgive me, please. Now I'll go."

Lara watched with her eyes full of tears through the window as his car pulled away from their house. She was in despair—she felt a pang of worry, remembering how much alcohol Derek had drunk that evening, he shouldn't be driving. She then felt ridiculous for worrying about Derek after everything he has done to her.

Derek was deep in thought as he sped down a dark, back road. The roads were almost empty as he passed by small villages, hamlets and empty fields. He had decided not to use the motorway but to take the more interesting route which would distract him from the problems he had caused. He blinked away his watery eyes, trying to clear his vision as he gripped the wheel. His lips were squeezed tightly, his body on autopilot as his mind churned through all the events that had led to this point.

He would go to his daughter Jane, and try to repair the damage to their relationship, then maybe something positive would come from today. He decided not to tell her about the events after the party. He hoped he could spend a few days with Jane and his grandson, which would give Lara some time to calm down and speak to him from her heart. Alex and Oleva will be leaving too soon, he thought. That will make it easier for them to have the difficult conversation about the sexual photos if they are not having to whisper and hide from the children.

Derek's tired eyes squeezed almost closed as the bright headlights from the car behind reflected off his mirrors into his face. He realised the car had been following closely for a while now. Was this the bloody Russians again, surely, they have had their fun by now? He became furious, who gives them the right to ruin a man's life?

Derek was swearing and hitting the steering wheel with anger as he sped up. He would take these goons on if they tried to overtake or stop him. The alcohol still in his blood made him brave, and the pain in his heart made him reckless.

Derek signaled a right and as feared the car behind accelerated alongside him before he could make the turn. Derek furiously swung the steering wheel to the right, his right wing crunching into the front wheel arch of the Russian's car. It shot across the road and onto the glass verge before the driver regained control just a few meters before hitting a tall strong pine tree. Once they re-joined the road they sped up again and were soon beside Derek again. Keeping their distance this time, the passenger lowered the window, and shouted, "Stop the car! I will shoot you if you don't."

Derek did not stop. In reply, he flicked them the middle finger and smashed into them again. This time, the Russians were ready and met Derek's action with their own. Derek looked across at the Russians, who were steering away from his car, thinking that has panicked them. His heart nearly jumped out of his chest when he saw the passenger take out a silver gun, stretch his arm out of the window and fire off a shot into his tyre. Derek felt the steering become heavy but pushed his foot on the accelerator as he fought to maintain control of the car. "You will not get me," he whispered under his breath.

Chapter 21

Major Kosinskiy and Captain Orlov were each sipping a beer shandy in a quiet corner of a traditional English pub while waiting for Derek to arrive. They had their doubts about if he would make an appearance at all. That would be easier on everyone, they thought. Easier for Derek to just get on and give them what they need, and easier for the two Russians who wanted to avoid what was heading towards a tense situation in a foreign country. Their diplomatic cover gave them a certain level of protection, but they were well aware of the less diplomatic reception they would receive from their superiors back in Moscow.

"The problem with the English is their lack of appreciation for vodka," remarked Ivan Kosinskiy as he gulped back another mouthful of shandy. Orlov smiled, replying "Yes, vodka washed down with herrings with onion. Try finding that in an English pub.". He smiled wryly.

"The sooner we sort out the situation with Derek the sooner we can enjoy a decent drink. We've relied on him too much," Kosinkiy said, making a point of looking at his watch for effect.

"Thirty minutes late, he's not coming, is he?" Orlov finished his drink and agreed with his Major. With that, the Major angrily slammed down his glass and stood up.

"We won't wait for him anymore! Stay here a moment, I need to report back, I'll head outside where it's quieter."

General Litvinov sat in his Moscow office with a sullen face as he listened to the report from the UK.

"Let me clarify," he interrupted angrily. "You are telling me that this operation is a failure. The invention is out of our reach and in the hands of the British. Is that correct?" He barked.

The general looked across his office at the picture of his president, hanging proudly on the wall. He pursed his lips and let out an exasperated sigh. The finality of the situation dawned on his face after a moment deep in thought.

"In that case, major, we have no further use for the businessman's services. In fact, we should make sure we never 'work' with him again. Do you understand what I'm telling you Major? Good! Also, you need to tie up loose ends with the student. I'll leave it to you to determine the way forward there, based on current situations. If the British are guarding him then you will need to be one step ahead, be cleverer than they are. This responsibility is yours now to finish this operation, I'm sure I don't need to tell you step by step what needs to be done now."

He replaced the telephone handset down gently. No use for anger now, there was not much he could do by this point. This was possibly the last operation he would oversee, and it would be a black mark on his career. But very soon he would be retired, and would enjoy flying to the Bahamas with his wife, his lengthy career behind him. A few months of relaxation and letting the sun warm up their elderly joints would be just what is needed to get over the disappointment.

But before that, he would need to face the final hurdle of accompanying his boss to see the president and verbally give his report on how the might of the Russian FSB failed a mission against a student in that foggy Albion. Whichever way he looked at the situation, he couldn't see a positive outcome.

"Captain, time to leave!"

Major Kosinskiy said as he re-entered the pub, seemingly in a rush. Reducing his voice to a whisper,

"We will continue to watch Derek for couple days more. But we got orders to close down this operation with the finality it requires. We lost the game, but there are still some actions required from us. Did you prepare the 'kompromat' on Derek, those 'sweet photos?' Good, then listen to me carefully. On Derek's birthday evening, we will deliver them to Derek's house and his beloved wife while he is out enjoying his birthday celebrations. On their return, they will see our 'Present.'"

He winked, taking pleasure in the imminent suffering he would cause Derek, feeling some enjoyment in the revenge he was about to take on Derek for foiling his plan.

Two days later, their black car was once again stationed near to Derek's house, the agents observing the comings and goings of Derek and his wife. Ivan Kosinskiy, feeling the effects of a long operation and the disappointment of Derek not playing by their rules was having difficulty staying awake. Without the adrenaline rush of a live mission, even his coffee was failing to rouse him from his tired state.

Orlov noticed that Ivan's alertness was fading and started a conversation with him to keep them both occupied. "Listen, Ivan, what can we do if we do not catch up with Derek tomorrow?" But there was no reply from Ivan.

"Let's call it a day and get some sleep perhaps? We can reassess the situation in the morning," Orlov repeated hopefully.

"No, we stay here overnight." Ivan replied lethargicly trying to hide his disappointment.

"Tomorrow we should finish our deals here and the day after tomorrow we should fly to Moscow.

"I did not tell you the bad news, our colleagues in the capital tried to catch Alex without success. The British secret services are looking after him well. So, as you see, there is no time to relax, Captain. By the way, you can move the car a bit closer."

He pointed his finger and yawned widely. "We'll have a better view from there."

After a brief time, they saw the front door open and Derek moving at a rapid pace, almost running to his car from the house. In seconds, his car was revving and took off into the darkness.

"Quick, Captain, let's move! Follow him!" Ivan was shouting panicked commands to Captain Orlov who expertly started the car, moved into gear and pulled away in what seemed like a single movement. He kept the car moving slowly until Derek turned a corner before accelerating with the aim of not letting him know he was being followed.

As they turned the corner, following the lead car, Derek had gained some noticeable distance between them. The two agents glanced at each other and shared a common thought, where the hell was Derek going this late in the evening. Alone, on his birthday, he certainly seemed to be in a hurry to get somewhere, but who knows where?

The Russians pushed on in silence for the most part. Keeping up with Derek, while not making it obvious they were following him, was stressful. They had followed Derek for some miles before he turned off the main road onto a very rural back road.

"Michael, more gas please, I want to speak to Derek through the window, get up alongside him and match his speed," ordered Ivan.

Captain Orlov dropped down a gear and floored the accelerator. Their car revved heavily and they felt themselves pushed back into their seats as quickly they moved up next to Derek's car, on the wrong side of the road.

"Stop the car, Harrison! I will fire if you don't!"

Ivan shouted at him twice, the second time more loudly and more threatening.

Derek's reaction was unexpected. He glanced sideways at the Russians for just a second, his face filled with rage and hate. Before the Russians could react, Derek jerked the steering wheel to the right, putting the wing of his car into the passenger door and knocking the Russian's car off the road. Orlov narrowly avoided putting his wheels into a ditch, but overcorrected and swerved back into the road, lurching onto the opposite verge before regaining control and making it back into the road.

"Again, again!" Ivan shouted above the roar of the engine. He pulled out his gun again as they pulled alongside once more.

They tried to use Derek's trick against him, swiping the rear end of his car sideways to try and spin him off the road, but the Jaguar was heavier than their car and quickly recovered, regaining speed. Frustrated, Ivan lowered his window, learnt out through it and fired directly into the tire of Derek's car. This did the trick, the rubber of the tyre shredded itself, flying off in all directions. The car, now driving on the rim of the wheel slowed down, clearly Derek was struggling to control it as sparks flew from the wheel.

"Michael, I am going to shoot him, make sure our car will be in the right position for me."

"Are you sure, Major?!"

"Yes, Captain, I am very sure!" he barked at Michael.

The Russians easily now overtook Derek's car, letting off several shots as they passed, and with increasing speed disappeared into the darkness of the empty road.

Ivan Kosinskiy turned back and had a long look over his shoulder. Derek car was laying upside-down on the side of road in a ditch, the flickering of flames of a small fire starting, probably from fuel leaking over the hot wheel rim he thought.

"Ok, now finally this damn mission is complete," Major Kosinsky made himself comfortable in his seat and started to look forward to putting the failed operation behind him. Now that operation Fulmination in England was accomplished, or at least as much as possible now they should think how to survive back in their motherland.

❦❦

Mr. Smith and his deputy John were sitting opposite the young man and listening with great attention to his story. They wanted to believe that everything he was saying is true.

"Alex, why did you decide to move to UK for work and bring your invention here?"

Mr. Smith was looking attentively towards Alex and was clearly enjoying the conversation. He felt immediately that Alex seems smart and honest and was open to answering any questions put to him.

"My decision was based mainly on our family circumstances, my mother married and moved here to live, in the UK. She asked me not to go to any other country, trying to keep our family together here. That was fine with me as I like this country."

He looked at them seriously. "But it is not the only reason why I made this decision about my invention. I think your country is a peaceful, friendly, generous nation, so your country will be able to use my invention on an industrial scale in the most effective way. And, frankly, I had a choice only between three countries..., Russia, Sweden, and England. And now, I've made my choice."

Alex hoped that his sincere words would be taken at face value.

Mr. Smith looked at John,

"Do you have any other questions for Alex. Ok!, if not, lets wrap up," he glanced cheerfully at Alex.

"Alex, we hope that you will keep our meeting discrete for now. I'm sure we don't need to remind you that as the inventor of such a significant source of energy it makes you a subject of interest not only to Russian intelligence but possibly other countries too. We would like to offer you some local bed and breakfast accommodation here in the capital, where it will be much easier to look after you. Do you agree? Good!"

The Director continued.

"You soon have a meeting with the government Energy Department, which we appreciate very much. After that we would like to talk with you again.

"But again, please allow us to bring you to that meeting in our 'taxi.'" Mr. Smith winked at him and continued, "We have credible information that foreign Secret services will try to kidnap you. So, one hour before your meeting at the Energy department, our car will wait for you at the entrance of your accommodation.

Do not leave the safety until you see we are waiting for you, and do not stop to talk to anyone else. You will easily recognise it, our driver will be in a yellow jacket and blue cap. We will use a password, you should ask the driver, "Are you a clown?" his answer will be, 'no, I am just eccentric!" If it does not look like our taxi, or anything else seems 'off' then stay in your accommodation and call us immediately," he pointed towards his deputy.

"At this stage, two of our agents will keep an eye on you. You probably won't notice them, but they will be there. So, my advice, be careful, don't travel more than absolutely necessary, and take this opportunity to catch up on some quiet reading or television."

They stood up, the Director of British Intelligence moved towards Alex and shook his hand,

"Alex, don't worry—everything will be ok and we will keep in touch."

With that he smiled at Alex and accompanied him to the entrance door.

Alex walked out of the meeting a little shocked. He thought back how his life had changed in the last few months and wondered where it might end. After all the talking, he wanted to find a quiet area of the airport to sit and think, and maybe have a bite to eat. With all the excitement, he hasn't realised he was getting hungry.

Soon he would meet with the energy department, and with some good fortune would sell his invention into trustworthy hands. This would be the most important thing he would ever do, and he realised he needed to put all the troubles recently behind him and be thinking clearly. It would be best, he thought, to stay away from his mother's home until the deal was done. Especially after recent conversations with Derek. It would be Derek's birthday, and he promised his mother he would attend. That should be fine he thought, just family and friends and less chance of confrontation while Derek was in a good mood. Besides, he was looking forward to seeing his sister and he always enjoyed a good party. He smiled to himself a little, it relaxed him to have something simple to look forward to. Perhaps after all this he would hear from the energy company about a job offer.

"Hi Mum, its Alex. I'm back from Stockholm. Yes, everything was fine, and you can congratulate me—I have my PhD in my pocket now!" He laughed, happy to speak to his mother. "Yes, I will come, but I have a few things to do first so I'll come straight to Derek's party. No, I have a B&B for a couple of days, I'll tell you more later. Don't worry, everything is alright. I'll call you later, love you."

Alex woke up late, and dressed quickly, before rushing outside to his 'taxi' which had been waiting for a while. Before he jumped in, with a racing heart and feeling a bit silly, he exchanged passwords with the driver. The driver already knew where he was going and seemingly, that he was a little late as he pushed his way through the traffic, making use of some well-planned shortcuts.

The car pulled up near an imposing tall and glassy building.

Alex suggested that the driver not wait for him because he wanted to have to some free time after the meeting. Alex jumped out, hurrying up the steps to an oversized glass door. He didn't glance back, knowing that somewhere there was likely to be multiple agents of different nationalities watching him. At least he thought.

The conversation with the British security services had calmed his nerves a little, it was nice to know someone was watching his back. While he could not be sure of their intentions, they had certainly been more open with him than any other the other agents he had encountered.

A stocky, pleasant looking man, with dark eyes waited for him in the airy, spacious lobby. He held a thick file in his hand. Sunlight streamed in from a huge glass dome many floors above them.

"Mr. Petrov?!" The man called him.

"Yes, I am!" Alex went towards the man and shook hands as they made their introductions.

"My manager is waiting for you in a room on the third floor. Follow me please."

They went into a roomy elevator and soon stepped out into a wide corridor which lead them to a conference room.

"Ah, Mister Petrov, welcome, if you do not mind I will call you just Alex! Welcome and join us, please."

The manager also shook Alex's hand and sat down. There were two other people beside the manager. As later became clear, it was the director responsible for the finance department and director of science and energy development.

"Well, Alex, we were expecting you with excitement. Believe us, when we tell you, you have caused quite a stir in the department. From what we understand so far about your invention, we think it could be a game changer."The manager started.

"Could you tell us please about yourself, who and what you are and, what is your invention, please feel free to be as technical as needed."

Alex sat more comfortably, looked at the panel of people listening to him then with smile started, "I was born in Russia…"

After an hour, Alex stopped his speech, took some water which was suggested, and finished. "It's up to you now to decide if you would like to buy the licence to my invention and how much you value it. If you, I mean the British Government, are not interested than next in the queue is Sweden and I believe my invention will help them to dominate world energy."

The room fell silent for a minute or so as people furiously scribbled notes and passed them to each other. A few glances and nods around the table, and then the manager with his assistants smiled.

"Mr. Petrov, Alex..." the Manager began. "I would like to assure you on the behalf of our government that we are...interested!

"To show our serious intent, we will put pressure on the Patent Office to consider your invention as soon as possible, bypassing the usual delays. We are absolutely keen to make a deal with you, something which you will be satisfied with—a very substantial offer. Together we will be the first in the world to produce cheap and ecologically safe energy.

"And in finishing our meeting, Alex, I would like to give you some very good news," the manager smiled to him, "we know through our channels, that you will be soon receiving an offer for the job in the nuclear company where you applied. So congratulations on the new job!"

Alex left the meeting in very good mood. He walked capital streets smiling inside, with a radiant face ready to embrace anybody who wanted it.

Later in the evening Alex decided to go to dinner at a nice cozy restaurant, he'd heard about from his friend. It was a short walk from his lodgings. He liked London, and a short walk would help him de-stress after the busy day. Time for some enjoyment on his last evening before he went to his mother's place.

It was really nice food, tasty and expensive. Alex was in his thinking mode, waking back along the street which was still busy with cars towards his B&B. He did not see as a car followed him then stopped some meters behind him. Two well built, middle age men jumped out of the car and with quick steps approached Alex from behind.

Alex flinched, caught by surprise as he realized that two men were grabbing him from both sides under his arms and pushing him towards the car. Even being stunned Alex tried to shake them off but quickly realized their grip was tight as a vice.

In the same minute, another car announced its arrival with squealing breaks. It pulled up close to the pavement, opposite to Alex and before he knew it, another two men were almost on top of them. They shouted, "stop! Police! You two, step back! We are…" They did not finish their sentence before the first two guys jumped back in the car and next second with engine revved, sped away, wheels spinning.

"Alex, are you OK?!" One of the men asked him. Alex was glad to see his British protectors had been true to their word in watching over him, and felt a little foolish about wandering around London on his own.

"It is very close to your place but we would like you give a lift to your entrance," said another officer smiling at him, "I think you want to avoid another Russian attempt to kidnap you. We certainly do!"

৩৩

Mister Smith rolled over in bed to face his wife, he placed his heavy hand on her waist and started quietly snuffling. His day was so busy, a lot of meetings and important decisions. So, when he came back home, all he wanted was dinner with his wife and his comfortable bed.

As he drifted off, a shrill phone ring tone woke him on the way to a sleepy nirvana.

"Yes, I am listening to you, John. Could you calm down please! Yes, yes, I understand."

He lowered his voice, "I will call now at once. Keep an eye on this and report to me as things change. I will not be sleeping until the situation is resolved. Tomorrow I will be in the Office first thing and we discuss next steps. Ok, I await your call"

He replaced the phone handset and immediately lifted it to his ear again. He tapped a number in from memory and asked to be connected to the Chief Inspector of West Midlands Police.

Mr. Smith briefly explained what had happened and asked the person on the other end of the line for his full cooperation and immediate action. He asked him immediately to block particular roads leading out of the forest zone to A5 and especially road B4636, and make all efforts to locate and arrest the two men who are suspected of the killing of Derek Harrison. He emphasised the highly important nature of their quick actions in this case, its urgency could not be understated. He also asked him to keep him appraised about progress. As soon as the men were arrested they should be immediately transferred to London for questioning.

With any chance of sleep now out of the question Mr. Smith let out a deep sigh of resignation. He went to the bathroom to freshen up his face before waiting for the phone to ring and inform him of the result by his deputy John.

His wife was awakening already, she murmured, "Darling, what is going on?" He bent down, stroked her ear and suggested softly, "Don't worry darling, sorry I woke you up. It's just something going on at work. I'll move to my office now to work on the computer. I'll keep the noise down while I wait for some further calls." He went to his home office and quietly closed the door.

After a sleepless night, the director of British Intelligence was back in the office. As always he was in a smart suit with tie, shaved but with visibly tired eyes. With great attention, he was listening to the reports of his agents and making notes in his notebook. Also in the meeting room was the rest of the team of key players in this operation. The director was not the only one with tired eyes, clearly a few others had been actively involved in the operation overnight.

"So, Robert, let us hear it. What happened and how last night? Also, did you managed to let the Russian slip away, as I understood, you now have no evidence or witnesses as to the exact moment when they presumably killed Derek Harrison.

"Yes, Sir. I prepared a brief report for this morning's meeting and I'm ready to explain what happened. Sorry, if I interrupt my speech by yawning but I did not sleep at all after this stressful night," he punctuated his sentence with a deep yawn.

All members of the meeting relaxed a little and there were a few smiles around the table. Robert continued.

"Yesterday evening we were on duty covering Derek, in future I will call him Object, we located ourselves with a view on his home. We did not expect any activity from the Russians because Derek and Lara came back home very late. Because of the device in his car, we can hear everything that is said in there. We saw in the distance the Russians car, they were relaxed and didn't look like they expected an action. Suddenly for us both everything changed. Object ran from house to his car, and took off. The Russians followed him straight away. We waited for them to move away, but once we started, we noticed that the tracker on the Russians car was not working, maybe the battery had died or they hit a bump and it had fallen off. Luckily we still had another device on Object' car so we could still see where Object was heading. Because we knew the Russians would be in close proximity to Object car we determined there was no need to stay too close and dropped back, following them by the tracking device.

We reviewed his intelligence file and thought that maybe he was going to see his daughter. Unfortunately, we picked up a nail on one of the front tyres and were out of action for about five minutes to change the wheel before continuing the chase. '

Robert stopped, and took a deep breath.

"After that we heard from the device in Object's car, that the Russians overtook him on a road which was in forest area, demanding him to stop, he did not, then we heard a banging noise, followed by several shots and then silence. We knew we couldn't cover all the exits from the area to prevent the Russians from escaping so we called John and asked for assistance to stop and arrest them. Soon, we reached the place where Object's car was, and found it overturned and already on fire. We stopped for a minute, removed Object's body from the car and called an ambulance. Then we continued the chase with hope that the roadblock had been put in place up ahead by the local police.

"Well, thank you Robert, take a seat and we will hear from my deputy John, can you report what happened from this point on?" The Director again scrawled notes in his book.

"I would say, you could call this the grand finale, because with quick help of the local police force we trapped the Russian team in our dragnet. As we speak, now they are sweating in custody, not too far from us." John, smiled to the team.

"So, our chief, Mr. Smith, after my call to him, worked with the Chief Inspector of the local constabulary to flood the area with police and put in place multiple roadblocks. Because they acted so quickly, they were left with nowhere to run. Predictably, they reached one of the roadblocks where they were arrested based on charges of several counts including the murder of a British citizen, Mr. Harrison.

"Everybody here already knows that Harrison was co-operating with Russian spies and now it seems his story, indeed his role in our case, will be ending without any further action needed from our side. I expect our director will make some final conclusions on this matter, in time.

"But for the Russians, they are unlikely to escape this so easily. We have enough evidence that any jury will stick them in prison for a long time. They claimed at the moment of their arrest that they have diplomatic immunity but I think it's a bluff, they are not known to us under the names they gave. Soon the truth will be revealed."

"Thanks, John," Mr. Smith, looked around all the team seriously and said, "I have some questions to the team who was on duty last night.

"How is it possible that just at the important moment, your tracking device did not work and you caught a nail in the wheel?!"

Robert was trying to say something in their defence, but the Director stopped him by raising his palm.

"Ok, I can believe that the Russians found your device and destroyed it and we all know there are a lot of nails on our roads," he shot an enquiring glance to Robert and Steve.

"Please tell me, did you record everything that Harrison said in his car?"

"Yes, Mr. Smith, we were recording everything from the bug. So, we have evidence that the Russians killed him. We have the gun found in the possession of the Russians, and we're confident of a ballistic match to the bullets we found in Derek Harrison's car," Robert replied.

"Very well then! Shall we continue our work? Night team, go and take some well-deserved rest but for the rest of you there is plenty to do with our arrested spies and securing and monitoring our young inventor."

The Director turned to John,

"Please could you stay in the room for us to discuss another matter?". The room emptied except for the two senior gentlemen.

"John, I'm asking you to take an unpleasant mission to visit personally Harrison's widow, Lara Petrova, she, actually, did not change her name to Harrison in her documents.

"I would like you to express to her our sympathy and condolences, OK? Also, take the opportunity to see if you can determine if she knows about her husband's relationship with the Russians."

John nodded but added in answer,

"I will go, but before I'll contact the local police to be sure that they don't make that visit before us."

"You are right, John, do as you suggest.

"And I would like to say that despite all we know about Harrison, her late husband, I still think that she is a fair and smart lady. Also, you know—she is the mother of our young inventor Alex Petrov, with whom we still should continue to work.

"I think, John, it would be fair, if you make a call to Alex tomorrow and tell him the truth about his stepfather Derek…He deserve to know.

"So, we did a good job in preventing him from being kidnapped by the Russians. I am very pleased about this,

John. I would like to say a big thank you for all your good work, and to the team under your leadership."

The Director smiled cheerfully to John, "You will see my thanks when you all get your annual bonuses." He pressed his lips together cheekily and continued, "I can see that you are exhausted. Just one more thing," the Director lowered his voice, "I would like to know in detail how the Russians failed to kidnap Alex, after your rest, I'd appreciate a full report.

"But for now, off you go, John."

The Director of the British secret services smiled and with a feeling of joy leaned back in his chair.

Chapter 22

It had been a sleepless night for Lara and she decided to get up early. After the previous day's terrible discovery of Derek's infidelity there was no point trying to sleep any longer. She wrapped herself up in her, cozy long grey gown and slowly made her way downstairs for her morning cup of coffee. In silence, she poured herself a coffee before sitting in her favorite chair by the large conservatory window. The pain in her heart would have been apparent on her face, if anyone had been watching.

Her marriage with Derek was on the edge, and she knew it, but she did not know what to do yet. There was a storm in her heart, in her thoughts, and in her head. She physically felt a pain like a glowing, pulsing in her head which was preventing her from thinking rationally. Her overflowing eyes were dropping big salty tears down her cheeks.

Where he is now, she wondered. *Why did he not call me in the morning even just to check that I'm OK? Possibly he went to his sister for the night and today later he will come back like a "bitten dog" with a present and flowers as a sign of accepted guilt and an apology for something he knows he should never have done? Or was he going to demonstrate to her some nasty behavior which would lead into a messy divorce?*

Too many questions. Lara realized these thoughts would just make her life miserable and sad, and possibly lead to loneliness, in that world where only unmarried, single, and unhappy people live.

She did not know what to do yet. She decided she would call him later to check to see if he was at least safe, then they would talk. She deeply sighed. She was not looking forward to picking up the phone, but at least for now she felt in control of the situation. Lara decided a bit or normality was what she needed now, she would get herself dressed and feed her children. They had arrived home very late last night in a taxi and went straight to sleep upstairs without noticing that Derek was not at home. So, now, after breakfast she was going to tell them the truth. It would be a day of difficult conversations, it seemed to Lara.

"Well, there is no choice for me," she thought and with a worried look on her face, went to get dressed.

The shrill sound of the doorbell momentarily shocked Lara, before she rushed to the front door, swiftly opening it.

"Mrs. Petrova?" Two police officers were on the doorstep, wearing serious expressions.

"Could we come in?"

Lara invited them in and started to tremble inside, her heart beating in her throat trying to guess why they come. Were the children ok? Or had Derek assaulted somebody in a drunken rage, all these thoughts ran through her mind in a moment but she tried not to show her worries to the slim police woman with blonde short hair and the big pleasant-faced policeman with his broad shoulders.

"Take a seat, please," she invited with an artificial smile.

They sat down, and the two police officers exchanged glanced before the police woman started to talk.

"Your name is Lara and you are the wife of Mr. Derek Harrison, can you confirm that is correct please?" Lara nodded silently to them with wide open eyes.

"Well, Lara, we're sorry to tell you that your husband has died," the officer paused for a moment before continuing. "Late last night, he died after sustaining injuries in a road traffic accident. We are very sorry for your loss," the officer looked genuinely sad to be breaking the news.

Lara covered her mouth first then, "Oh no! It cannot be. Oh my God."

Lara inhaled before involuntarily letting out a loud short scream…Then her head fell into her palms and she began to sob.

This was a black day for Lara. The officers stayed with her for a short time, making sure she had a cup of tea and her children were around her to support her. The children were also shocked at the news, and were trying to find a way to ease the pain for Lara. They tried to hug her, and be around her but Lara needed time and her own place to cry out her sorrow. She was crying not only for her husband who had been so good to her and brought her to a new life but also for his cheating and that she would never hear him explain and apologise. Now there were just broken hopes on her once bright future with him. He would never have the chance to earn her trust back. She asked the children to give her some time alone and agreed they would speak again in the evening. She went upstairs to mourn her loss alone.

"Mama, I am with you, with all my heart in your sorrow." Alex was sitting near his mother in the evening, he put his hand on her shoulder. "Mama, please, stop crying, you are tearing our hearts out, and you Oleva, stop sobbing! Let me get you both a nice cup of tea."

He had found a way to stop them sobbing, at least temporarily.

They nodded, "Yes," and Alex went to prepare the tea and to take a look at what was in the fridge, maybe a light snack would help them.

Outside it was dusk, and Alex could tell his mother was still processing the bad news. He could see that her mind was in agony and she was struggling to think clearly. Lara got up from her chair and quietly said, "Children, I am going to bed now, I'm sorry that I cannot spend the evening with you both.

"You can arrange something to eat from the fridge but I do not want anything. I would like to be on my own now." And she slowly went upstairs.

"Wake up, wake up, mother." Oleva rubbed her mother's shoulder, trying to wake her up. Lara had been in bed now for over 15 hours and Oleva was getting worried.

Lara opened her eyes, saw her worried daughter and son behind. Her eyelids wanted to droop down again but she made the effort to force herself to answer the children and get out of bed.

"Mama, we made a nice breakfast. If you hurry up it will be still warm. We'll see you in the dining room in a few minutes. Ok?"

Lara nodded to them, she would be there. She was pretending that she had been sleeping all those hours but she had barely slept at all. She had a lot of tears, heavy thoughts about regrets, about doubts, about what the future could bring her now.

Lara thought that maybe she had overreacted about Derek's dirty secret, possibly if she had reacted differently than she did then Derek would not have left in such a hurry and now he would be alive. Should a one-night stand really have cost him his life? Lara let out a pained moan.

"We have a lot to do today, Mama," Alex said as he sat down in a chair in the conservatory. The three of them were finishing off their lunch with a coffee.

Alex decided to take the lead in helping his mother and started to plan what needed to be done in the next few days before Derek's funeral. The legal and financial things should be sorted as soon as possible, he thought. But first he should agree with his grieving mother about what to needs to be done.

"Well my dears," Lara looked tiredly at her children. "I am lucky that you are with me now, it helps me to get through this terrible time. Could you please note down a list of things which we need to do this week and we can look at it together to work out who will do what. But firstly today, if you could call everybody needs to know about Derek death. His sisters, daughters, his business friends…"

"Mum," Alex interrupted his mother, "Listen to this carefully. I would like to tell you something you should know. Your husband was not such a simple naive man, and possibly he was not honest with you and he did not like me, I thought you should know the truth…"

Alex took a sip of coffee, while looking at the garden. He admired the beautiful green, shrubs lit by solar posts through the glass wall of the conservatory. He waited for his mother's response.

"Why are you saying this, my son?" Lara turned angrily to Alex.

"Because mum, he was cooperating with Russian Intelligence against me—the KGB or the FSB or whatever they are called these days! He wanted to help them to take my invention, because he was involved in economic espionage, that is why mum!

"I presume, I hope, that you were unaware of all of this. I was talking on the phone yesterday with a man who told me that Derek was killed by Russians, because his usefulness to them ran out. My invention is already in the hands of the British Government.

"Sorry, mum, I've had no chance to tell you about something what happened to me when I came back from Sweden. But I will, later.

"Sorry to say mum, but also Derek told me to leave the house as soon as he knew that the prototype and documents were submitted to the Patent office. It was quite unpleasant for me but I did not tell you because I did not want to create a rift between you and Derek. I know you probably don't want to hear any of this right now, but I hope, in time it helps you to deal with this."

Lara was sitting still in her chair and with wide open eyes she was staring at Alex. She was shocked and did not know what to say. Slowly, as Alex's words sank in her sadness was turning to anger.

"Darling! Son, I'm speechless! I cannot believe it! You should have told me about this earlier—as soon as you found out about it. But, thank you son, you gave me a chance to rethink something important and review my life."

"Mama, and you Oleva, I must tell you about my personal plans. In two weeks, I will start my job at the nuclear energy company which, I think, will make me very happy and the company will send me to Paris. I am going to to there for one month for mandatory induction training straight after I start the job," he smiled at both of them. "It sounds very good, doesn't it?!

"So, mum, I will help you with everything, to organize the funeral and then I'll have go.

"Oleva, you told me, that your husband Michael will come here in a few days to stay, and then take you back home to Sweden?" he turned then to mother.

"What do you think, mum, about being alone here in the house soon? Will you cope? If not, we will change plans, isn't that right Oleva?"

"Yes, yes, brother we will." She nodded.

"Children, you are my rock and wall behind of me and I love you both to bits," Lara said in sad and low voice.

"As you said, son, I will be glad of your help over the next few difficult days. After the funeral, then, off you go both of you, go on with your lives. I know, you will not forget me and visit me often and it will make me happy. I promise you, I will survive here and I hope, will cope with my widowed status." Then Lara looked at Oleva,

"When will Michael come darling?"

"In two days, mum."

"Ok! Now, Alex, shall we make a list of the jobs and actions we need do?" Lara said in a weak voice and returned to her grieving, sitting in her chair in silence, gazing into the garden.

One week before the funeral Lara got a call from Derek's daughter Jane. Every day since Derek's death, Lara had visitors who tried to support her with help or a kind word, also the phone rang regularly which helped Lara feel that she wasn't alone in her grief, she had not realized how many friends she had, or were they just people being nosey? Lara believed her internal instinct, as a former director working with lots of people, she thought she could recognize who is a real friend who is not. But this call from Jane was something she did not expect.

"Lara! I will not take a lot of your time. I just want to tell you that it is you, who is the cause of my dad's death. Yes, you are. I never liked you but now, I hate you, and I want you to tell me now when we will be invited to dad's lawyer to hear who will get what, inheritance, business, house, money. I am sure you know all about his will and I hope you get nothing because you only just married him!"

"Stop, stop it, Jane! I do not want to listen to the nonsense! I do not expect any love from you and to be honest, you are not my cup of tea either, as woman, or as a daughter, You just think a little about your behavior toward your father for a minute, you never visited, supported, or helped him, never.

"So now, Jane, I know the will, your father did not make secrets about it and it is in his lawyer's hands. I advise you to be patient until he calls all of us, to a meeting in his office. You will get what you deserve from your father. I do not want to speak to you again and I would not be disappointed if you didn't come to the funeral but it is up to you. Goodbye!"

Lara threw back the phone handset onto the base with a racing heartbeat and seething anger. She could not believe that his daughter talked to her in this manner. She had not done anything bad to Jane, in fact, she'd always tried to smooth Derek's heart and mood towards her.

She knew how disappointed Derek was and upset after each conversation with this daughter, now she demanded his money even in death, so it was not for her to judge anybody. *That is a real shame. Impudence! I should tell Anne, Derek's other sister about this,* Lara thought.

Her children were sitting in another room and heard their mother's conversation. They looked at each other with raised eyebrows.

Several days later, just a couple of days before the funeral, Lara decided to make a call to Jim in Scotland. Sometimes, especially after Derek death, she was returning to the secret part of her soul and thinking about Jim, about what he said and why he said it, last time they met. Today, since she woke she'd had a nagging remainder asking her to make a call to Jim without delay. She expected it would be a nasty surprise for him and although it was short notice, she owed him the opportunity to come to the funeral.

"Hello Jim, did my call surprise you. No?! I have some shocking news, my husband and your old friend Derek has died. Yes, Jim. That is what happened.

Lara's voice started to tremble before turning to full sobbing.

"Ok, ok, Jim, sorry, I am still in a bad state. He died in a road accident at night. I will tell you later about the details but not now, if you will forgive me. I just had a thought that if you wish to come to his funeral then you are very welcome. I will give you the details of where and when.

"No, thank you, at the moment I have great help from my children, but later if you wish you can help me after the funeral. Yes, it would be nice. There are plenty of B&Bs in our area, it's easy now with the Internet. Let me know when you are coming and where you are planning to stay.

"Ok, OK Jim. Thank you very much, Jim."

Unexpectedly, a lot of people turned up to Derek's funeral. Lara, in her black dress with elegant black hat and veil was greeting people and trying to hold back her tears. Around her were her children in black suits, only Oleva's husband was not in black, he didn't own one but wore a nice dark blue suit. All was going well, people one by one expressed their condolences to her and with the busses Alex had arranged they all arrived on time at the crematory. After the service, everyone was brought to a pub where food was already laid out on the tables and the bar was fully stocked.

After some drinks people became more relaxed, talking more loudly and laughing. She thought that some guests even forgot that it's not a party but a funeral. It's supposed to be a sad gathering of family and friends in memory of a lost friend or relative. The lawyer approached her with his condolences and suggested that the reading of the will would be ready in three days and he would like to announce Derek's Will to the family in his office. Lara nodded confirming she will be there.

For Lara, it was an unusual Wake. The children were sad, wearing somber faces, Jim stayed not too far from Lara. He made sure she always had a drink if anyone tried to talk to her about different things but not about death.

Lara remembered what Derek asked her seriously before he had died. So, she had prepared a surprise for the people here. Derek had requested of her, in case if he died first then she should play a specific piece of music at his funeral.

There was a famous Russian waltz which he liked terribly. He requested that all people who came to his funeral should listen to it but not dance. He hadsaid that he would be jealous in his coffin if they would be dancing, Lara smiled at his dark humour.

"Attention, please." Lara stood up from her chair, took her little goblet of white wine, and looked around all the guests.

"Shall we have this drink for the soul of Derek who left this world, and me, too early.

"For Derek, my husband!." And without sipping, she drank her small glass of wine empty.

"Now, all our respected guests," she continued, "I would like to introduce you to a piece of music beloved by Derek, which he asked me to play for you at his funeral, in case of his death. But he asked you not to dance please, just listen."

Lara could see inquisitive faces staring back at her. "This is a famous Russian waltz. Enjoy it, please." Lara said and took her place.

Jim bending to her ear said, "well done, Lara, you have arranged a fitting send-off for Derek."

Three days after the funeral all of Derek's family were in the reception area of the lawyer. They were all invited in and after exchanging pleasantries and condolences once again, the lawyer looked at each of the family members before looking down and slowly started to read Derek's Will.

During his reading, the temperature in the room was rising, nothing was said by the family, but the atmosphere in the room changed perceptibly. Derek's daughter Jane was furious with her father's Will and when the reading was complete she jumped up from her chair and dramatically left the room. Her face was screwed up with anger and she was murmuring something negative under her breath. Her father had decided to give the house to his wife Lara, and the business would be divided up between his two daughters and his wife. Lara's part would be more than the two sisters together, so Lara would keep control of the business. Of the money, he had left half for his wife and half for his daughters. Also, surprisingly he left a small amount for each of his brothers and sisters. By now both daughters were furious and had left the room while his brothers and sisters were happy. Lara too was happy and a little shocked because it appeared that Derek had changed his Will three days before his birthday and untimely death. The Lawyer said that he had wanted to make it a nice surprise for his wife, Derek has mentioned nothing of this to Lara.

Lara realized now that she has her own place to live and would have some money to live on with more to come from the business. She should now be prepared to find a candidate to run the business and invest in a good manager. She was not ready right now to sit there in the office, to control and run the business where she had little experience. She already knew who she wanted that man to be.

Her children had left her the day before, as they agreed, and now she did not know what to do with herself. In her state of grief, she was mostly sitting at home and doing nothing. Jim was still staying in town and every day he come to the house trying to lift her mood and her soul, inviting her here or there, but Lara did not want much of any activities. Jim did not try to make any private approachs to her so she believed he prolonged staying in the city for other reasons, he said he has some business to do in town so he would stay longer so she sincerely believed him.

But today she received an invitation from him to come to a restaurant for a meal in the evening. She did not refuse, she decided to go, he was very pleasant company, why should she sit at home alone, in deep sadness, sobbing.

Lara and Jim were driving to the best restaurant in her area, which he chose for them. They took their places at a window table overlooking the little lake with swans and ducks. They were beautiful surroundings, Lara sighed deeply, gave Jim a nice smile and then again turned her eyes toward the lake. Jim periodically glanced towards Lara and while making his choice from the menu, tried to guess what Lara was thinking about.

They finished their delicious five course tasting menu, followed by coffee and were having a quiet conversation. At one point Jim looked at her softly, meaningful and suddenly for Lara said,

"I would like to invite you to come and stay with me in Scotland, in my house. Maybe just for a few days or weeks but if you wish you are welcome to stay for longer.

"You would be my most welcomed guest, Lara. You know I have plenty of space, you can choose your bedroom. You don't need to do anything there, the exact opposite in fact, you can tell my cook what you want to eat and he will prepare it for you!

"The fresh Scottish air is good for the soul, and getting away from here and all these memories for a while will help. It will give your mind a chance to recover from all the stress, and of course you can spend some time keeping me company."

He smiled at her. "Am I good company or not, it's for you to decide."

"Jim, you are good company, for sure, and you are a very good friend to me. I feel you are sincere when you talk to me and I value this very much." Lara looked at him seriously.

"My answer is—I will go with you to your beautiful home—but first I need to make sure that the business will be left in good hands so I won't worry about it while I am away. It'll take me a couple of days to sort everything out hopefully, I need to put someone in charge who can be trusted and who isn't going to need lots of instruction in how things work."

"Do you have anyone in your mind?" Jim wondered.

"Yes, Jim, there is a hard-working man who has been operating all the machinery there for many years. He's an engineer but he knows the place inside and out.

I know that he can do any kind of job there, even dealing with new customers, and I trust him, his name is John. So, I need to offer him a promotion to manager and just hope he accepts."

"Lara, I am so glad you will stay with me, you are a great lady whom I was lucky to meet."

Jim's demeanour became noticeably upbeat,

"You won't regret it! I'm going to show you a lot of interesting places in Scotland. I will try to impress you, dear Lara."

He smiled at her with his happy face, took her hand and kissed it meaningfully.

"So, shall we start to prepare to leave this town for a while? If you would like any help with your business arrangements you only need to ask. I have a quite good understanding of paper work!"

"Jim, did you finish your business here with your friends?"

She looked him screwing up her beautiful eyes with cheeky lips.

"Very nearly, just a few more errands to run, I'll be finishing up just as you will, I'm sure." Jim tried to be serious but Lara noticed a glint in his eyes…

It started as a bright sunny day in Scotland with Lara sitting at her dressing table doing her morning cosmetic routine, then she stopped and started to look outside through the large window onto the garden where the rolling lawns were dotted with ancient English Oak trees. It was such beautiful scenery that Lara was bewitched.

A knock at the door interrupted her observation,

"Come in!" Jim's housekeeper entered with a breakfast tray. Smiling to Lara, he explained that Jim woke up very early to a phone call and he had to take a trip to Edinburgh. He made sure Lara was comfortable, telling her how Jim had instructed him to make sure she was well looked after and that Jim planned to return in the early afternoon and, he promised to take her on a trip on his return to apologise.

"Yes, I would be happy to, and thank you bringing me breakfast here, but I will be happy to come down to the dining room tomorrow!" He nodded and smiled at Lara in response.

Lara had been in Jim's Manor for three weeks already. She had spent some wonderful days with Jim who took her to the many different beauty spots around Scotland. They visited the main National park, the rugged mountains of Black Mount, and historic Sterling Castle. On their travels, they saw all kinds of wildlife and Lara remembered the breath-taking experiences at the seal sanctuary and the otters on the shores of the old lake Loch Linnhe. Lara was so impressed by the beauty of Scotland. Also, the unforgettable cruise from Oban to the Island of Mull.

She could tell that Jim was keen to impress her, and make her happy.

But despite all the amazing trips of the past weeks, in the evenings, after the inevitable delicious meal, Lara would return to her bedroom on her own, and sit sobbing and feeling very alone. She thought about the hope of a happy, peaceful life with Derek, now destroyed. She still felt betrayed by him. But every new day she awoke in the morning with new optimism about her future life. She remembered how Jim had told her the trip to Scotland would help her see things more clearly, and he was right.

Occasionally over the next few days, she started to think about returning to her sad home, to the memories of what could have been with Derek. These thoughts made her scared, in contrast to her care-free time in the Scottish manor. She wondered how she would fill her days alone, how she would learn to live life without a beloved man to support her in adjusting to what was still a new country for her. All these thoughts would, now and then creep into her mind and leave her deep in thought.

Even Jim noticed her changing mood, her vacant, worried gaze.

"Lara. What is troubling you?" He asked her softly.

"I am thinking about returning home and returning to reality," she sounded very sad. "It's time to try to stand on my own feet, without any support."

"Dear Lara, stay another couple of days and then if you insist I will take you home. I was trying to keep in as a surprise, but I wanted to take you to the famous Edinburgh Tattoo. I remember you mentioned you had wanted to see if for a long time, and it's such an impressive show. Well, I already have us a pair of tickets!"

He was encouraging but with sad eyes that smiled at her,

"Do you remember a few weeks ago I had to make a trip very early in the morning? That is where I, and another member of the Committee for organizing the Tattoo needed to take care of some urgent tasks because one of our members was suddenly taken ill. It was almost a disaster, but we managed to recover the situation. As a thank you, we now have tickets for two of the best seats."

Jim had been right before, and she trusted him. She thought she was too confused to make any big decisions and decided to lean on Jim and take his advice. She knew he was an intelligent man and he wanted the best for her.

Three days later Lara and Jim went to a room on the top floor and out onto a big West-facing balcony. To Lara's surprise, his housekeeper had prepared a round table with a bright white table cloth and two chairs, Lara gasped in amazement at the romantic setting. It was mid-evening, with good weather, still very warm and quiet. It was a perfect place for them to watch the stunning sunset together. Lara was glad she had worn a green summery dress which complimented her green eyes. Jim wore a dark blue suit with a white shirt which made him look very elegant. In front of them stretched a panoramic view of the Scottish mountains and some little lakes. It was remarkable how much more impressive the views were from the top floor. Lara expressed her admiration of the location and Jim with an understanding smile nodded, He loved his home and was proud to have someone to share it with.

The housekeeper started to serve dinner just as Lara's mobile phone rang.

Lara excused herself, explaining that Alex was calling.

"My dear son, I am so glad to hear from you. How is Paris? Oh, I'm so pleased that you like it. How have the first days been in your new job? Excellent! I am so proud, for you darling. Yes! I am still staying in my friend Jim's house. I love to be here, it's an excellent place. Also, he has shown me a lot of Scotland. It's a blissful land, but I am returning back home tomorrow.

"What—what?! Son, you met a nice woman? Oh! You are thinking about marrying her! Son, you know that I will support your choice if she is your sweetheart. I hope you will respect, love, and care about her. Do you understood what I mean, my son? And she must love and respect you the same way, look after you as I have done. Ok-Ok, son! I just said what I am really thinking. I hope this is important for you.

"That is good. Before you make a proposal, please, I hope you will introduce us? Very well, my son."

Lara switched off her mobile and with twinkled happy eyes looked at Jim. He heard the conversation and understood.

"So dear Lara, soon your family will be increased by one more, a Parisian girl?! I am glad to hear this. Your family is very international now and will soon be even more so."

"Yes, I am happy that Alex has found his other half, it is the first time he has ever mentioned the word 'marriage,' he has had several girlfriends but never one that he wanted to marry. This girl must be really special, well, to him at least!

"We will see! Any way I am glad that my boy can start his family life and will be settled. But you my friend," she nodded to Jim, "I hope will have the opportunity to see her too and have your own view."

"Really? I'd very much like that if you would be ok with it," Jim looked serious.

"Yes, I would like that and I will' Lara answered looking in his eyes.

The two of them, not young but not too old were sitting comfortably on the balcony after dinner sipping their Champagne and coffee.

The big orange ball of the sun started to go down below the horizon, the sunset was beyond beautiful, and neither of them could look away as they watched the sun disappear.

And suddenly for Lara, Jim slowly got up from his chair, keeping his eyes on Lara. He decided to do the one thing which he wanted most in his life now. Jim took a couple of steps towards her and knelt down on one knee.

"Lara, would you like to be my wife? I promise you to love you, to care for you and share with you everything I have. And your children will be for me as my own."

Jim lowered his eyes awaiting her answer.

She was caught totally by surprise. Her eyes, twinkling even more than usual, started to fill with tears, she was shocked to hear the words, but she felt happiness wash over her. Lara already knew her answer, she wanted to be with this kind and wonderful man who offered her his heart and asked for her hand. She got up, put her hands in his and looking in his waiting eyes said, "Yes, darling, I do, I would like to be your wife, my heart feels you."

About the Author

Larysa Rychkova is a new author, a debutant in the writer's world, now looking in her later years to achieve a passion she has harboured for many years—to write and publish a novel. She was born in the former Soviet Union, in the territory of the Ukraine. Although an exceptional student in her study of mathematics and precision work, she was very creative and had a love of the arts. Her university degree in mathematics and computer programming took her to the very Far East of Russia, learning many new skills within the new culture of Russia and dealing with people from different layers of society. After that next chapter of life, and with two children already, brought her to a successful twenty-year career as a director of the government job centre in Ukraine.

With time, her beloved son and daughter, already in higher education, moved to a university in Sweden, achieving their masters degrees in Stockholm, and have since moved to successful careers in London. A very new experience also brought Rychkova to England eighteen years ago as a newlywed with a British husband, where she has settled and begun to write in her retirement.

Who does not like to read, to swim, to travel, to paint? But the most fictional chapters of her novel, A Clash of Forces, were planned while participating in her love of swimming. Having a huge life, job, experiences, it was easy for her to write intriguing insights in a real Russian's life, with interesting glimpses about the world where possibly many readers have not been. This story hopefully will eliminate the myth about women from the eastern part of Europe, who search for love, and also make us believe that sometime, someone, will invent something which makes our world a greener place and to live without a dependency from current energy sources which will change the world forever.'

Lightning Source UK Ltd.
Milton Keynes UK
UKHW020652150622
404464UK00011B/1079